NOVEL ENTERPRISES

The LaSalle Street Murders

Written by
Carol Sissom

"The LaSalle Street murders were a "riveting" incident, and the dedication and relentless pursuit of Carol Sissom, reminiscent of a trained detective, undoubtedly has led to a positive conclusion."

- Sgt. Ken York (Ret.) Indiana State Police.

"A perfect combination of detail and suspense. As chilling as a read, I couldn't imagine living it."

- James Hall, Indianapolis, Indiana

"A new Ann Rule on the literary scene; follow Carol Sissom on her frightening personal search for the solution to these murders."

"Carol Sissom, with no previous experience in detective work, takes you step-by-step on her frightening search for truth."

"Carol Sissom is proof that one person can make a difference; and what a difference she makes in this decades-long unsolved crime."
- JoAnn Green, Indianapolis

"I loved the book. I had a hard time putting it down. Ended a lot differently than I expected."
- Gary Jennings, Indianapolis

Dedication

To my best friend,
who sticks closer to me than a brother.

THE DISCLAIMER PAGE

This is where I get to disclaim anything and everything, apologize for anything and everything, and tell you that I am not responsible for anything in this book that may harm, offend, defame, libel or injure anyone.

THE LASALLE STREET MURDERS is the true story of my life and the relationship I had with the one and only man arrested for the most sensational, celebrated, gruesome, unsolved murders in the history of the city of Indianapolis, Indiana.

The story you are about to read is true. Absolutely every effort has been made to verify facts and make sure every part of this book is accurate. However, in some instances – such as recreating some conversations and scenes and dialogues of the deceased and murdered victims this was impossible. The names, scenes and characteristics of some individuals were changed for their safety and to protect their identity and the identity of their families. Some names, characters, places and incidents are used fictitiously. Any resemblance to actual persons, living or dead, events or locales is entirely coincidental. Some parts have been fictionalized in order to move the story along. Therefore I am not responsible for anything in this book that mistakenly portrays anyone or anything in an inaccurate or unfavorable way. It was purely unintentional. I am not responsible for anything that harms or injures anyone in anyway, including those who are not alive to defend themselves.

I would like to both thank and commend the Indianapolis Police Department, The Marion County Sheriff's Department and both of their homicide divisions, including the countless homicide officers and others who worked endlessly on this case for years, even decades. There are those of you who not only lost sleep over this case, but you sacrificed yourselves, your health, your marriages, your families, your privacy, your friends and even your reputations all for the solving of this triple homicide. You missed weddings, Christmases, birthdays, graduations, promotions, anniversaries, vacations and even lost money and your sense of humor over this case – all for the pursuit of justice in The LaSalle Street Murders.

A special Thanks to Actor Steven Seagal.

About The Author

Carol Sissom is a freelance writer, investigative journalist and a contributing writer/reporter that has written for the following media organizations on various projects: The Saturday Evening Post, Indianapolis Magazine, Indianapolis Woman Magazine, Indianapolis Monthly Magazine, Nuvo Newsweekly, The Indianapolis Star, The Fine Line Christian Newspaper, Charisma Magazine, The Zionsville Times, The Zionsville Mainstreet and Lifestyle Magazine.

Her detective writing has been featured in The Wall Street Journal, Indianapolis Monthly Magazine, many television and radio programs, Geraldo, The CBS Evening News, Inside Edition, Hard Copy and The 700 Club.

Along with the above, Carol Sissom has freelanced as a correspondent and feature writer for Newman Video Services in San Jose, California, which produces documentaries. She has been a writer and correspondent for Charisma Magazine in Lake Mary, Florida. Her most recent article for them was her story on "Former President William Jefferson Clinton." Carol has received a first place national award at The National Federation of Press Women Conference for her cover story feature of a USAIR crash survivor. She has received the Thomas R. Keating Feature Writing Award twice. The first occasion was in 1986 for Best Deadline Feature – "Drug Dealing in Indianapolis" and the second time in 1991 for Best Overall Winner, Feature Writing – "Cab Drivers" – "Teenage Suicide" – "Battered Women." She has received the Eugene Pulliam Scholarship twice. Carol received a bronze medal of honor, an award in 1995 from The National Vidocq Society, in Philadelphia, for "Outstanding Contribution to Law Enforcement in The United States" for her contribution in helping to solve the oldest murder mystery in the history of Indianapolis, Indiana.

In 1996, Carol won another law enforcement award from The Vidocq Society, a gold plaque titled, "EVERYONE LOOKED, BUT ONLY YOU SAW." She is also the author of a book "Pure

Heart: The Biography of "One Man's Message to America" (the true story of a young man known to be one of the greatest youth pastors in America – killed in 2001) which is being written for the Richard M. Bourke Foundation.

Carol Sissom
P.O. Box 17247
Indianapolis, Indiana 46217

Dear Reader

In 1991 I was a freelance journalist and a single mother when I wrote a 20-year anniversary story about the greatest unsolved murder mystery in the history of Indianapolis, Indiana – the LaSalle Street Murders – on December 1, 1971.

The slayings of three good-looking bachelors who had their own microfilming company, ties to organized crime and The White House – plus a romantic contest to see who could have the most women in one year – was a notorious, grisly, sex-driven triple homicide that launched the most intense investigation in the history of the Indianapolis Police Department.

I quickly became addicted to the case – and after writing my article, I began to uncover leads and witnesses that the police overlooked in 1971. I eventually developed a suspect that I hoped would be profiled on the television show, Unsolved Mysteries.

Overwhelmed with an abundance of my own research and material, I decided to write a book about the murders. In the midst of my research, I met an elderly man who claimed to have ESP – an ex-husband of one of the lovers of the victims. We shared a common interest about the murders and the grandfatherly figure insisted on helping me write my book. He told me that I had identified the correct killer – confirming it with his alleged psychic abilities - and offered other priceless information. I admired his knowledge - he knew more details about the murders than anyone I had ever met. Together, we penned several chapters together and he helped me in my attempts to solve the case. We became a good co-writing team. Over a period of several months we became good friends – until one day, to my horror – I realized my original suspect was not the LaSalle Street mastermind – the real killer was my friend and co-writer of my book – GRANDPA!

I reeled at the thought that I had been writing a book about a triple homicide with the killer!

But not for long, I immediately began my own intense undercover assignment – determined to get grandpa behind bars – when I realized the police had no intention of – and possibly a secret agenda against – arresting this man.

With a handful of police officers that believed in me, I fought a lonely battle against a political system for four years until one day I achieved success. The story you are about to read is a true account of my journey – and a chronology of my life – as I detail the relationship I had with a suspected killer – and the dangerous odyssey I embarked on in order to get him in jail and solve these murders.

I have a voluminous amount of material to share with you. I tried to pick out the best parts of my life with such a limited amount of space. I omitted many facts and culpability that would affect the case or a police investigation. I wanted you to truly share in all of the suspense and intrigue with me – as I tell you what happened during my journey. Amazingly, the most bizarre part of this story is how the killer and I both changed from the first chapter to the last. You will see how our relationship transformed by the final chilling chapters. You will see what drove both of us to the edge – and an unsuspecting end.

Stay tuned, and please make sure your doors are locked before you start reading this.

- Carol Sissom

Foreword

The woman had a hideous look on her face when Rock pried her
fingers away from the glass she was holding. She didn't even drop
it when she died, Rock noticed with surprise. She had held onto it
so tightly. For dear life, actually. It was the look of horror - laced
with amazement - on her face before she died that he pitied. It was
such a shame she didn't want to spend time with him tonight. She
could have stopped it all, that's for sure. But she *had* to argue with
him.

It was her fault, Rock admitted, shaking his head.

Now he'd have to bury her in the basement - with the others.
Now she could lay quietly with them - in peace.

He gently pulled her auburn hair away from her face and
tucked it underneath the collar of her blue and white pinafore
dress. Her apron had an aqua blue background with a pattern of
delicate white circles in the shape of pinwheels all over it.

It was all so dainty-looking, he noticed. He could tell it was
made of a sturdy material, though. Something very nice to be
buried in, he thought. It would protect her from all of the dirt.

The kitchen floor was a mess. It would take a long time to
clean it up. Dark red blood was smeared all over the pale blue
linoleum - right up to the edge of the white cabinets lining the
south wall. It was so thick it looked like chocolate syrup. He
noticed it was starting to run down the metal register in the floor,
near the last cabinet. It undoubtedly would drip all the way down
to the basement below.

He hoped it wouldn't smell like the others did. He knew he'd have to burn extra incense tonight.

He looked at his watch. Only three more hours to go and she would be calling. The young reporter called him every night and every morning like clockwork. He was always waiting for her - with baited breath. The game was so challenging, so fun. He looked forward to it nightly.

"Pretty One," he said to himself as he tidied up the place. "It's a shame you weren't with me tonight. If you were - this wouldn't have happened. Now I'm going to have to find another housekeeper."

1

THE KILLINGS

November 30th, 1971

On this wicked and cold Tuesday morning, the LaSalle Street killer woke up hungry. He was thirsty for blood – for a human life begging for mercy at the end of his fingertips. He could taste blood on his lips and on the tip of his tongue – even the roof of his mouth was tingling for it. He knew that he could kill again – tonight would be easy because he'd done it before. He knew how to punish people for their sins. He knew that even tonight wouldn't be his last time to take a life – there were others that would have to pay for their transgressions. He was so looking forward to it – that he practiced the scene over and over again in his mind – excited at the thought of getting even – finally. Tonight would be his chance to get revenge. Punishment would be paid to the man that had betrayed him. The debt would be paid off with the expertise of his right hand and the long, sharp knife he was taking with him.

As he walked down the long sidewalk to his car, he moved with calculated steps one at a time. He counted his footsteps in his head as he listened to himself breathe with excitement. He visualized how much fun he was going to have doing it – he knew exactly what time he wanted the man to suffer. He was anxiously waiting for the hours to escalate to the time of doom.

Hours rolled by into minutes, and finally, shortly after 5 p.m. he began his journey into death. He loaded up a shotgun, a type-writer, a box of rope, duct tape and memories. He set off to take a man's life. He licked his lips with anticipation – salivating almost as he drove to his destination. By the twilight hours of December 1st, 1971, the job was done. He had a smirking, dirty smile on his face as he carried the knife – still dripping with blood and the remains of human vertebrae on it – and got rid of it. When he was finally driving home, it was bitterly cold, about 20 degrees out-side, and a tiny flurry of snow splattered on his windshield, hint-ing that Christmas time was just around the corner. But he wasn't cold at all. In fact he was burning up inside – bursting with adren-aline and excitement for what he had done. He was happy with how the night had gone. He had gotten more than he bargained for – at least three men had suffered under his knife tonight – the more the merrier he decided when he got there.

2

ONLY THREE MILES AWAY......

I had no idea that I was going to come face to face with the LaSalle Street killer.

I was just seven years-old and I had an innocent look painted with freckles, dimples and long, tender eyelashes. I wore shiny blond hair in pigtails and homemade cotton dresses way past my knees. I was a second grade student at Grassy Creek Elementary School on the far east side of Indianapolis. It was a small brick building nestled far out in the country where farmers raised pigs, cattle, corn and tomatoes they sold at the City Market on Wednesday mornings. It wasn't unusual to see a cow grazing by my window when I was taking a spelling test. The smell of manure was rich and full whenever I played outside at recess. My teacher, Mrs. Malstrom, a delicate woman who smelled of special perfume and wore expensive clothes, said that she recognized I had an unusual, unique talent right away. I penned an award winning story about alligators and she submitted my work to a larger competition. I won the first of many trophies at the end of the year. To her delight, this inspired me to develop a hunger and a thirst for writing and journalism.

It would never go away.

Unfortunately, it would lead me into a lot of danger some day.

3

BRUTAL MURDERS

It was an especially nasty homicide.

A dark and ominous chill flirted with the air on the afternoon of December 1st, 1971, as a man by the name of John Karnes found three businessmen slaughtered in their home on LaSalle Street on the Eastside of Indianapolis. Not only was he a member of the Indianapolis Police Department – he was one of their closest friends. What he found devastated him for the rest of his life: a massacre that was the most gruesome, grisly, unbelievably horrifying murder case in the history of the Indianapolis Police Department.

His friends, the victims, were Robert Gierse, 35, Robert W. Hinson Jr., 27 and James Barker, 26. All three men were best friends and they had more in common than anyone realized. They were good looking, clean-cut, suit and tie-wearing executives, well-known and loved in the community. They worked in the microfilming business of photocopying top-secret records. They had connections to nearly every bank, insurance company, real estate entity and upscale business in the city – as well as ties to Washington, the CIA, the Pentagon and the underworld.

While they were men they were still boys at heart – *playboys* in fact, known to be Casanovas who romanced women all over the city, leaving broken hearts both in the pubs and the suburbs. They were legendary as lovers who stole hearts coast to coast.

Gierse and Hinson, who both lived together at the house they were murdered in, had just formed their own microfilming company. They called it B&B Microfilm Company. It was on the north side of East 10th Street, adjacent to an Alert Cleaners and right across the road from the Merchants Bank and a Burger Chef Restaurant. James Barker was to join the duo in their newly founded business in January, 1972.

The LaSalle Street Murders quickly gained the reputation as the *greatest* murder case in the city's history because of the brutality of it. Each of the men were bound, gagged and tortured. They had their throats slit from ear to ear. The police officers who discovered the dead men said it was the most ghastly, ghoulish crime scene any of them had ever encountered in their entire careers. It sent more than one man to his knees vomiting. Blood was everywhere – on the walls, the furniture, the hardwood floors and the hallways. The slimy red plasma even flooded the bathroom where one of the men was found. It looked like a rainstorm with human remains had made a torrential downpour inside the tiny home.

The incredible story about the macabre slayings made headlines at the Indianapolis Star every single day for close to a month, with breaking news topping the paper for decades. The sensational story even reached national and international news outlets. To sum it up in a sentence: *The LaSalle Street Murders rocked the city and rocked it hard.* The senseless cruelty of it sent residents reeling in shock, fear and disbelief.

"What happened?"

"Who did this?"

"Why?"

These questions were on the lips of nearly everyone in Indy, both young and old alike. The sweet little farming town, nicknamed the Crossroads of America because of it's latitude to

Chicago, Nashville, Los Angeles and New York, was now a famous place on the roadmap of death, danger and chilling suspense.

The case went unsolved for days, weeks, months and years, stumping the local Indianapolis Police Department, the FBI and even the CIA. It baffled the most intelligent of the bureau's investigators because of the incredible number of possible motives: Business, robbery, sex, jealousy and the most unusual news, Robert Gierse was politically involved. The police interviewed over 1000 people – most of them attractive women who were lovers of the dead men. The case was publicly compared to the Charles Manson murders and Truman Capote's *In Cold Blood* story.

The LaSalle Street Murders became more than notorious. It became a part of Indianapolis history. From barber shops, beauty salons and sidewalk cafes to even the concrete playgrounds of the most innocent schoolyards - it was the most talked about murder case in the city – for over two decades.

*While most people thought it was strictly a crime of business – with all of the top secret microfilming records involved – a key suspect was formed. A former employer, a man by the name of Ted Uland, was the beneficiary of a $100,000 insurance policy on Gierse and a $50,000 policy on Hinson. He refused to take a lie detector test. (The former employer called the dead men twice on the night of the murders.)

*It was the victims' sexual encounters – most specifically those of Robert Gierse and Robert Hinson – that caused the most suspicion. It was a time of "free love" and the sexual revolution – the 1970's – and sex was on the minds of everyone…whether they approved of it or not.

*The greatest irony in the case was the fact that Robert Gierse did meet and know former Teamster Jimmy Hoffa in 1966.

*Gierse met Hoffa in Chicago. It is said they met because all three murdered men used to live in Chicago. They all worked for a Chicago-based microfilming company, Bell and Howell.

*Gierse's boss while they worked in Chicago was Senator

Charles Percy. He was from Chicago. Percy's twin daughter was also a victim of murder in 1967. Police for several years thought there was a connection.

*Robert Gierse was involved in the Republican Party. He worked on several election committees for several years.

*Robert Gierse did microfilming work at the Pentagon. It was confirmed that he was doing microfilm work in Washington at the time of his father's death.

*The police verified there was microfilm missing from the death scene, according to Gierse's brother.

*Gierse's brother, Ted Gierse, St. Louis, had been eliminated as a suspect to the cops early on. He declared his brother was extremely intelligent, a man who had an excellent photographic memory. "I wonder if Bob saw something he wasn't supposed to – on microfilm," he said.

*There were suspicions that the murders were related to the slayings of several other microfilm salesmen. An Indianapolis microfilm salesman named John Terhorst was murdered in March, 1971 when he and his 1966 black Corvette disappeared. He was a friend of Gierse's and Barker's. He was found shot to death in Eagle Creek.

*There was also concern about another salesman found shot to death – he was discovered with Robert Gierse and Robert Hinson's business cards on his body.

*Ted Gierse said, "When my brother Bob died, someone at the police department told me, "THIS COULD BE SOMETHING REALLY BIG!"

The Indianapolis News

FRIDAY MARCH 22, 1996

SUNNY
Clear and cold tonight. Low 16. Mostly sunny and
cool Saturday. High 37. Page B-4.
1 p.m. Temperature 33

THE
INDIANAPOLIS
NEWS
SINCE 1869

"Where the Spirit of the Lord Is,
There Is Liberty." - II Cor. 3:17

THE GREAT
HOOSIER
DAILY

ICING
THE CA
With season
coach readie

Blue Streak

25 years later, a murder charg

Grand jury indicts ___ 69,
in grisly 197_ ___ngs

"*Headquarters Detective* magazine,
Sept., 1973 issue"

James C. Barker   Robert Gierse   Robert Hinson

n a house on the 1300 block of
orth LaSalle Street on Dec. 1,
71, their hands and feet bound
and throats slashed.
"It's one of the ___
murder cases in ___

solved. To have the original investigators bring it to this conclusion
is really a relief," said Detective
Jon Layton of the Indianapolis Police Department. He began investigating the case in 1993.
The original investigators included former Marion County
Sheriff Joseph G. McAtee and IPD
Lt. Michael Popcheff, who testified
before the grand jury late last
year.
They had pressed for a grand
jury investigation several years
ago.
But it was not until Prosecutor
Scott Newman took office last year
that a decision was made to have

grand
"We'r
prosecu
and let
Layton
the gut
dence a
We're r
News
questio
instead
stateme
"Alth
challeng
the fact

Clubbed, Bound And Slashed To Death

Detective Magazine 1

NUVO Magazine

PULP FICTION?

IT'S STRANGER THAN FICTION. IT'S THE CONTINUING STORY OF 1971'S LaSALLE STREET MURDERS

By Carol Schultz

PULP FICTION?

COVER UP?

THE FAMILIES

NUVO Magazine

Cover Story

March 10-17, 1995

DEC. 1, 1971
2:26 P.M.

The front door was ajar, the porch light was on, and the morning paper was still on the steps.

When John Karnes came to the white bungalow on North LaSalle Street to look for friends who hadn't shown up for work, he expected to find three bachelors hung over from a night of partying.

Instead, he discovered the most gruesome bloodbath the Indianapolis Police Department had ever encountered.

"It's something you remember for the rest of your life," says Karnes, now an IPD detective.

Robert Gierse, 34, Robert Hinson, 27, and James Barker, 27, had been clubbed, bound and gagged, their throats slashed ear to ear. Blood dripped from the ceilings and walls.

"They didn't bleed to death," recalls Marion County Coroner Dennis Nicholas. "They asphyxiated when their spinal columns and windpipes were severed." IPD Patrolman Michael Williams was the first on the scene.

"There's been a triple homicide on LaSalle" he radioed to an unbelieving dispatcher. "Send me a coroner. And identifications. Send me a coroner this you can?"

The investigation, which involved the FBI and experts from around the world, was the longest and most intense in IPD history. Details of the murders reached news outlets from Canada to London and dominated the Indianapolis Star's head lines for weeks.

"A reporter from Washington told me this was the biggest thing since Manson," remembers Gierse's brother, Ted Gierse.

Police received 1,500 tips in the first week. IPD homicide detectives Mike Popcheff and James Strode found themselves overwhelmed with too many clues, too many motives, and no witnesses. The victims of the so-called "Nice Guy Slayings" had left a trail of intrigue.

The young executives recently had left a microfilming company to form their own firm, B&B Microfilm. They took clients from their former employer, who collected $140,000 in life insurance and refused a polygraph test after the murders.

In fact, the three apparently were involved in a sexual conquest game, a race to see who could sleep with the most women in a year. An address book found in the house listed more than 40 women's names, leaving the police sometimes jealous boyfriends, husbands and fathers to interview.

A week before their deaths, the victims had been seen arguing with a suspected organized crime figure at the Executive Health Club, an elite men's organization. They also were associated with a local gambler who ran junkets to the West Coast.

The trio were associated with two other murder victims, John Terhorst and Bobby Lee Atkinson, who also had suspected ties to organized crime.

Terhorst, a friend and microfilm salesman, was found shot to death in Eagle Creek six months before the triple murders. He had disappeared after going to sell his black 1966 Corvette to a "Hobby" on the East Side.

"I strongly believe the Terhorst murder was related to the LaSalle murders," says former State Trooper John Swearingen. "It was the only unsolved homicide in my 15 year career."

Atkinson, a known underworld burglar, was found shot to death in Morgan County three weeks before the LaSalle incidents.

"I am certain the triple murders are related to Atkinson's death," says former Morgan County Sheriff Paul Mason.

Although detectives Popcheff and Strode worked endlessly, no strong leads surfaced and no arrests were made. IPD became the target of cover-up rumors, especially after most of the evidence was thrown away inadvertently during a 1986 cleaning of the department's property room.

Any hope of cracking the case was very slim.

MARCH 1991

As a correspondent for The Indianapolis News, I wrote a story about the local taping of a segment for TV's Unsolved Mysteries. I decided to write a sidebar on Indianapolis' biggest unsolved mystery, and the LaSalle case was definitely the most notorious. Every policeman I interviewed remembered where he was — whether eating lunch or waiting at a stop sign — the day of the LaSalle ...

NOVEMBER 1991

Six months passed before the case for six months before I write a 20-year anniversary story. When I interviewed Popcheff, now an IPD businessman, he told me the intriguing details and mentioned there had been a recent tip, "a one-in-a-million shot." He didn't have time, but he suggested I check it out.

Popcheff said a waitress at the now defunct Thomy's Starlight Palladium had seen the owner talking to a man with "dark, crazy eyes" on the night of the murders. The description matched a tip from a ...

young Bible student ... three men — are ... drinking ... LaSalle Street ... murders ...

I spent thousands ... senses, with a ... on. I found ... prison. The ... Michigan family ... danger ... said "No or...

I learned ... reporter the ... identified the LaSalle ... ings, the police never acted on his ... series. The police never acted on his ... Theatre ... remote Florida town ...
who ...

I now believed there was reporting the murders, and they accepted it as ...

With months to wait before the show was scheduled to air, I tried to find more of the trio's relatives and associates, as well as many of the women listed on the "score card." It wasn't easy; many had married and moved away.

I also began retracing the strange lives of Gierse, Hinson and Barker. They were bartenders and womanizers with shady business connections but had also worked as special-education teachers and in-home volunteers.

With some help from friends — Tom Leyh, a photographer and research associate, and Michael Rogan, a bounty hunter who accompanied me on potentially dangerous interviews — I interviewed nearly 1,000 people. My home was filled with boxes and files of information on the murders.

I kept a picture of the man with the crazy eyes on my refrigerator for more than a year. But by the time I finally met James William Smith in December 1992, I was convinced that he had no part in the killings. Police agree that he is not a suspect.

Although the promising trail eventually proved to be a dead end, those eyes drew me into the case. I had become obsessed with the senseless, grisly murders of the three good looking bachelors.

JULY 1992

With my wealth of information, I decided to write a book. A man whose name had surfaced in my investigation — a wonderful, elderly war hero who claimed to have psychic abilities — offered to help me.

This man, who I'll call "ESP," was the ex-husband of one of Gierse's girlfriends. He said he had met Gierse once and had ...

B&B
microfilming
service co.

Bob Gierse's office on East 10th Street, where B&B Microfilm was founded in 1971.

Robert Gierse

Robert Hinson

James Barker

NUVO Magazine

B&B Microfilm housed the most top secret documents in Indianapolis.

4

TWENTY YEARS LATER

My name was Carol Schultz when I solved a triple homicide. I
was only 28-years-old. Some people say it was by accident, others attribute it to my relentless, persistent devotion to the case.
Some say it was because I became obsessed with the LaSalle
Street Murders. They are all probably right, but either way, I stand
firm that it was because I had a passion for adventure and a fear-
less streak inside me. I was afraid of doctors, hospitals and the
dentist - not gangsters, crooks or serial killers. I just liked solving
murders. I still do.

I stood five-foot-five inches tall back then – I always wore
high heels – and weighed no more than ll9 pounds. I had long,
curly blond hair, blue eyes and dimples. I was dainty, feminine,
enigmatic and full of questions. I was divorced and I lived alone
with my 10-year-old son in a secluded farmhouse, hidden by a forest of bushes and trees. We were nestled in a corner lot set far

away from the street – very few people knew where we lived.

I loved being a single mother, my country home and writing. I had won several journalism and writing awards while in college, which landed me a job as a newspaper correspondent for the largest evening newspaper in the state of Indiana, *The Indianapolis News*. My strength was in feature writing and investigative journalism. In 1991 I wrote an article about federal bounty hunters, which gave me my first taste of police work. When I learned that one of the best, most intense bounty hunters in the United States lived in Central Indiana, I couldn't wait to get an interview with him. Talking to Trent Marsh, a mysterious man that even the FBI relied on to catch their most dangerous fugitives, was a challenge in itself.

During our first meeting Trent was more than aloof. He was tall, strong and good-looking. His dark eyes were piercing and he wore his long black hair in a ponytail. I couldn't help but notice that he was the spitting image of the Hollywood actor Steven Seagal, both in looks and personality. From what I learned of him he lived an incredibly dangerous and intriguing lifestyle. He caught his criminals, dead or alive. He didn't have a girlfriend and didn't want one because of his career. Most of his friends and relatives - even the US Post Office - didn't know where he lived. I was instantly fascinated with him and the art of bounty hunting. I admired the way he made his living - putting the most violent escaped criminals back in jail where they belonged.

My bounty hunting story ran on the cover of the News' Extra Section. (I later won a prestigious award in feature writing for this article.) After it went to press I went looking for something even more unusual and interesting to write about. Police work had caught my attention.

It didn't take me long to find it. I heard that the television show "Unsolved Mysteries" was coming to Fort Wayne, Indiana, which was about three hours north of Indy. I learned that they were doing a segment on Big Brothers – Big Sisters of America and were profiling baseball legend Hank Aaron. I called Aaron's press agent and scheduled an interview. It was while I was covering this article for the Indianapolis News that I got a bright idea. I wondered what Indiana's greatest unsolved mystery was. I thought it would be good to write a short sidebar story about it to go with my piece on Hank Aaron.

How would I find Indiana's biggest mystery?

I made my very first inquiry at the Marion County Public Library. It was there that a woman told me about a sensational murder case that happened when I was just a small school girl.

"You've never heard about the LaSalle Street Murders?" the librarian asked me in a shocked voice. She was amazed that I hadn't heard about them.

"No," I told her.

"It's by far the greatest unsolved mystery this city has ever known," she told me, drawing a deep breath to be dramatic. "You have *got* to read about it. I promise you will not want to put it down once you get into it. It's so bizarre you will hardly believe it's true."

I took her advice and started reading as many articles I could get my hands on about this historical case. It captivated me from the moment I read the very first paragraph in the very first story. I knew instantly that this was it – the subject for my sidebar story. It was an incredible tale about three good-looking bachelors senselessly murdered only a few miles from where I grew up.

5

I couldn't help but think of Bob Gierse as anything but handsome. He was terribly attractive and I couldn't imagine why anyone would want to slit his throat – for *any reason.* I shook my head as I read more gory details of how he and his two best friends, Bobby and Jim, were executed and hacked up like animals.

I was hooked on the LaSalle Street Murders – from day one.

After reading several more articles on the slayings, I decided I had to do more than a small, 12-inch sidebar to accompany my Hank Aaron piece. When I looked at the calendar I realized that the 20-year anniversary of the LaSalle Street Murders was coming up in a couple of months. I felt confident that writing a 20-year anniversary article was what I should do. The story compelled me, drew me, from a deeper dimension.

I had to learn and tell more about it.

First, I telephoned the Indianapolis Police Department. In case there was any doubt in my mind, a detective confirmed that I had positively identified the greatest murder case in the Indianapolis Police Department's history. He oohed and aahed about the particulars of the slashings until I'd had enough. I knew it was time to go to work finding the venerate policemen who first tried to unravel this mysterious case.

I was told that Indianapolis Police Department Lieutenant Mike Ryker was the original detective on LaSalle Street back in 1971 – and he was still on the department working as a cop. He was now an honored lieutenant. I found his telephone number at the Shelby Street Southside District and called him. A civilian receptionist intercepted the call on his behalf. When I told her I was requesting a media interview with Mike Ryker, she checked with him and promptly replied that he had agreed to talk to me. An appointment was set up for the following Saturday morning. We arranged to meet at a restaurant near the scene of the LaSalle Street Murders.

I was excited.

6

November, 1991

When I walked into the Waffle House on East Washington Street it was shortly before 10 a.m. I scanned the crowded restaurant looking for the Indianapolis Police Department's Lieutenant Mike Ryker - the same veteran police officer who once led the city's greatest homicide investigation. He was tall, dark and Greek. He had an olive complexion and wore a crisp white Lieutenant's shirt, navy pants and a gun on his left hip. He had shiny black shoes and a polished appearance. He fit the stereotype of a police officer one hundred percent – I spotted him because he was drinking coffee and smoking a cigarette.

As soon as our eyes locked, I knew it was him and I waved.

I gave him what I hoped was a not-too-nervous sort of smile and he reciprocated with professionalism, warmth and interest. Mike appeared just as he had described himself over the phone. He even looked like one of those television homicide cops, only without the trench coat. Quickly, I took my seat in the booth across from him. I noticed that he smelled like Obsession cologne.

"Wow," I said right away. To me, Mike Ryker was a hero.

Mike smiled with humility.

"I am honored that I finally get to meet the original homicide investigator of the LaSalle Street Murders," I said with admiration. I wanted to ask him for his autograph.

Mike smiled again. This time I decided he seemed almost shy, but I quickly realized that he thoroughly enjoyed the attention I was giving his lifetime passion. I could tell he was a cop who had seen it all. He seemed to go down memory lane as I asked him to rekindle memories of the most important era of his career – and his entire life. I could tell it had been a long time since he had talked about it.

"Do you think the LaSalle Street killer is still alive?" I asked, point blank.

"Oh, yes," Mike told me with assurance. "Not only do I think he's still alive and well – I believe he will confess before he dies. It might even be a deathbed confession."

"A confession?" I asked. "After all these years?"

"Definitely," Mike said, staring at me with determination.

Intrigued, I conducted my first interview about the sordid details of the case swiftly and painlessly. I fired questions at Mike left and right, and he carefully and meticulously described the day he first set foot in the tiny white bungalow on LaSalle Street. The more he opened up to me, the more I could tell it was just like yesterday for him. When he told me how he observed the gaping throat wounds of Robert Gierse, Robert Hinson and James Barker, a cold chill ran through my body. All of a sudden, I felt like I could see him, shaking his youthful detective-head way back then, taking mental notes of what would be the most gruesome killings in our city's history.

"It was definitely a bloodbath," Mike said with a grimace. "More blood than I have ever seen in my life."

Mike told me how he was careful to secure the crime scene and how he and his partner, James Strode, took steps to go through the nearly 1,000 leads that would pour into the department over the next few weeks. The Indianapolis Police Department was undoubtedly overwhelmed, I realized. It was at a time when they didn't have an answering machine device to take the voluminous amount of calls that flooded IPD.

It was a case that would consume Mike's life for years – a case that almost destroyed his family, I learned.

"We worked this case every single day, 24-hours a day for weeks," Mike explained. He worked right through Christmas and New Years Eve that year, and he and his partner barely had time to get a couple of hours sleep and eat each day. Mike even missed his sister's wedding, which she still hasn't forgotten, he mentioned.

"I ate, drank and slept the LaSalle Street Murders," he said. "I was never home."

Mike explained that his biggest hurdles were the countless multiple motives for the crime:

It could have been sex. Within a few hours, he learned that the men were having a contest to see who could have sexual relations with the most women in one year. He told me that an actual scorecard was in the house – with 63 women's names etched on it.

The men, especially Hinson and Gierse, it was learned, had tallied their conquests up on the night of the murders.

"Really?" I asked.

"Really," he said.

"What a contest," I commented.

I was amazed that this kind of thing even happened. It became clear that there were likely many jealous lovers, boyfriends and husbands who wanted these men dead.

"Yes," Mike agreed. "The motive could have easily been jealousy. There were literally *hundreds* of jealous husbands, fathers and ex-husbands to interview.

It also could have been a crime executed by the quietest of our city's organized crime leaders in the community. It was learned that Gierse and Hinson were associated with local hoodlums and well-known gangsters – both in and out of state.

The business motive left even more endless possibilities for Ryker and Strode to pursue. They explored endless possibilities with Gierse's and Hinson's newly formed B&B Microfilm Company. The executives had an uncanny ability to discreetly copy the most top-secret records for some of the most high profile people and organizations in town. The most intimate details of the wealthiest Indianapolis residents fell into their laps. They had open accounts with Merchants Bank, Indiana National Bank, AFNB and several local insurance companies at the time of their murders.

What was dangerous about this? Robert Gierse was known far and wide to have a photographic memory. What he read stayed in his mind forever, it was said.

The men lived a life of cliché's. Gierse, Hinson and Barker were into fast, shiny cars, good-looking, fast women and having a lot of money. They were also into health and fitness. They were big men – each of them was the size of a football player, weighing nearly 250-pounds each. They belonged to a very special club in Indianapolis, where only the elite worked out. It was called *THE EXECUTIVE HEALTH CLUB.*

The CIA and the FBI were called in the very next day after the bodies were found. It is believed the CIA was in attendance at the two funeral services held for the men. The dead men maintained their playboy reputation *after* their murders. They left behind countless sobbing women who claimed to be their girlfriends. There were babes of all shapes and sizes – most of them very attractive. They were lovers who were devastated, uncontrollably wounded. Their hearts were broken. They were still madly in love with the men.

Even the Feds and the CIA agents shook their heads. They didn't know what to make of the brutal triple homicide, observers reported.

The city of Indianapolis never grew tired of hearing more details of the crime. Ryker became a celebrity on the local news as fearful residents hung onto every tidbit of information offered to them. He lived on the adrenaline of the case, which kept him going night and day.

The city of Indianapolis, with roughly over 700,000 people, quickly became chaotic. Mike and his partner had to make sense of it all. It was not an easy task. It was a "complete circus" of leads. Everyone thought they knew someone who knew something.

"In spite of it all, do you think this case is still solvable?" I asked Mike, as I wrote every word he said on a large yellow legal pad.

"Oh, yes," Mike said, sitting straight up in his seat. He seemed indignant for a split second. "There has been a new clue in the last couple of years. It's a very strong lead."

I looked up at him.

Mike went on to say, "This is a clue that could crack the case."

All of a sudden the Waffle House became so quiet you could hear a pin drop. Or so I thought. Dishes rattled and conversations continued again in an instant, but I believe the world stopped for just a second when Mike told me it was a priceless, "one in a million" clue.

I thought about it for a moment. This was a case that had stumped the city, *even* the FBI and the CIA *for two decades.* Why would a new clue surface now?

"They (the Indianapolis Police Department) would never give me detail to go and check it out," Mike said, looking me square in the eye as he spoke. "Why don't you go investigate it?"

I put my pen and paper down and stared at him.

"What?" I asked him.

"Why don't *you* go check it out?" Mike repeated himself.

"Me?" I asked.

"You," Mike said with finality.

I looked at him suspiciously.

"What's the clue?" I asked.

"Dark, evil, crazy eyes," he said.

"What?" I asked. I didn't understand. "Dark and crazy eyes?"

Mike talked like he was an announcer on a radio program. His dictation was perfect. He spoke with both confidence and precision.

"There was a man who came into the bar, Tommy's Starlight Palladium, the night of the murders," Mike explained. "This man went directly into the back of the bar and talked to the bar's owner, a man everyone in Indianapolis knew as *"The Expert."* It was a pretty intense conversation, he said. A waitress at the bar that night said she saw him come in and talk to *The Expert.* Her name was Angel Summer.*"*

I eyed Mike with both of my eyebrows raised as he continued. I was more than intrigued. I was captivated.

"I ran into Angel Summer recently," Mike explained. "A couple of months ago. She's now a go-go dancer but she remembers the night of the LaSalle Street Murders like it was yesterday."

"This man – the one who came into the bar to talk to The Expert that night – he had dark, evil, really crazy eyes," Mike said.

My mouth fell open as I followed what he was saying.

"This matched a statement we received from a young Bible study student who was going for a walk that night. He passed by the death house on LaSalle Street right around the time of the murders – about 9 p.m.," Mike explained.

The Bible study student's name was Michael Wray. He said when he walked in front of Robert Gierse's house that night, right about the time the murders were probably going on inside, he saw a man sitting in a car out front – *just watching* the house."

I waited for Mike to tell me the punch line.

"The young Bible study student said the man sitting in the car had incredibly evil, dark and crazy eyes," Mike told me.

My mouth fell open.

"There is no way that both the waitress and the Bible study student would both describe this man's eyes as 'dark, evil and really crazy' unless he was the same person.

"So this is my clue?" I asked Mike. "Dark, evil, really crazy eyes?"

"Yep," Mike said, looking at me as he took a drink from his cup of coffee. "You should check it out. See if you can find this man. He may not be the killer, but I would bet he'll lead you to some answers in this case."

I stared at Mike for a minute, then I looked away. I jotted in my notebook with the speed of a court stenographer.

I couldn't give Mike an immediate answer, but I was fascinated with his challenge.

"Call me after your story comes out," Mike said, flipping a couple of one dollar bills on the table for a tip. He stood up and walked to the cash register to pay the tab as I followed him. He walked me out the door.

"Get with me after the holidays are over if you're interested," he said, nonchalantly, and disappeared to his squad car. I couldn't tell if he was teasing me or daring me. Or maybe he was just joking, I thought.

I said "Thank-you," and waved good-bye to him, more than intrigued. With a Christmas scarf wrapped around my neck, my notebook and tape recorder tucked under my arm, I ran to the car to get out of the harsh wind that was biting at my face. I chewed on my bottom lip as I jumped in. I had never thought about investigating something as dangerous as a murder – but now that the clue was dangled in front of me, I knew I couldn't resist.

7

January 1992

The 20-year-anniversary story I wrote about the LaSalle Street Murders received more attention than I had anticipated. To my surprise, it ran on the front page of the evening paper.

"This murder was the talk of the town in 1971," Wanda said with a drawl. She was a petite store manager with coal black hair. She clerked at a Crystal Flash convenience store around the corner from my house. She sized me up and down as I purchased ten newspapers all at once. I explained that I needed multiple copies for my files, but Wanda still looked at me like I was more than a little strange as I bought them out.

"I remember this case like it was yesterday," she said from behind her cash register. "It was just awful."

My published story seemed to re-open an old wound about town. It reminded people how the Eastside had once been blanketed with fear. My editor at *The News*, Mark Ridolfi, called me at home the next morning to personally thank me for doing such a good job on the story. I seemed to have an uncanny ability to relate to the victims. It was as though I knew them, somehow.

It was no surprise to me, that, after Thanksgiving and Christmas was over, I couldn't quit thinking about the "clue" that Lieutenant Ryker had told me to investigate. What if the veteran police officer was right? What if the most famous murder case in the state's history really was still solvable – and it all hinged on this one lead? It really could all rest on *my* shoulders, I believed.

I decided to check it out or I would never be able to quit thinking about it. After New Years Eve and New Years's Day passed, on January 2nd, 1992, I began my search for the man with the dark, evil, crazy eyes.

"Where, oh where do I begin?" I asked myself. "How do I find this strange man who had incredibly dark, evil, crazy eyes?" I wondered what his name would be, if and when I found him.

"What do dark, evil, crazy eyes mean?" I pondered. "Were his the eyes of death? Eyes of evil? Eyes of Satan?"

I decided the first thing to do was to find the young Bible study student who lived near Bob Gierse's house in December, 1971. I found out his name was Michael Wray. Why not start with someone who saw him?

Lieutenant Ryker said the young man who was passing by that night lived by the nearby creek that ran adjacent to LaSalle Street. It was a wet, murky valley of waters that streamlined the neighborhood. How would I find the man who followed it like a mouse in a maze - right to the path of a sinister crime, twenty years later? What if he had moved out of state? Gotten married? Traveled out of the country? What if he was dead?

After relentlessly scouring the telephone book, line by line, calling every single person with the last name Wray, I found him! One of his relatives lived on a surrounding street. After a lengthy telephone conversation, I was able to obtain his phone number at his home in Michigan.

When I telephoned him, the Bible study student, now an older gentleman with a warm, Christian voice, was genuinely surprised to hear from me. He was congenial and offered what information he could. I couldn't wait to tell Lieutenant Ryker.

My second goal was to find Angel, the waitress at the bar, "Tommy's Starlight Palladium," in 1971. This is the woman that

Mike Ryker said saw a man with dark, evil, crazy eyes come into Tommy's the night of the murders and talk to the bar's owner, The Expert. Matched with Michael Wray's testimony, it could lead me to the unknown man with dark, evil, really crazy eyes!

One week later, I found out that the bar was only eight blocks away from Gierse's house. The dead men were known as regulars there because it was so close to home.

With a little tenacity - and the speed of the fingers on my right hand dancing on my telephone keypad, I found Angel! She was a go-go dancer at a seedy establishment near South Meridian Street, not too far from downtown Indianapolis. She was a very nice woman. When I questioned her, she was extremely helpful. She spoke with a throaty, cigarette-smoking voice and she was enveloped in warmth and sincerity. I liked her immediately. She remembered bumping into Lieutenant Ryker recently and telling him what she remembered about the wicked night of December 1st, 1971.

She wanted to help me.

I was pumped with adrenaline!

My third goal was to find the bar's owner, The Expert. I knew this one wasn't going to be easy. I put a call in to Trent Marsh – the mysterious bounty hunter I wrote about for *The News*.

"Be *very* careful with this guy," Trent warned me immediately. "The Expert was a former bail bondsman who also ran a car lot on East Washington Street. He was known to write bonds out of his car. He is supposed to be *very* dangerous."

Trent told me The Expert supposedly went to jail for mail fraud sometime in the 1980's. After a quick call to the Federal Bureau of Prisons, I found the Expert at a federal penitentiary out of state.

I sent him a letter – and to my amazement, a few weeks later, The Expert wrote me back. His letter was simple and typed on a sheet of sheer white typing paper. It had a prison return address.

A short time after I read The Expert's non-descript letter, he called me.

The Expert talked to me in an achy, throaty voice. He was extremely aloof but he was also thorough and polite. He was amicable and said he wanted to help me – he sure didn't *seem* dangerous. He definitely didn't seem like a criminal. I thought he sounded like a sweet man who ran the corner market down the street. But I couldn't ignore Trent's stern warning. When I questioned him extensively, The Expert denied owning Tommy's Starlight Palladium or even being in it the night of the LaSalle Street Murders. In fact, he denied knowing anything about *anything to* do with the LaSalle Street Murders. He didn't want to talk about Tommy's Starlight Palladium either.

Period.

So there. I had it. I had found all three of the people Mike Ryker had told me to find.

The Bible study student.

The go-go dancer.

The gangster.

These three people definitely did not lead me to a man with dark, evil, crazy eyes.

But they did wet my appetite to find more.

****

February, 1992

I couldn't wait to meet up with Lt. Ryker and tell him everything that I had found.

I made a list for him, documenting every single thing I could remember for his files.

I scheduled another Saturday morning meeting at the Waffle House near the Target Shopping Center on East Washington Street. It was a bright, happy little yellow building near the front parking lot of the L.Fish and Levitz Furniture Stores. This time, I wasn't too nervous to eat. I ordered a cheddar cheese omelet and dry toast with orange juice.

Lt. Ryker didn't seem to mind meeting me in person again. He smiled when he saw that I was armed with a briefcase and three notebooks.

"You're really serious about this, aren't you?" he asked.

I nodded eagerly, flipping through my papers as I looked at him. When I told him I had some exciting news, he had a new peace flash across his face. He complimented me on my story and shared some comments from some of his co-workers. I was bursting inside with all of the new information I had. I couldn't wait to tell him about all of the people I had met and interviewed.

"I can't believe it," he said. I could tell he was traveling down memory lane.

When I told Mike all of the neighbors and acquaintances I had found, he shook his head with amazement. He said he couldn't believe I had uncovered all of the people he had told me to find.

I surprised him with a list of contact phone numbers and he had a little surprise for me, too.

He let me look at the dead men's coveted telephone and address book.

I was in awe!

When I leaned over and touched it, I fingered the textured cover for a moment before I caressed it in my right hand.

"I can't believe I'm actually holding their little black book," I told Mike. I closed my eyes and could almost see Bob Hinson dancing with a beautiful woman on a dance floor. I pictured him to be charming, smelling of musk cologne, sweeping the most elegant woman in the room off her feet as he whispered romantic nothings into her ear.

Mike handed me another surprise. It was a small ledger. It was Robert Gierse's bank book. I looked at it and snapped back to reality.

I was more than awestruck. I was honored. I held the book in my hand like it was something from an historical museum. Like Elvis Presley's diary or something. It was small, about the size of my hand, navy blue and had the words *Indiana National Bank* engraved on it.

"Wow, Mike, this is incredible," I told him. "This really helps me get a feel for who they were."

"How did you do it?" he asked. "I mean, finding everyone so fast?"

I really didn't have an answer for him. I stabbed my eggs and looked up at him, fluttering my long eyelashes. "All I can say is it had to be adrenaline, Mike," I said.

I could tell he really didn't expect me to take him up on his "dare".

For a moment, I thought maybe he wasn't serious when he suggested I pursue the new lead, after all.

"You're the one who told me to do this," I reminded Mike with a direct look. I thought for a second he thought I had gone too far.

"I talked to all three of them at length," I said, showing him a large spiral notebook full of notes.

His eyes grew wide open.

"Angel Summer was great," I said. "You're right. She really did know what she was talking about."

I shot him another, independent look.

"What do you think her intentions really are, Mike?" I asked him. "Is she really trying to help solve a murder?"

Mike didn't seem to be responding to my comment about the former waitress. Instead, he seemed to be sizing me up.

"Are you mad that I did this?" I asked him. I couldn't figure out what was wrong. "Am I in trouble? Am I going to jail?"

"No, no," Mike said, surprised. "I'm glad you did. I told you the Department would never have given me the time to pursue this. I'm – I'm just surprised you found everyone so *fast*. You did a great job."

I smiled at him.

"What's next?" I asked him, eager for more to investigate.

He stared at me for a moment, like a doctor reading a report before he talked to the patient. He was a bit distant, which disappointed me. But I knew it was because he was tempted to go back on the LaSalle Street Murders as a full-time detective again. After all, it was a case that had once consumed every waking moment of his life. I could tell he was proceeding with as much caution as a school bus full of children traveling through an intersection. I realized he was hesitant not to let the case mesmerize him again.

He finally smiled back.

Perhaps he was amused with my tenacity, I'm not sure. But at least he flashed an accepting grin. I took it as a sign of approval.

"You need to find the guy with the crazy eyes," he said matter-of-factly. "You need to find out his name. Find out everything about him. Have you looked through any of the old Indianapolis Star articles yet?"

"Well, a few of them," I answered.

"They did a lot of stories on this case back then," he said. "And I mean *a lot.* There's probably something in one of those articles for you to pursue."

"Done," I told him. "I'll do the research by next Saturday. But next week I'm going to need some more clues about the case, okay?"

I chugged the last of my glass of ice water. "I need to learn more about these playboys on LaSalle Street, Mike. I'd like to start getting in touch with all of these women who were in love with them. I think *one* of them knows something."

Mike appeared to be lost in his past.

"Yeah, I bet they do," he said. "Maybe they'll talk to you now. Back then all they did was cry. My partner and I couldn't get any concrete leads out of any of them."

"How about their little black book?" I asked him. "Do you know if they each had one? If they did – I'd like to read it."

"Let's see how you do with this guy with dark and crazy eyes," Mike said, grinning at me.

I gave him an approving nod and a wink.

"If you can actually find him I might give you some more leads," he promised.

"Okay," I said. "See you next Saturday."

"You got it," Mike said.

Little did I know - our Saturday morning meetings would occur nearly every single week for almost a year.

With Mike's help, I was able to examine the large case file at IPD headquarters. I arrived at the Marion County City County Building on Alabama Street shortly after 9 a.m. It was a short ride in the east wing elevators to the IPD homicide unit. Once inside the arid cubicle, I shook the hand of the head of the Homicide

Division, (1992) for the first time, as Mike introduced him to me.

"Carol Schultz, this is Lt. Pink, he's in charge of all of the homicides in the Indianapolis District," Mike said.

I winced at Pink's firm handshake when he picked my dainty hand up, gripped it and gave me a hearty "Hello and welcome."

I sized up Lieutenant Charles Pink in a second. He wasn't anything like his last name. Pink sounded like the name of a Mary-Kay cosmetic sales rep. But Lt. Pink looked more like a championship wrestler. He was very masculine and extremely muscular. He carried himself tall, wore a shock of curly brown hair and I couldn't help but notice he was stout and respectable.

Lt. Pink asked me a lot of questions about my book, but he was smiling so much I didn't think much of it. He seemed to be sizing me up and down, like a new puppy on display at a pet shop. Everyone in the room was. They seemed to be intrigued with the new `LaSalle-Street-Murders-writer'.

Pink chatted with Lt. Ryker for a bit and then he disappeared down a skinny, musty corridor. He returned after a few minutes with the "THE BIG BOOK" - the original LaSalle Street Murders case file.

"I see there's a nice layer of dust on this," I joked, fingering the black ledger that was about 12-inches thick.

"Do you want me to wipe it off before I look at it?" I said, grinning.

Pink and Ryker both laughed.

"Yeah, nobody's looked at this for a long time," Pink said, looking across the room at Mike. "Glad somebody's finally writing a story about it."

When he handed it to me, I gingerly took it from him and set it down on a long table. I immediately flipped through the pages with awe and determination. I felt like a tourist on a European pass. I absorbed everything on every page. Everything was so surreal. I felt like I was in the Holocaust Museum in Washington.

I was honored to be looking through something so important in Indiana history.

After a while, Pink disappeared and returned with another large book. I couldn't believe my eyes. It was full of crime scene photos of the LaSalle Street Murders! I gasped and covered my mouth as

I took it from Pink's hands. I looked at the dead bodies of Gierse, Hinson and Barker for the first time. Page after page, it was truly fascinating. I realized that the men were nearly decapitated.

I felt overheated for a minute as I looked at their faces. The look of horror on Robert Gierse's and Robert Hinson's faces grieved me greatly. I knew their expressions would stay with me forever. It nauseated me.

Gierse, Hinson and Barker were memorialized like statues in a wax museum.

I was so caught up in the reality of the book I was reading, I didn't realize that Pink had moved behind my chair. He was standing next to me, watching over my shoulder as I looked at everything. When I glanced up at him, I noticed he had these incredibly intense eyes that absorbed every ounce of my being. It made me a bit uncomfortable – just for a split second.

I could see that he was amazed with the expression on my face. Was he enjoying it?

Pink was intrigued with *my* intrigue.

I saw that Mike was standing across the room, watching me as I took notes. He had to have noticed that Pink was guarding me and the LaSalle Street case file like a hawk. I appreciated that he was giving up his own personal time to help me.

For the next two hours, with Lt. Pink's approval, I dug deeper and deeper into the books.

The brutal reality of the slayings fueled me to want to solve the case and find the man who murdered Gierse, Hinson and Barker. I was more determined than ever to find the man with dark, evil, really crazy eyes.

By noon time, I folded up the book and handed it back to Pink. I was mentally and emotionally exhausted. I stood up, stretched for a couple of minutes, sipped on a cold can of Sprite and moved through the room, interviewing several other IPD homicide employees. I spoke with anyone and everyone who would talk to me, both male and female. I took down phone numbers and memorized case-file numbers. I moved on to evidence and fingerprint technicians, forensic specialists and even the property room manager. Everyone was extremely cooperative.

The case ensnared me. It had endless avenues for me to explore. I knew in my gut – I *had* to find out who was behind this senseless crime.

8

The following Monday I was at the downtown Marion County
Public Library on St. Clair Street by l0 a.m.

Indianapolis was a first class city with a first class library system. I was ready to spend the day investigating, so I loaded up an
assortment of apples, peanut butter crackers and boxed orange
juice in my backpack. I drew up plenty of pens and a big empty
notebook, prepared for anything and everything I might find.

I was ready to crack a murder.

I went up to the fourth floor and researched as many of the old
Indianapolis Star articles on the LaSalle Street Murders as possible. I learned everything was stored on microfilm. Gathering the
multiple boxes of reels was no easy chore, but a library clerk
helped me out and soon I was whizzing through the stored files
without a glitch. I was fascinated as each story sped into my sight,
all with the flip of my wrist on a tiny dial held between my right
thumb and forefinger.

I studied every page and meditated on every headline. I felt
like a scientist dissecting a small animal. I spun the wheel again.
A weird feeling went through my body as I read intently. I felt a
haunting chill as I scanned each article. It was amazing how so

many different stories on the triple homicide had captured the front page for so many straight days. The *Star* headlines were impressive – they even booted President Nixon and his trips to China to the back of the paper and the bottom section. The LaSalle Street Murders were just as dramatic and captivating as the assassination of John F. Kennedy in 1963.

I started to feel like I personally knew Bob Gierse, Bob Hinson and Jimmy Barker because I had read so much about them.

The personal photos of the men were just as inviting. Some of them were so engaging they made me want to cry. I turned my head sideways and nearly stood on my elbows to get the best angle to view them all.

I wished I had been a reporter in 1971. I wondered what it would have been like to have met the men.

"If I was Bob Gierse's age in 1971 – would I have been some-one he would have dated?" I thought.

It was obvious my hometown was once just as absorbed with the men as I was. The police investigation continued to dominate every newspaper for the rest of 1971 and the early months of 1972. It appeared to have gained the same attention as the Charles Manson slayings had. There were even surveys, asking people what they thought about the case.

I observed that the majority of the articles were written by four reporters at the Indianapolis Star. Their names were John Gibson, William Anderson and Harley Bierce. The more I read I noticed that the majority of the pieces were written by John Gibson.

I learned that he was *the* one and only John Gibson who was the lead reporter on an investigative team that wrote a series of articles in 1974 about corruption within the Indianapolis Police Department. The first article in John's series was published on Sunday, February 24, 1974. John's series won the Star a *Pulitzer Prize* for special local reporting in 1975.

Undoubtedly, his byline caught my attention. To me, John Gibson was a hero in Indianapolis. I was honored to talk to any reporter who had won the coveted Pulitzer Prize.

I decided to call him.

"Yes?" John Gibson answered when a Star operator transferred me to his extension at the Indianapolis Star that afternoon. He had a dry, vacant voice when he picked up his line.

I hesitated for a split second.

"Can I help you?" he asked, as though I was bothering him.

I told him that I was working on the very old LaSalle Street Murders case. I told him what I had been doing.

He didn't waste much time setting me straight.

"What are you doing messing around with the cops on this case?" he said, sounding thoroughly disgusted with me. "I solved that case a long time ago. Have you read any of my articles yet?"

I had to admit that I had not completely read them all.

"Well, *read* them," he said. I thought he sounded disgusted with me. *"Read them all."*

I was taken aback by his sharpness.

"Well, Mr. Gibson," I said with respect. "If you actually solved this case a long time ago, then why didn't you work with the police and get it officially solved?

I didn't give him time to answer.

"What about an arrest and a conviction?" I asked him. "Why didn't you help the police get an arrest?"

"Humph," Cady said, mumbling something in direct difference to my suggestion. He let me know that any kind of unity between the police and the press was not favorable. Not in this town.

"Call me back when you're more informed," Gibson said with wisdom. I thought that he was growling at me.

"Okay," I said, but I felt offended when I hung up the phone with Mr. Gibson. I knew that he was a decorated journalist. In spite of his offensive bedside manner, I agreed to read all of his articles.

It was another trip to the downtown library the next day - and another backpack of peanut butter sandwiches and fruit for ammunition - that proved more than helpful to me.

When I printed out John Gibson's articles, I couldn't believe my own eyes. The veteran journalist wasn't joking. He named three men – obviously hoodlums and reputed thugs – as the LaSalle Street killers in his article. He clearly alleged that they were involved in the murders. He even had photos of the gangsters to go with his story.

I couldn't believe my eyes.

One of the men had dark and crazy eyes!

I asked an assistant at the library to copy and blow up the article. I enlarged it by 300 percent.

Unbelievable!

One of the men pictured, a man by the name of Johnny Wilson Dough, had DARK AND CRAZY EYES! The eyes looking back at me were incredibly EVIL!

I was speechless. I couldn't wait until the next Saturday morning at Waffle House, so I could show Mike Ryker what I had found!

I thought that I might very well have found the LaSalle Street killer!

9

March, 1992

I waited until Mike had finished his breakfast that Saturday morning before I showed him the picture of Johnny Wilson Dough.

I watched him intently, careful to capture his expression when I showed him John Gibson's article and the photo of the man with dark, evil-looking eyes.

Mike's expression was dull. His dark brown eyes fell across the photo. When he was done studying it, he looked up at me. He was not as excited about the picture of Johnny Wilson Dough as I was.

He seemed *more* upset about the conversation I had with John Gibson.

"So, let me get this straight," Mike said with blatant sarcasm in his voice.

I was prepared for the worst.

"He solved the murders back in 1977?" he asked me in a dry, monotone voice. I could tell he was irritated.

I nodded, still excited about the picture.

"Why didn't he call *me* when he solved these murders?" Mike asked pointedly.

I felt uncomfortable in my seat. I said nothing to the cop who was upset.

"If he found the LaSalle Street killer then why didn't he bring the information to us so we could make an arrest?" Mike asked me. He was very offended.

"What does it matter *who* solves it – as long as it gets solved?" he demanded.

I stared down at my scrambled eggs. I tried to make circles in them with my fork, so I wouldn't have to look Mike in the eyes. I scooted my whole wheat toast around my plate to keep busy.

Mike continued to stare at me, shaking his head. I shrugged my shoulders in reply. I was disappointed that he didn't share my enthusiasm. I couldn't answer Mike's question, but I offered him a suggestion.

"It's either hostility or pride," I told him. "And probably a little bit of both."

Mike gave me a dirty look on John Gibson's behalf, but he softened a little, to let me know he wasn't mad at me.

"But Mike," I said, pleading with him. "I want to *help* you. I want to help the *police*. And I really think this guy Johnny Wilson Dough could be **the** guy. Gibson could be right! Come on, Mike. Just look at this picture. Look at these eyes! They are so penetrating they could cut steel! And they are definitely dark, evil and crazy eyes!"

Mike just shook his head. Even the waitress pouring him his third cup of black coffee looked at us sympathetically. We were becoming a regular on Saturday mornings.

I told the Lieutenant I had an idea.

"Mike, I still have the phone number of Katherine Kavich at Unsolved Mysteries. She was a really nice woman that I worked with when I was doing the story on Hank Aaron last year," I said. "How about I give her a call and tell her what I've found. If this guy Johnny Wilson Dough really did do it – then maybe they could come out and do a show on the case. They could help us find this guy and even flush him out!"

Mike just looked at me.

He was suspicious.

"Come on," I said, feeling like I was pulling my son's arm to leave the playground. "Unsolved Mysteries is supposed to have amazing results in helping police solve cases."

He shrugged his shoulders and gave me an unassuming look.

"You can if you want to," he said. "But I doubt it will do any good."

"I think it will really help, Mike," I said, trying to encourage him and hide my excitement at the same time. "This case is going to be solved. I just feel it."

"You do?" he asked. I could tell he didn't know what to think at this point.

"I really think so," I told him, trying to sound positive. "I'll call Katherine first thing Monday morning."

10

The second Monday morning in April, 1992

I kept my word to Mike. I was so anxious I was up at dawn to make myself some Maxwell House instant coffee and scan the Indianapolis Star. I had to while away the time until I could call the show's California phone number. I waited on the sun and for the city to wake up. It was always refreshing for me to pad outside in my bare feet in the morning. I liked to dip my toes in the wet grass saturated with dew and nature. I prayed to God that Katherine would agree to do a story on my case.

A few hours later I finally reached Katherine on her private line. She was amazed at what I told her. She said she couldn't believe all that had gone on since I had last talked to her.

"Yes," she said. "We'll do it. I love it, Carol. If I can get an approval from my superiors, we will definitely come out to do a story."

I almost screamed with delight.

"What kind of people do you have that we could interview on the show?" she asked.

"Oh, Lieutenant Ryker for one," I said. "And then there's

Robert Gierse's brother, Ted. He lives in St. Louis. And James Barker's mother, Endress. She lives in West Virginia. Who else would you like to talk to? I could probably find a dozen or so other cops to come on the show."

"Women," Katherine said.

"What?" I asked her. "Women? You don't like men?"

"Yes," she laughed with a little girl's laugh. "I like men. I'm married to one. But I want to see some of the girlfriends these LaSalle Street boys had. I want to see what they look like now – if they're still carrying a torch after all these years. I want to find some of them to go on the air and talk about what great lovers these guys were."

"You got it," I told her. It was a major task, yes. But I knew I could do it. Women are extremely difficult to find because they change their names, hairstyles and they can gain and lose weight so easily. They are masters of disguise. I promised her I would find as many girlfriends of the dead men as possible to go on the air. ASAP!

Excited, I called Mark Ridolfi, my editor and friend at The News.

"How about a story about Unsolved Mysteries coming to town?" I asked Mark, explaining a new slant I had on the Murders. I was confident that he would be just as excited as I was.

But I could hear Mark shaking his head.

"I'm sorry, Carol," he said, trying not to disappoint me. He didn't share my enthusiasm. He was all journalism. He didn't want to tell me, but I had overstepped my bounds. I was more concerned with solving a murder than writing about it.

He said I was starting to sound more like a cop than a reporter.

"Carol," Mark said gently, but with a firm voice. "We can only take so many news stories about the LaSalle Street Murders."

I fell solemn and quiet. You could hear a pin drop.

Suddenly, I realized that I had had more fun meeting with Mike Ryker on Saturday mornings – and being an amateur private detective - than I ever did writing newspaper articles as a hobby. I realized that I hadn't written about anything else but the triple homicide since last Christmas.

Mark was encouraging.

"Why don't you take all of this material you have and write a book about the murders?" Mark suggested. "You've got *so* much information."

Immediately, I tingled all over. I visualized the dozens of manila file folders I was collecting in my bedroom. I remembered all of the files I was gathering on my computer.

"You know, I think you've got something, Mark," I said.

"I think you could write an excellent book," Mark insisted. "I'm looking forward to reading it."

"Thanks, Mark," I said.

That very afternoon, I drove over to the death house and parked my car right in front of Robert Gierse's former house. I spent at least an hour, just staring at the tiny gray bungalow. It had been professionally remodeled with new paint and happy-looking shutters. It obviously had a fresh coat of camouflage that weakly covered up a permanent stamp of horror. It had a decorative nuance, but underneath, the house screamed "AMITYVILLE HORROR." Even from the nearby curb where I was parked, the house gave me an eerie feeling. I wondered why the new owners had revamped and restyled the house. I wondered what kind of creepy things they heard in the middle of the night when everyone went to bed.

That night, I wrote the first chapter in my book. I wrote about a Saturday night of dancing and partying that the three bachelors had just before they died – at the bars near their home – the Idle Hour, The Hi Neighbor and the Palomino Club.

When I was done, I titled it, "Dark and Crazy Eyes on LaSalle Street."

I could hardly go to sleep.

11

April, 1992

I was on a mission.

I had to find the women.

I needed to locate Bob Gierse's, Bob Hinson's and Jimmy Barker's former lovers as soon as possible. Time was of the essence. I had to move quick. I needed to find them not only for the camera, but for my book and for myself. Unsolved Mysteries was scheduled to come out in September, only a few months away. If I started immediately, I figured I could have the women all lined up – Kleenex boxes still in hand – for the camera crew and producers to capture their grief – twenty years later.

I had it all figured out in my head. I just *knew* this would make a good program – and ultimately produce good results in helping the police solve the murders. I was determined to expose Johnny Wilson Dough and have him arrested. I thought sure he was our killer!

Besides, I could always kill two birds with one stone. I could find women to interview for the show and for my book at the same time! I sifted through my notes and photographs and decided to start with the most important women in the men's lives.

After much scrutiny, and a tender photograph of Robert Gierse's 34th birthday party only 12 days before his brutal death, I decided on one woman.

Diane Norton.

I had to find her.

She was the most important woman because she was Robert Gierse's main girlfriend at the time of his murder. He was the most important victim because he left behind the most suspects. This was because he was the oldest, he was the owner of B&B Microfilm Company, he had extensive political ties with the Republican Party, he had once done work for the Pentagon, he had known Jimmy Hoffa and he was the one that owned the house where all three men had been slashed to death.

Diane was more than just Bob Gierse's Saturday night date, however. Even though he blatantly dated other women, Diane was Gierse's confidant. She was his lover. His passion. The woman he trusted his deepest secrets with. The woman whose breasts he laid his troubled head against at night. The one he felt most comfortable with. The one he slept soundly with during the midnight hours – when others thought he was somewhere else.

Diane was the only woman Bob Gierse said had captured his heart. Forever. Even though the executive bachelor had been married before – and even though he had turned the hearts of many others to Jell-O, Diane was the "only" one he said he had ever really loved. In fact, she was the woman who had planned and orchestrated his final birthday party – held only two weeks before he was murdered. I knew I couldn't stop until I found her. There were too many clues to be researched at that birthday party. It was said to be exotic *and* erotic.

I had read that there had been rumors of pornographic movies made by the murder victims.

After exhausting the most obvious resources to find the sophisticated, elegant beauty, I realized it was going to take extra-ordinary efforts to find her. I pressured myself because of my promise to give Unsolved Mysteries exceptional interviews with the men's lovers. I even shared with my friends that I had great hopes that the filming of this show in September would help police put the case to rest. One night, I even dreamed of Johnny Wilson Dough surrending to police on the night the show aired.

Unfortunately, two decades had left more than an ugly scarlet stain on the once carefree Indianapolis. I feared that Diane, under the heavy cloud of rumors that her boyfriend was the victim of an organized crime "hit", had plenty of time to change her identity and virtually disappear.

Amazingly, one sunny spring afternoon, I received a supernatural miracle. It was the hook I was looking for. Irony played a definite role in my search for Diane Norton.

I was getting ready to get a tune-up on my car. I drove a royal blue Honda Accord that I had purchased brand-new off the showroom floor in 1990. I paid $11,000 for the first and only new car I'd ever owned in my life. I always kept up with the scheduled maintenance at the dealership, protecting it's newness as though it were a precious piece of jewelry.

I telephoned the dealership to make an appointment for my regular maintenance. I spoke with the receptionist who answered the dealership at Ed Martin Honda at length. I was shocked to learn that her name was Louise Henderson. She was the very same woman that I had read was Robert Gierse's secretary at B&B Microfilm when he died!

It was more than ironic! We talked and agreed to meet somewhere away from the car dealership. We met at the Ground Round on East Washington Street and Shortridge Avenue for coffee a few nights later.

I learned from Louise that the murders of her employers had devastated her, leaving a permanent scar on her broken heart. It was easy for me to see why they had hired Louise. She was beautiful, in every sense of the word.

"They hired me for my legs," Louise said, smiling sheepishly. Indeed, she had the gams of Marilyn Monroe. Her beautiful brown eyes were as captivating as Princess Grace and her figure – at 50 years old – was that of a 30-year-old. In spite of the grief the LaSalle Street Murders had caused her, she carried her age well. I was so impressed when I met Louise Henderson, I gave her a big, warm hug when we were at the restaurant.

"Thank-you for pouring your heart out to me," I told her.

I could tell Louise wanted to cry. She reached into her purse for a tissue. She broke down and confessed that she was still deeply in love with Robert Gierse, Robert Hinson and James Barker. The murders were so vicious and so senseless, she was mystified. She encouraged me to do everything I could to solve them.

Approximately one week later, destiny – and Louise Henderson – helped me find the lead I was looking for! The voluptuous and attractive Louise Henderson led me straight to Diane Norton!

I thought about how competitive the women were with each other back then. Louise Henderson was a good-looking, eye-stopping woman for her age. She smelled of expensive perfume and carried herself like an educated model. Even though she was a good Christian woman and the mother of seven small children in 1971 – she was still constantly surrounded by men.

It was no wonder Robert Gierse had taken her in. She would have been an asset to any corporation.

I wondered if and how well Louise Henderson and Diane Norton really knew each other. I wondered how jealous all of the women involved with the good-looking executives were of each other. How many of them knew about each other and how many were kept in the dark?

What kind of love triangles did the dead men keep?

12

"Ed Martin Honda, may I help you?" Louise Henderson said when she answered the telephone the very next Friday afternoon when I called the auto dealership. I needed to have my tires rotated and the Honda people knew my car so well, I decided to have it done at Ed Martin's.

"Yes, you can help me," I answered Louise. It was a beautiful day full of promise. The birds in my backyard were singing and I had fresh laundry drying in the sunshine on my clothes line outside. I was in a good mood and ready for a miracle.

There was a pregnant pause on Louise's end.

"Yes," I said again. "I'd like Honda service, please."

"Is this Carol Schultz?" Louise asked, sounding surprised to hear from me again so soon.

"Yes. This is Carol," I said. "Hello, Louise."

I still couldn't get over the coincidence that Louise worked where I had my car serviced. What a small world.

"How are you today?" I asked.

"I'm fine," she said, so country you could almost see apple blossoms when she talked.

"How's your book coming?" she asked.

"Good. Good," I said. "Do you have anything new to tell me?"

"Nope. Nothing new," she confirmed with her thick Kentuckian accent.

"But I did have a question," she continued before she transferred my call to the Service Department. "Are you still trying to find Diane Norton, Bob Gierse's old girlfriend?"

"YES!" I said, without hesitating.

"Well, I think I might have a clue," Louise said. She was for real. I could tell she wasn't teasing me.

"A man by the name of Mr. Rock Norton calls in here all the time to talk to Mr. Ed Martin, the owner of the entire dealership," Louise informed me. They were not friends, but Rock did a lot of business there.

"I think he is Diane Norton's ex-husband."

"You're kidding!" I said. "Tell me you're kidding, Louise!"

"No, I'm not," Louise said. "Do you want me to ask Mr. Martin to see if he can get his phone number for you?"

"Yes!" I answered without hesitation.

"Okay," she said. "I'll see what I can do."

"Oh, Louise, you're a doll," I said. "This will be good. If you speak to him, and he doesn't want to give you his phone number, feel free to go ahead and give him my telephone number, just to protect *his* privacy.

"Okay," Louise agreed. "I'll call you back later."

"Okay," I said, and peeked out my window to look at my shiny blue, four-door Honda Accord sitting in my driveway. My car was like my sister. She was three years old and had never given me a bit of trouble. I was always careful to take good care of her. I never missed a scheduled checkup or tune up.

Not only had my car been dependable, now I believed she was bringing me good luck.

13

It was almost 4:30 p.m. when the telephone rang in my living room.

I was taking a bath on the other end of the house, in my tiny blue and white ceramic bathroom that I had decorated with blue and yellow flowers. It was the most cheerful room I had – cropped with daisies and lilies and powders and crystals and every kind of sweet smelling scent imaginable. Even though I was immersed in the sauna-like heat and had silky bubbles up to my elbows, I knew instinctively this was a call I needed to take. I quickly slushed and slurped out of the tub, slinging water puddles around me as I glided across the floor. I scooped up a yellow terry towel from underneath the sink and raced to the living room.

"Hello?" I said, out of breath as I answered the phone.

"I am looking for Carol Schultz," said a solid male voice on the other end of the phone.

"This is she," I answered, patting my right calf dry as I wiggled the telephone cord around my toweled body.

"This is Rock Norton," the voice said, dictating into my ear like a military sergeant reporting for duty.

"I received a message from a one Louise Henderson at Ed Martin Oldsmobile to call you," said the militant voice on the other end of the telephone.

"Oh, yes," I replied with surprise as I plopped down on my sofa and tossed my son's jacket across the room and onto a chair.

"Thank-you for calling me, sir," I said. I was surprised that he had called me so soon after my conversation with Louise.

"How can I help you?" asked the warm male voice, his tone softening with my attention.

"Sir," I began honestly, "I am desperately looking for a woman by the name of Diane Norton. Louise Henderson suggested to me that you might be the man once married to *the* Diane Norton who used to date a Mr. Robert Gierse in 1971. He was famous because he was a victim in one of the most horrible murders in this city's history."

The silence that followed my announcement was without reproach. I could have whispered, "A penny for your thoughts" out loud.

"*I* would be the man that you're looking for," Mr. Norton said with gentle sincerity. "May I ask why you are looking for Diane?"

"Because I am writing a book about the LaSalle Street Murders," I said, proudly.

It was almost as though the men on LaSalle Street belonged to me now. They were like family. They were a part of me. I wanted Mr. Norton to know why I wanted to trespass in his past.

"Do you remember the LaSalle Street Murders very well?" I asked the stately gentleman. From the sound of his voice, I pictured that he looked like the actor Roger Moore in the **James Bond – 007** movies.

"Yes, I do," he said with the poise of an articulate, educated gentleman. "I remember them *quite* well. It was a very famous case in this city's history."

I was impressed that he knew of the case that I was so immersed in. "Do you think you could help me come up with a phone number for Diane Norton?" I asked him.

There was another deep, thoughtful silence.

"Well, she's moved to Florida," Rock explained. "And we haven't spoken to each other in years."

There was another repetitive silence.

"But I think I can coax one of my children's grandparents into giving me the number so I can give it to you," Rock gestured with true helpfulness.

"Oh, thank-you," I told Mr. Norton. I was both overwhelmed and grateful.

"So, tell me more about this book you're writing, Mr. Norton said with a genuine curiosity. "I've always been fascinated with this case. What's the title of your book?"

"Well, I think I'm going to call it, `**Dark and crazy eyes on LaSalle Street**," I told him. Then I shared the tale of how Unsolved Mysteries was going to come to Indiana to profile this case. For some reason, I trusted the sound of this man's voice. In an odd sort of way, Rock Norton sounded just like my own father, who died when I was just fifteen years old. There was an immediate connection between this man and my own father. Even the inflection, tone and pitch of their voices were the same.

"Really?" Mr. Norton said, his voice elevating with concern. "I'm certain Diane would want to know about this."

"I hope so," I told him. "I really want her to be on the show."

With no disrespect to the elderly man I was talking to, I shifted the conversation off of myself and onto him.

"So, what do you do for a living?" I asked Rock. I guessed him to be about 60 or 65 years old. He sounded the same age as my father would be, if he were still alive.

I was pleasantly surprised to learn that he was in the car repair business – *just like my father was!* My Daddy owned his own auto body repair business that flourished on the Eastside in the 1970's.

"How do *you* know Mr. Ed Martin?" I asked Rock.

""Oh, I've known him for years," Rock said. "I've been in the business of automobiles for 40 years."

"Really?" I asked him. "So was my Daddy. He used to work for Miner's Body Shop over on 30ᵗʰ Street near Keystone Avenue. Have you ever heard of Miner's?"

"Why, yes, I have," Mr. Norton said. " A man by the name of

Ben Miner used to own that, didn't he?"

""Oh, my God!" I said loudly, covering my mouth because I almost shouted with excitement. "Ben Miner was *my* Daddy's boss!"

"I know a lot of people in this town," Mr. Norton said. "I've been in this town for a long, long time."

"Wow," I said. "I don't believe it."

Mr. Norton changed the subject this time.

"So, tell me more about your book," he prodded. "The LaSalle Street Murders affected my wife seriously. I mean, it almost put the woman in the nut house. She has never been the same since."

I identified with Rock Norton's fatherly type of voice. I felt like he could be trusted like my own father. Or maybe it was because of his automobile-industry background that he was so easy to talk to. Whatever the reason was, *I immediately felt safe with him.*

"Oh, there's so much to tell, I don't know where to begin," I told Mr. Norton. "I've been snooping around this case for almost a whole year now."

"Really?" I could hear his voice pitch raise ever so slightly.

"Yes," I confided in him. "And I think I know who the LaSalle Street killer is, too!"

"No kidding!" Mr. Norton replied with amazement. He wanted to hear more.

"Yes," I said. I let him know the truth as though he were my very best friend.

"It's a long story, but I even know his name! I've been follow-ing him for months. I've been working with the original homicide detective on this case for a while now."

"Is that right?" Mr. Norton asked, intrigued.

"Yes," I told the male voice that instantly made me feel encour-aged. "I've got a lot of information. That's why I started writing a book in the first place. I have *too much* information, in fact. Way too much for many more newspaper articles. So I just decided to take off and write a book about these murders."

"So who is your suspect?" Mr. Norton asked me casually.

Just then, there was a knock at my front door. Startled, I apologized to Mr. Norton and said, "Excuse me! Could you hold on for a moment?"

"Of course," he said.

I appreciated the distraction. It gave me a chance to put the phone down, toss my towel on the couch, throw on a pair of Levi's blue jeans, a cotton T-shirt and answer the front door. I couldn't imagine who it could be, this time of day.

14

I could hear metal screaming against concrete and the clatter of business-goings-on in the background as I picked up the receiver to talk to Mr. Norton again. He didn't seem to mind being put on hold for nearly five minutes. I could hear a silence that listened for me with a hungry intrigue. He was patiently waiting to finish our conversation.

"I'm back," I said, apologizing for interrupting our talk. "It was the paperboy."

"So," Mr. Norton began again, apparently undistracted by my brief absence. "Tell me more about this book you are writing. Tell me more about the murders."

"Oh my," I said as I thought about how impressed I was with this man. He seemed to be genuinely interested in my favorite topic.

"It all started with a very simple little story I wrote about Hank Aaron," I said, repeating the story for the umpteenth time.

I could almost hear Mr. Norton leaning forward in his seat, his full attention on me.

"Hank Aaron? The baseball star?" Rock asked me. He sounded

impressed.

"Yes," I explained, taking a sip of water so I could tell my story with moist lips. "You see......I was a correspondent for the Indianapolis News when I wrote a story about Unsolved Mysteries coming to town to do a show on Hank Aaron and Big Brothers/ Big Sisters of America.

I wondered if Mr. Norton were taking notes.

"So I got to meet and interview *the* one and only Hank Aaron," I relayed. "He even gave me an autographed baseball. I also became friends with one of the producers of Unsolved Mysteries. Being an investigative journalist, I thought it would be really neat to write a sidebar story about *Indiana's* greatest unsolved mystery – to go with my Hank Aaron piece."

I had to stop and take a breath.

"So, I had to find out what Indiana's greatest unsolved mystery was in order to include it with my story," I told him.

Mr. Norton was listening to me politely.

"So I began making calls," I said, practically telling Mr. Norton my life story. "I started out with the library, the police department, the Marion County City County Building, and with anyone and everyone I could think of. *"What's the biggest unsolved mystery in the State of Indiana?"* I asked everyone.

"And everyone came up with the same answer," I revealed to him.

"Is that so?" Mr. Norton commented.

"Oh, yes, definitely," I told him.

"It was funny. I had heard about the LaSalle Street Murders when I was a little school girl," I told Mr. Norton.

"I can remember my Daddy taking me for a drive in his big black Chevrolet Apache pickup truck," I said, telling him about my favorite fishing story with my father.

"I can vividly remember Daddy and I driving by LaSalle Street," I remembered. "I knew without a shadow of a doubt – I had the right mystery for my story. The LaSalle Street Murders."

The response on the other end of the phone was an appreciative, "Hmm."

"So, I began researching the case," I told Mr. Norton. "All on my own."

"Really?" Mr. Norton asked. He seemed to be cheering me on.

"I talked to a man by the name of Spencer Moore who was the head of the Crime Stoppers Division at IPD," I told Rock. "He confirmed what I had just found out. One thing led to another and then another. Before the day was up I'd found a half-dozen people to talk to me about the LaSalle Street Murders.

"It was weird, Mr. Norton," I said, keeping my face close to the phone. "It was just like talking to people about where they were the day President Kennedy was shot. Everyone seemed to remember *what* they were doing on that famous day – December 1st, 1971 – in Indianapolis. It was downright *spooky*. This story absolutely fascinates me, in a creepy sort of way."

"Me too," Rock Norton said, agreeing with me.

"My God," I continued. "This case had it all. The men were good looking playboys."

"Well, I don't know about *that*," Mr. Norton chipped in.

I smiled at his gesture. "They had dozens of playboy girlfriends – both married and unmarried. And they were executives. There was talk of organized crime. Even the CIA and the FBI were involved. And these men – they led some really interesting lives. I couldn't put the newspaper articles down!"

I heard a muffled shuffling of papers on the other end of the line. I wondered if Mr. Norton was getting bored with my talk.

"Before you knew it, I found myself driving by that house on LaSalle Street just to get a feel for where they were murdered," I shared with Mr. Norton, certain I still had his steadfast attention. "And a feel for this spooky case that stumped every cop in town."

I heard a soft chuckle on the other end of the line.

"One thing led to another and after writing a 20-year-anniversary story about the murders last year – I began writing a book about the LaSalle Street Murders. My boss at the Indianapolis News, Mark, suggested it after he said he could only publish so many stories about the case," I informed Mr. Norton.

"You know, I was inside that house once," Mr. Norton said quietly. He was popping up with information out of the blue.

"You are kidding," I said, pronouncing each word carefully. I was shocked at his announcement.

"No, I am not kidding," he said.

"How? What happened?" I asked, astonished.

"Well, the day of these murders, my ex-wife was missing and I was extremely worried about my two children, Steve and Misty" Rock explained.

"So I drove over to the house where it happened. The news was all over the radio – the street was jam-packed with people gawking, trying to get a look at what happened. Well, when I got there, I just walked up to the front door and told the police officer guarding the house who I was and he let me inside," Rock told me.

"I told the cop I knew the men were international spies," he said.

"Wow," I said, in awe of someone who had actually been inside the death house on LaSalle Street.

"Well, I saw it *all*," Mr. Norton said. "The house was indeed what you call a bloodbath. I saw a body with a white sheet over it – and red blood was seeping through," he said.

"Your detective-friend, Lieutenant Ryker wasn't joking when he told you it was a bloody nightmare. There was blood EVERY-WHERE. Those men were slaughtered like pigs."

"That's incredible," I told Mr. Norton, wincing as I pictured it all. "You have my full attention, sir."

"What else did you see?" I asked him.

He appeared preoccupied with someone talking to him from the shop he worked at.

"Well, you know I don't quite have time to go into that right now," Mr. Norton said. "But I would really like to get together with you on this. Maybe we could have dinner and talk sometime."

I was flattered. This stately gentleman wanted to meet *me.*

"Where do you live?" he asked. I imagined he had a pen and paper in hand when he asked me.

"On the Eastside," I answered him without hesitation.

"Good. Good," he said. "So do I,"

"I've got to get going here," he said. "But tell me this. How many people do you have helping you write that book of yours?"

His question took me off guard.

"Well, no one really," I said. "I meet with the detective, Lieutenant Ryker, about once a week or so to go over everything I find. I'm trying to get the book done by the time Unsolved Mysteries gets here to tape the show this fall."

"Interesting," Mr. Norton said. "You don't have much time."

"I know," I said.

"I could really help you with this book you're writing if you're interested," he offered.

"Are you a writer?" I asked him.

"No," he said. "But I do have something called total recall. Do you know what that is?"

"No sir," I admitted.

"I can read an entire, 600-page book and then turn around and recite it all back to you – start to finish," he explained.

"WOW!" I exclaimed.

"I was in World War II and I was able to help the military do a lot of things," he said. "I even won the purple heart."

"Oh my goodness," I said. "I am honored to talk to you!"

"I also have what is called extra-sensory perception. ESP," he said, continuing to explain his qualifications to be my co-writer.

"You are kidding!" I said, praising my new friend with his astounding abilities.

"No, I am not kidding!" he said, almost profoundly, like he was making a public advertisement. "I could really help you in a lot of ways. I know *a lot* of information that could help you write a best seller."

"Really?" I asked, believing him.

"Really," Mr. Norton said. "You sound like a very intelligent – and probably very attractive – young lady. I'd like to help you out. And I'd like to hear more about this detective – what did you say his name is...Detective Dumbo?"

I giggled. "No, it's Ryker," I said. "And it's Lieutenant."

"Hmm," Mr. Norton said. "Well, I have to go for now. If you're interested, we could get together and I could help you out."

"That would be *awesome,*" I told Mr. Norton. "I've never met anyone besides Mr. Ryker who knows so much about this case. You are *so* helpful. I am very grateful."

"Oh, you'll be surprised at what I know," Mr. Norton said. "I really do have ESP. I could probably help you solve these murders you're writing about. In fact, if you stick with me, I may just help you win the Pulitzer Prize."

Pulitzer Prize?

I was speechless. I didn't know what to think of what this man was saying. I did believe in miracles, however.

"Mr. Norton," I asked. I was listening to him with my eyes closed. "If you truly do have ESP – what can you tell me about the murders right now? Right this very minute! What happened to Robert Gierse?"

"Well," he began. He seemed impressed that I would ask his opinion. "This suspect you have – the one with the dark and crazy eyes – I believe he is your LaSalle Street killer. He's the one who masterminded the whole deal. You are on the right track."

"Wow!" I told him. I was immediately impressed by Rock's alleged psychic abilities.

I gave him a challenge.

"Do you think you could get your ex-wife, Diane Norton's telephone number for me pretty soon?" I asked.

"Yes," he said. "I'm sure I can get it out of the grandmother of my children. I'll call you back this evening or tomorrow."

"Thank-you, Mr. Norton," I said. "Thank-you *so* much."

"Thank-you," Mr. Norton said. "Just talking to you has made my day."

15

***

Spring and summer, 1992

For the next six months, Rock Norton and I worked closely together. We had to. We had a book to write together. A bestseller, Rock insisted.

Rock had been a tired old man, until he met me. When I came into his life, he seemed to perk up. He was indeed phenomenal. He knew more about the LaSalle Street Murders than anyone I'd ever met – even Lieutenant Ryker. In spite of my religious beliefs, I began to wonder if he didn't have some sort of psychic ability. He knew *so* much about the killings. He was even able to go into a psychic trance and describe just exactly how the men were bound and gagged, with their feet tied up, before they died. He told me who was killed first, second and last. He even described how they were tortured with vivid photographic detail. The police didn't even know who died first – *but Rock Norton did.*

Rock told me that the men were held up with a shotgun before they had their throats slit from ear to ear. He even told me what the men had to eat before they died: Pizza. He told me many intimate things that even "God didn't know," Rock insisted.

"That Robert Gierse - he left his big fat wallet lying on the coffee table before he had his throat slit," Rock told me.

"Really?" I asked, impressed with his insight.

"Really," Rock said. I thought I could hear him nodding.

"You are absolutely amazing," I told Rock. "How do you know all of this?"

Rock sounded genuinely humble. "Well, for one thing, remember I was *inside* that house after the men died. This big huge police officer – he stood about 6-foot-six inches tall – let me in. I told him I knew these guys were international spies and he let me right in the front door."

"That's awesome, Rock," I said, giving him a verbal pat on the back.

"I *had* to get in there," Rock explained. "I had to find out what happened to my children. My ex-wife was involved with that bum and I was worried about my kids."

"Your children?" I asked again.

"They were my life, and I was desperately worried about them," Rock said. "But apart from that, I do have a gift. I am able to know things that other people don't know. In a supernatural way."

I listened to Rock carefully, with respect.

"The gift I have is called Extra. Sensory. Perception," he explained.

Although I had no desire to participate in any psychic avenues myself, I continued to be amazed by Rock's ability to recount the lives of Gierse, Hinson and Barker before they died. He did this on a daily basis. We talked on the telephone every single morning every day. Sometimes it was several times a day. He always had something incredibly grisly to tell me about the case. It was as though he enjoyed captivating me with gore. If he didn't have anything from his memory for the day – he turned on his ESP to help me figure it all out – no matter what it was I needed to know.

In the meantime, Rock was checking *me* out. To him, I wasn't just an eager little reporter, hot on the LaSalle Street trail. He told me he wanted to know everything about me. I told him everything I could think of.

I usually called Rock at 6 a.m. If I was busy, I'd call him in the afternoon. After my son went to bed, usually around 9 p.m. I stayed up into the wee hours of the night, composing chapters. It seemed fitting – writing when the night was dark and only the hooting owls or the slaves of the midnight hours could hear me type. Sometimes I frightened myself as I crafted chapters based on Rock's knowledge of the murders. Some nights, nightmares followed my slumber as I fell into an eerie, foggy sleep. Sometimes this was only seconds after my head hit the pillow.

Daily, Rocked seemed as anxious to talk to me as I was to him. Each chapter was a promise of an even more exciting chapter. I seemed to satisfy a need in him to be heard, recognized, believed and admired. I made him feel important. He made me feel like I was doing the city a great service – answering questions that had been unanswered for twenty-some years.

Ours was a friendship that grew quickly. We handled each other respectfully and delicately. We had one vital thing in common – we were both passionate about the same thing – the LaSalle Street Murders.

"We've got to get this thing solved," Rock told me one afternoon in May. "We've got to work harder at it."

"You're right," I told him, agreeing with him wholeheartedly. "The time is at hand to solve this case once and for all. I feel it in the air."

After a lot of hard work and research, I finally located the man I suspected had committed the murders, Johnny Wilson Dough. The man with the dark, evil, crazy eyes. The man that the go-go dancer had said came into Tommy's Starlight Palladium to talk to the bar's owner, The Expert.

Johnny Dough was still alive and well, I learned. He was a former Teamster who was arrested and put into boy's school at only 15-years-old. I looked up his photo as a youth – he was scary looking and even had dark and crazy eyes back then! I was so convinced that I had found the right man – my original suspect – that I hired my bounty hunter friend Trent Marsh to drive by Johnny Wilson Dough's house in Florida while he was on a bounty hunting trip. It was the first weekend in June.

I was very nervous when Trent took off on his business trip. He honked and pulled into my driveway at an angle, his back tires still in the street. He knew I wanted to talk to him before he left town. I ran out to his car in a pair of blue-jean shorts and a flannel shirt. I felt like Daisy Duke in "The Dukes of Hazzard" television show. I stood in the gravel, barefoot, looking at him for a minute before I handed him a thin yellow manila folder full of information. Inside it there was a white envelope full of money. I paid him for his private detective services - I believed that a man is worth his hire. There was also an excellent photograph of Johnny Wilson Dough inside, directions to Dough's summer home, a number for the nearest law enforcement agency in Welaka, the name and address of a bar I believed Dough frequented, a few license plate numbers and Dough's vital statistics.

Trent took the paper from me and flipped through it for a second. I glanced inside his big white Lincoln Town Car. There were red leather seats and a digital console. I caught a glimpse of a row of handcuffs underneath the dashboard near the steering wheel. Near the passenger door, I saw a brown tip with a black handle. I knew instinctively it was a loaded shotgun. Trent was prepared to drive over 1,000 miles to catch a slew of "skips" that had been evading him, his partner, Keith, and the law for months.

Trent knew he had to bring them back "dead or alive."

I was honored that he wanted to help me out with my case while he was down there.

Trent could tell I was nervous. He shut the envelope and looked up at me.

"It's going to be okay, Darlin'," he said as I reached in the window and gave him a good-bye hug around his shoulders. With my face next to his neck, I could smell Trent's Laugerfield cologne. For just a split second, I got all emotional – like women do when they're being women. I suddenly realized how dangerous it was going to be for him. After all, if Johnny Wilson Dough was the killer I thought he was – Trent's life could be at stake.

Trent gave me a knowing squeeze around the arm.

"This guy can't be all bad, Carol," he said, making light of a serious situation. "He drives a Harley Davidson motorcycle. Anybody who drives a Harley has to have *some* good in him."

I smiled at him and he gave me a comforting wave good-bye.

Within five seconds, he had backed out of my driveway and disappeared around the corner.

I wondered if I'd ever see him again, alive.

16

Four days later…..

I wanted Rock Norton to be the first to know that I found Johnny Wilson Dough. I called him before I even thought about calling Lieutenant Ryker.

"I think I found Johnny Dough! I think I found Johnny Wilson Dough!" I said, raising my voice with excitement when I called Rock Norton at his auto shop that afternoon. "At least I found *a* Johnny Wilson Dough. I don't know if he's the same one in Dick Cady's articles, but I think this is the guy!"

Trent had called me from Florida on his car phone about 6 p.m. Tuesday night. He had spotted Dough that afternoon. He said Dough was coming out of a local market when he saw him. Trent flashed a few snapshots, took down the pertinent information I needed and was headed back home. He said his own trip had been successful and he had two fugitives handcuffed in his backseat. He was headed straight to the Marion County Jail on Alabama Street.

"I gotta get these boys' in the backseat here a steak dinner, and I'll be home," Trent said on the phone, joking. I laughed with him

– for just a moment - at his dry humor. I knew he meant what he said. He often bought his skips a steak dinner after a long, hard chase. He said he felt they both deserved it. When I hung up, I was glad he had a good trip. The mission was successful for both of us.

"You're kidding!" Rock said when I relayed the news. He sounded almost as excited as I was. I could tell he wasn't just pretending to be happy for me.

"I've traced him down to a trailer park in Welaka, Florida," I told Rock, sharing information on how I hired Trent to do a quick surveillance on Dough. "He's near Old Shell Harbour Road. It's pretty Close to Clearwater, Florida. He's about twenty minutes from Tampa."

"Really?" Rock said. He was silent for a moment and then I thought I heard him humming. He sounded like someone going into a psychic trance. I knew he was getting ready to use his ESP again.

"This will be great for the show Unsolved Mysteries" I told Rock, still excited.

"My ESP is telling me you are right on target," Rock said. "I think you've found your killer. We had better talk about this in person. Can you meet me after I get off work tonight?"

"Of course," I said. "How about the Ground Round?"

"I'll be there," Rock said. "Should I wear a suit and tie?"

"Oh, for goodness sakes," I said. "You can wear whatever you want. Don't dress up on my account."

"I like to dress up," he said. I could hear him smiling over the phone. "Besides, we have something to celebrate – finding this man Johnny Dough is a great accomplishment. He's a hardened criminal and *you* found him."

I didn't say anything to Rock's praise.

"But I do have a bit of criticism for you," Rock said, changing the tone of his voice.

"What's that?" I asked.

"I think you need to change the title of your book," he said.

"It's *our* book," I told Rock. "You're the one helping me write this thing. I can't overlook all you've done for me. I should share the byline with you."

Rock said nothing. I could just imagine him grinning.

"But why do you want to change the title?" I asked before he could respond. "I think "*Dark and Crazy Eyes on LaSalle Street*" is perfect."

"Well, I think I know of an even better title," Rock said. He had a mysterious edge to his voice. "I think you should call it, "WHO-DUNIT.""

I laughed out loud. "WHODUNIT?" I said, giggling. "I think someone else has already done that."

"Okay," Rock said, firmly. "Then you should name it – "Let's Call It Whodunit," Rock said. He was adamant that I change my title.

"Let me think about it," I said, pondering. "It is kind of a catchy title. I think I like it."

I pictured Rock grinning like a Cheshire cat on the other end of the phone.

He seemed to love helping me.

"See you tonight, Pretty One," he said.

"See you tonight, Rock," I said, flattered that he was calling me a 'Pretty One.' "Don't be late."

"Oh, I wouldn't miss it for the world," he said. "I'll be there."

17

I was very disappointed when Rock called me at 5:50 p.m. to cancel our dinner date.

"I can't make it tonight, Pretty One," he said. He sounded completely breathless on the other end of the phone. I heard a lot of rattling of what sounded like – tin cans ….and….was it bricks being shoved around?

I was shocked. I had spent most of the afternoon doing my hair, nails and makeup. I had pressed a fine black suit to wear and picked out an elegant black and diamond necklace to wear with it. I was ready to make a professional, good impression on the co-writer of my book. I couldn't believe he was canceling.

"I have to go bury someone," he said, offering more information than I expected.

"Bury!" I said, startled. "What?"

"Bury," he said, repeating himself. His voice sounded like he was indeed mourning something or someone. I assumed that one of his beloved pets had just died.

"Let the dead bury the dead," Rock said. "That's in the Bible you know. Check it out."

"I'm sorry, Rock," I said. I was truly disappointed. I was so looking forward to our first meeting.

"There, there, Pretty One," he said. "There will be other times for us to get together. I have important business to take care of this evening. But rest assured – your time *is* coming."

Then the phone went dead. For a split second, I thought I heard Rock Norton laughing softly on the other end of the phone.

Disappointed, I spent most of the evening writing another chapter. I telephoned Louise Henderson and interviewed her again. Afterwards, I scripted what I thought was one of the best chapters I'd ever written about the dead trio. She shared a scene about the first time she ever met her boss, Mr. Robert Wendell Hinson. I may have been mistaken, but as I wrote from the scribbled pen marks in my notebook that night, I wondered if maybe Louise hadn't fallen in love with her sympathetic boss. She said he *always* looked and smelled good.

I wondered what would have happened if Bob Gierse hadn't hired her as his secetary?

Does Louise know something she's not telling me?

18

September 1st, 1992

The next day, I received a call that I will never forget as long as I live.

It was a phone call that pierced my afternoon with both excitement and terror at the same time. It was about 2:20 p.m. and a brilliant, sunny day. There was not a cloud in sight anywhere.

When the call came through, I felt darkness all around me.

The man on the other end of the line sounded like he was a native from the South. I thought maybe he was from North Carolina or Alabama. Perhaps Tennessee. He sounded like somewhat of a mountain man. As soon as I heard his voice I pictured him in a deep woods, deer hunting and fishing for a living.

His voice permeated my entire being, like a bolt of electricity, when he told me his name was Floyd Michael Chastain.

He said he had received a letter from me, a letter I had written earlier this summer. A letter asking him to call me.

"I know things about the LaSalle Street Murders that no one else does," he said, enticing me with information.

For a moment I was startled. I looked around for a moment to see if my front door was locked. I didn't remember contacting the man. But then I recalled it – Rock Norton had encouraged me to contact a guy he had called a "dangerous criminal" – someone named "Mike" who might have a few leads about the LaSalle Street Murders. I remember I took his advice. I knew that Rock Norton was a powerful man with dangerous friends on the "inside."

I fired a short letter off to the man named Floyd at the address Rock provided. Then I forgot about it.

Until now.

"I know who the LaSalle Street killer is," I had told him in my handwritten letter. I let him know I was writing a book and asked if he had any information that could help me. In order to protect my privacy, I had signed my name with a pseudonym, Betty Thompson.

"Thank-you for getting back to me," I said when he called. "What more can you tell me?"

"I don't think you know who did it, Miss Betty," he said.

I told him what I knew and who my suspect was. Johnny Wilson Dough.

"You know a *lot*," Floyd said. "But not *enough*."

He said I didn't have the right killer identified.

"What do you mean – I don't have the right killer?" I demanded. "If I don't, then *who* is the LaSalle Street killer?"

"Ma'am, I can't tell you," Floyd said carefully on the other end of the phone. "I can only tell you if you come down here."

"What?" I said, almost shouting. "Down where?"

"To where I am at," he explained. "I'm in the penitentiary at Punta Gorda, Florida."

"Mr. Chastain, I can't come down there," I told him.

"Well, that's the only way I'm going to tell you," he responded.

I could see where this was going. No where.

"I'll see what I can do," I told him, stalling. I knew I couldn't leave my son and travel out of state at this time.

"Can you at least give me a clue?" I said, feeling my veins fill with adrenaline.

"Johnny Dough. Can you tell me if Johnny Dough is the LaSalle Street killer?"

"He is *not* the killer," Floyd said.

"What?" I asked. "Is the killer still alive?"

"Yes, ma'am," he said.

"Give me another clue!" I yelped. My heart was racing.

"He doesn't live in Florida, he lives in Indianapolis," Floyd said.

"Who is he?" I pleaded.

"Ma'am, I can't tell you," the man said politely.

I was starting to get impatient. I started to guess.

"Can you tell me what he does for a living?" I asked.

Floyd didn't respond.

"Is he a policeman?" I asked Floyd, hinting at corruption in the Indianapolis Police Department.

"Oh, no, no," Floyd said, adamant that he was correct.

"How about a lawyer? A doctor?" I said, guessing. "A dentist?"

"No," Floyd was firm.

"A judge?" I asked.

"No," Floyd said. "You are *way* off."

I felt like I was playing a "Hot or Cold" game that kindergarteners play with their parents.

"How about cars?" I asked Floyd, starting to guess no where in particular.

"Yes, ma'am," Floyd said.

"Wait a minute!" I said, my mind flooding to the obvious. I gasped for air.

"He is in the car business," Floyd confirmed.

I started to guess someone who was a driver at the Indianapolis 500, but Rock Norton's voice suddenly came to me like a trumpet sounding on Judgement Day.

"It's not Rock Norton, is it?" I asked Floyd.

Silence.

"FLOYD!" I almost screamed. I felt myself starting to hyperventilate. My mind raced to my son! His safety! What about the front and back doors of my house! Were they locked!" I wondered.

I felt like I was going to pass out!

"Is it Rock Norton?" I demanded. "Is *he* the LaSalle Street killer?"

"Yes, ma'am, he is," Floyd said quietly.

I couldn't even talk; I was in so much shock. I had been writing a book with a murderer! No wonder Rock knew so much about the case! He did it!

"That's all I'm going to tell you," Floyd was insistent. His voice stilled to almost a whisper. I wondered who was standing next to him as he talked to me.

"Floyd, I am writing a book with this man!" I screamed.

Floyd continued to be silent.

"You have got to be kidding!" I shouted.

But Floyd confirmed it like a judge pronouncing a sentence.

"No, ma'am," Floyd said with pristine authority. "I am *not kidding*. Rock Norton is *the* LaSalle Street killer. No doubt about it. I know because I saw him do it. I watched him kill Robert Gierse with his bare hands. I watched it with my own eyes. He slit his throat with a big ole' knife."

I was speechless.

"I am serving time here in prison today because I covered for Rock Norton," Floyd said. He wanted me to know the truth.

"Rock Norton killed the man, not me. His name was Reynolds. Al Reynolds. And Rock Norton beat him to death with a board over the head on December 2nd, 1982. I didn't kill the man, but I took the blame for it – covered for Rock Norton because he promised a lot of things if I took the rap for him. I did it because Rock *told* me to."

Floyd emphasized how Rock Norton was a cunning con artist who manipulated him into taking the blame for his murder. He gave me the name and number of a police officer in Florida to contact – a man by the name of Wayne Porter – someone he said would know of his Florida case.

"I am an innocent man serving time for a murder I didn't commit," Floyd told me.

I was glad I was tape-recording this call.

"And I know about the LaSalle Street Murders because I drove the getaway car that night," Floyd said softly, volunteering information regarding his involvement in the case.

I couldn't believe my ears. Here I thought the LaSalle Street killer was Johnny Wilson Dough, all this time!

"Floyd – I have to ask you one thing," I said to the man with a gentle voice over the telephone.

"Am I in danger? This man – Rock Norton – he knows where I live! He knows everything about me! We have been working on this book about the murders together for months! How much danger am I in?"

All of a sudden I felt very dizzy.

"I would say that you are in a lot of danger," Floyd said calmly. "This man is extremely dangerous. He not only killed those three men on LaSalle Street – he is a *serial* killer. He has been claiming lives all over the United States for the last 20 years."

Our time was up.

I heard the prison operator come on the phone and interrupt our call like a robot.

We had only one more minute to talk before the prison would disconnect our call.

"Miss Thompson," Floyd said, repeating my pseudonym carefully. "You have got to come down here to Florida to meet me. If you do, I will tell you the entire story from start to finish. Don't waste any time. This man could kill again. Soon.

I was speechless.

"You could be his next victim," he said.

And the phone went dead.

19

Needless to say, my day was shot like a rocket coming out of a cannon. September 1st, 1992. It was a day of divine intervention – a day that I would remember for the rest of my life. It was a slice of eternity to be recorded in Indiana's history books.

I immediately hung up the phone and tried to call Mike Ryker at IPD's South District. A secretary told me that he was gone for the afternoon. I started to panic. I knew I couldn't wait until the next morning to tell Mike what happened.

I started pacing the floors of my farmhouse like I was a victim in the movie, "Cape Fear."

Finally, a light bulb went off in my head! I called Don Campbell, the private detective! I had contacted him earlier in the summer as a source to interview for my book. He was someone I knew I could trust. He had been a homicide cop in the 1970's – when the LaSalle Street case was hot in the department. Don had become famous for solving the Tony Kiritsis hostage case. He was someone the other detectives in the department came to for advice. He was a former US Marine and one of the most intelligent men I'd ever met in my life. I just *knew* he could help me.

"DON! THIS IS URGENT!" I said into the phone, leaving

several messages on Don's answering machine. Darkness was ebbing around my house like a tomb. I was getting more frightened by the minute. I sent my son to his grandmother's house for his own safety. I flipped through the yellow pages, looking for a good hotel to stay at for the night.

I knew what I knew about Rock Norton could endanger my life.

"This is Don," said the confident voice on the other end of the phone. "Leave your name and number and I'll get back with you as soon as possible."

"Don!" I practically screamed into his phone recorder. "This is bigger than anything that's ever happened on this case in twenty years! Ever!"

"Call me right away!" I said, looking over my shoulder as I spoke. The room was empty, but I felt like eyes were peering at me from behind the bushes surrounding my living room windows.

"I have to talk to someone now!" I shouted into the receiver.

20

October 1992

Don and another former IPD sergeant, a kind man with sensitive eyes, silver hair and a warm smile, were at my house by 9 p.m. that night. He was a friend of Don's and a former IPD hostage negotiator. I could tell by his demeanor that he could probably talk anybody out of anything. I was glad he was there to witness what I told Don Campbell.

They didn't wear uniforms, guns or badges. They were wearing leather jackets and solemn, curious looks on their faces.

I pulled out my black and gray tape recorder, planted it on my coffee table and watched their faces as I hit the PLAY button. I let them both hear the tape of what Floyd Chastain told me.

I watched both of their eyes as they listened to it. I saw them shoot darting glances back and forth between each other. Afterwards, Don shook his head and asked me one question.

"You do have a gun, don't you?" he said.

"No, "I told him, surprised at his response. "I have a child in the house. There is no way I'd keep a gun here."

He looked at me seriously.

"I'm not joking," he said. "This man has gotten away with this for twenty years. What do you think he would do to you if you made him go to jail after all of these years?"

I looked at Don and then I looked at my front door. I shrugged my shoulders, but I knew the answer.

"I'll tell you what he would do," Don said, looking me square in the eye like any Marine would do. "He wouldn't think twice about killing you in the same way he killed those three men on LaSalle Street. *Your* throat would be slit from ear to ear."

I felt tears of fear swelling in my eyes.

Don looked very concerned for my safety. "I suggest you look into getting a gun. And learn how to use it."

"I'll make a couple of phone calls in the morning," he said, trying to comfort me. "I know just the woman you need to talk to. Her name is Lonnie Trader. She works in the Marion County Prosecutor's Office. I'll make sure you get in to see her right away."

I nodded, agreeing with everything Don told me. He was certain that, once Lonnie Trader heard my story, she would issue an arrest warrant for Rock Norton right away.

His instructions were simple.

"Keep your doors locked," he said. "And call this guy Rock Norton back in the morning. If you have been talking to him every day for this many months, NOT calling him could cause him to be suspicious. That could put you in immediate danger."

"Okay," I said. I felt myself starting to tremble.

"Keep your cool," Don said.

I stared at him with fear in my eyes.

"You'll be okay," Don said, encouraging me as he walked out the door. "Just don't let him know that you're on to him. If you do, I'm certain he'll be at your front door. And he won't be bringing you a pizza."

I nodded in agreement. I knew I would be sleeping with my Bible tonight.

"Thanks," I told him.

"You're doing a great job," Don told me as he left. "You may have just solved a triple murder."

21

Within one week I was seated in the office of Marion County Deputy Prosecuting Attorney Lonnie Trader.

She was a tiny, short woman with long, dark hair. To me, she was as famous as Princess Diana because she had just successfully prosecuted the Championship Fighter, Mike Tyson, for rape.

I looked up at her like she was Wonder Woman when she walked through the door.

She looked down at me like I was Betty Boop.

Trader's gaze fell across me like I was an illegal alien. She examined, scrutinized and interrogated me. I gave her information and tapes of Floyd Chastain and I talking. I handed her several other tapes of Rock Norton and I engaged in conversation about the LaSalle Street Murders. In the tapes, Rock and I were talking about the book we were writing together about the murders.

Lonnie, in the company of another Marion County Grand Jury investigator, was fair, generous, kind, polite and to the point.

She wasn't interested.

22

October 1st, 1992

I couldn't believe the Marion County Prosecutor's Office didn't want to arrest Rock Norton!

I figured I must have watched too many Columbo episodes as a child, because I naturally assumed that a) when you find a killer b) you go to the cops c) they go out and arrest him d) the bad guy goes to jail e) everyone lives happily ever after.

I was wrong!

Unfortunately, it was quite the opposite. A few days after I presented my entire campaign, a very compelling story to go out and arrest Rock Norton, I found myself pitted *against* this very powerful woman – Lonnie Trader. She had a reputation for her role in prosecuting Mike Tyson. I couldn't' figure out why she wouldn't just run out and arrest Rock Norton. After all, I told her he was a serial killer!

Undoubtedly, I was in for a rude awakening. I learned that, just because you know someone is a killer, (a *serial* killer no less) , it doesn't mean the authorities will arrest him.

End of story.

There are a lot more politics involved in arresting murderers than is portrayed on television and the movies, I found out.

Not only would Lonnie Trader *not* arrest Rock Norton, it soon appeared to me that this woman had an agenda to make sure no one else arrested him – ever. It almost seemed to me that NOT arresting Rock Norton was more of a priority than arresting him.

Her door was closed and so was her heart.

I was confused, frustrated and upset.

I had to find someone to listen to me.

I couldn't accept the fact that a political system was keeping Rock Norton – a man I was 100 percent convinced was the LaSalle Street Killer – from going to jail. Weren't these people concerned about innocent lives at stake here? An alleged serial killer is loose in this city! With my pleas for Rock's arrest being ignored, I was more than discouraged. I couldn't sleep at night – knowing I believed Rock Norton had slit Robert Gierse's throat.

And likely many other people in his lifetime, according to Floyd Chastain.

23

The next day, Rock Norton finally forked over his ex-wife Diane's phone number. He seemed a bit mysterious when he gave it to me, but I graciously thanked him for it anyway.

I called her immediately. It was a long distance telephone number somewhere in Ft. Lauderdale, Florida. I didn't get much information from her, although I was impressed with her grace and overall presence. I could tell she was an intelligent, elegant woman. And she was still a *broken* woman. A woman who was still in love with Robert Gierse. When I told her I wanted to talk about Bob's death, she started crying.

I didn't have the heart to keep pressing her, but I had one important question before I hung up.

"Did you ever think your ex-husband, Rock Norton, killed Bob?" I asked.

There was a deadly silence on her end of the phone. The kind of silence that comes from a tomb.

"I – I – I don't know," she whispered.

Enough said. I didn't need to hear any more.

That night, I fell asleep early. I was too upset to eat dinner and too restless to even write chapters. Things were not going as well as I had planned with this case. Just a few months earlier, I was focused on Johnny Wilson Dough – a premiere show with Unsolved Mysteries and a book with an ending – the arrest and conviction of Johnny Wilson Dough.

Now, I had the *real* killer practically in my arms and no one wanted to arrest him. When I told the producers at Unsolved Mysteries what was happening, they said they wanted to see if Rock was arrested before they put out the expense of flying a crew out to Indianapolis. I was so disappointed!

Somehow, I was in the middle of a tangled web of love that was frightening. I didn't know what to do. I tossed and turned most of the night.

I slept with the light on.

****

About 2 a.m. I woke up from a bad dream. I had been sweating. I recognized the perspiration – it was from fear. My chest was beating so hard I thought I was having a heart attack. For about ten minutes I even thought about calling 911. Instead, I just lay still, trembling. I couldn't tell if it had been a real premonition or a figment of my imagination. Either way, I knew it was just one of those passing dreams.......

By the end of fall I had one more witness who came to me in secret. It was a beautiful woman. She had information about Rock Norton and she appeared to be in a state of panic. The information she had was unexpected. She wanted to help me solve my murder case. I was willing to let her.

The witness was a nurse who lived on the Southside of Indianapolis. Her name was Elizabeth George Anne Purdy. Her looks were a mirror of her last name. Elizabeth was in her late 30's and she had long, silky black hair and a fair complexion. She had a polished appearance and wore designer clothes. From reading her impressive resume I could see she went to Indiana University about the same time I did. She was in the IU nursing program. I was in the IU school of Journalism. We probably had lunch together a time or two in the basement of Cavanaugh Hall and didn't even know each other.

I learned that Elizabeth had been a director of Nursing at Community Hospital East, a place where I had surgery in 1983. She was undoubtedly a part of a team of intensive care nurses who had taken care of me. She appeared to be somewhat of a socialite, even though she was born and raised on a questionable side of town, the 1300 block of LaSalle Street, in the 1960's. She traveled extensively, taking her 19-year-old daughter Alexandra to Europe every Spring. It was obvious she didn't want for money – she was an heir to a multi-million dollar estate in Massachusetts due to the tragic death of her uncle. Bernard Purdy was a prestigious physician who was killed in a plane crash in 1972. he was her mentor and a very dear friend. Bernard's death devastated her.

I was so excited I could barely contain myself when I learned how Elizabeth had met Rock Norton. It was on that fateful, dark and wicked frozen night on December 1ˢᵗ, 1971. Elizabeth was coming home from Methodist Hospital where she worked as a surgical tech in the operating room. She was having car trouble and had stopped to check her tires in the parking lot of a convenience store near Washington and LaSalle Streets shortly before 2 a.m.

When she pulled her 1968 Oldsmobile Cutlass up to the curb, she looked up. The headlights of Rock Norton's car had scanned her innocent face with an eerie glow. Squinting as she shielded her eyes with her forearm, she was able to tell Rock Norton had entered the same parking lot where she was parked. He was driving a large, impressive vehicle. She said the first thing she thought when she saw him was that he was a limousine driver. She watched him get out of a large black Cadillac with long, graceful fins and walk to the end of the car's left rear quarter panel. He stopped with amazing precision when he reached the trunk. He slipped something out but she couldn't see what it was. It had a reflection from the streetlight. She thought it looked like a metal briefcase.

To her surprise, she watched Rock throw the briefcase away in a loaded dumpster on the other end of the parking lot. Elizabeth observed how odd Rock Norton's behavior was. She couldn't' resist the temptation to watch him, even though she feared he might notice her and come over to silence her. She said her heart was beating so fast at that moment she thought she might have a heart attack.

In spite of her fear, she slouched down in the seat of her car and kept watching him. After his trash was deposited, she watched Rock run to his car like a child chasing an ice cream truck. Rock jumped inside the Cadillac, fiddled with the interior lights for a moment or two, then bolted out of the parking lot and headed west on Washington Street. Gravel was flying behind him everywhere. She knew he was "going at least" 50 miles per hour, she said.

She waited to make sure no one was watching her. She pulled her car close to the dumpster. She slipped out of her car unnoticed. Like an eagle sweeping down on top of a mountain, she crept up to the dumpster, swept the metal briefcase out of the bin and slid it across the vinyl driver's seat in her Cutlass. She sped off, her treasure next to her, breathing heavily as she kept an eye on her rear view mirrors. To make sure she wasn't followed that night, she drove three times around Monument Circle in Downtown Indianapolis before heading back to the Eastside. Rock Norton's face had left an impression on her she will never forget, she insisted.

"Evil," was the single word she used to describe him.

Instead of going to the two-story double she shared with her mother on LaSalle Street that morning, Elizabeth was smart enough not to go home with her prize. She knew instinctively that she had retrieved something that was one of two things.

Top Secret or Dangerous.

And absolutely valuable.

****

24

I continued calling Rock Norton every single day, just like Don Campbell told me to do. I believed an arrest was imminent and I was going to do everything I could to help turn Rock over to the authorities. I believed Don was right when he told me if I quit calling Rock he would become suspicious of me. Besides, I was still determined to write book chapters even though I *knew* he was the LaSalle Street killer.

It was just difficult not to let on that I *knew*, however.

The main thing on my mind was getting him arrested. In the meantime, I figured, why not kill two birds with one stone – and write some incredible chapters together?

"No wonder he knew so much about the LaSalle Street Murders," I thought sarcastically each time I dialed his number in the morning. Like clockwork, I called him each day between 5:30 and 6 a.m. This was the best time to catch him before he left his house for work. He was pretty perky and full of new information for me. He seemed to look forward to my phone calls.

I decided I had better let my bounty-hunter friend, Trent Marsh, know what was going on. I called him at work and told him everything.

"Darlin' – you sure got yourself in a jam now," he said, serious yet still light-hearted on my behalf.

"Thanks," I told him, whispering over the telephone. I wasn't sure if Lonnie Trader was tape recording my phone calls or not.

"I will help you in any way I can, Darlin' " Trent said. "You can count me in as your bodyguard. I'm not afraid of that old man. I'm sure I could outrun him and I am certain my arsenal is bigger than his."

"Thanks, Trent" I told him. "That means a lot to me."

I told Trent it was time to meet Rock in person.

He offered to give me personal protection whenever and wherever I decided to go. This made me feel safe, just knowing Trent was around the corner.

I called Rock and told him I would meet him for dinner at the Ground Round at 6 p.m. Trent told me he would sit outside in his car in the restaurant parking lot while we dined.

Just before noon, I drove over to my mother's house and let her know what was going on.

"He's a cold-blooded murderer," I told her as she stood in the kitchen, busy with her usual fall baking. She was making a Dutch apple pie from scratch and she didn't take her eyes off the green apples she was peeling as we talked.

"Floyd says he's a serial killer and I'm beginning to think he's right," I told her.

My mother didn't seem bothered by the fact I was talking about eating dinner with a serial killer. She just sighed and looked at me with the same look she had when I wanted to run away and get married. I was only 15-years-old.

"If you know the truth, don't give up," she said, quoting a Bible verse to me. "The truth will set you free, you know."

I hated it when my mother had a Bible verse for everything, but this time I had to admit she was right. I couldn't go on like this – tormented by the fact there was a killer running loose in Indianapolis. I *had* to pursue the truth.

25

I glanced at my watch. It was ten minutes after 6 p.m. on a windy Tuesday night.

It was the first time I ever laid eyes on Rock Norton.

We agreed to meet after work at the Ground Round restaurant on the Southeast corner of Washington Street and Shortridge Avenue. It was right across the street from Cub Foods and a block away from the Post Office and a Baptist Bible College.

I wore a smart trench coat, pearls, off-black silk stockings, high heels and a short-sleeved black wool dress, cut just above my knees. I set it off with a simple gold watch that was timed like a stopwatch to Trent's Rolodex. I was ready for the unthinkable – including running out the door at any second if I became scared.

When Rock walked into my sight, I knew it was him. He wasn't dressed in a suit and tie, but then again it didn't matter what he wore. In my opinion, Rock Norton was the ugliest thing I'd ever seen in my life. Of course, this was in human terms, only.

If I had to describe him, in a cautious sort of way, I'd say that he looked like a troll. He had a thick, egg-shaped head and cunning, arched eyebrows that framed his deceptive, blue-green eyes. He wore a strained face that was so weathered with a painful life that it reminded me of a flesh-colored gravel pit. He had a twisted, wicked smile and his bottom teeth (six or seven originals, I think) swayed a bit. Just like a snowman, he had an indignant, fat nose that was quite poignant. It seemed to have a personality all its own. It was a schnozz that Jimmy Durante would have been proud of. A few sophisticated, wiry nose hairs flared to accent the look. It was gross.

Once seated, Rock and I both asked for something to drink. Perhaps we were both a little nervous and thirsty. We had a dainty, friendly waitress and I told her I wanted a cold Sprite with lots of ice and Rock ordered a Coca-Cola. We both eyed each other suspiciously as we waited for the giddy woman to come back and ask us what we preferred to eat. I couldn't get my mind off the dead bodies of Gierse, Hinson and Barker. I knew I was supposed to be firing questions at Rock, but I just couldn't. Tonight would just have to be a "warm-up" night where we both sized each other up.

I tried not to stare into his sinful eyes – I didn't want him to think I was looking at him with adoration.

He ordered a steak, rare, and I asked for a baked potato and salad only. I was prepared to nibble. If I ate a full meal, I couldn't concentrate. I saw a sign in the lobby that said, "A penny a pound" for our meal. I thought how tacky it was to be eating dinner with an alleged serial killer and to be charged "A penny a pound."

When we were eating, I noticed that Rock's bottom chin came to a squared off point. Distinguished silver and white whiskers went every which way but up. Maybe he was having a bad hair day and forgot to shave – but there wasn't much to offer except the trim around his odd-shaped ears. He strutted some sassy and pink full lips that were forever protruding – as if like every moment of the dinner he was ready to kiss *any* damsel in distress. And his breath, unfortunately, smelled like motor oil (only on Tuesdays and Thursdays, he insisted). I couldn't help but notice his aroma.

Deception was a way of life for Rock Norton. I could tell it immediately. There were gray, sunken shadows beneath his eyes.

He looked at me from behind an old-fashioned set of silver, wire-rimmed glasses. He had piercing green eyes that were constantly aware of his surroundings. I imagined Rock already had the license plate number of our waitress's car. He was a cunning, calculating Cobra. It didn't take much to figure it out as we shared small talk about the weather and our fine city. I knew he was evil from the first second I laid eyes on him. He was strong, short and stout. Like a shark. Nimble but proud. He had these extremely long fingers that I imagined could lock around an engine and successfully thrust it out with little effort. His hands were hairy, scarred, winding and blue. They alone were a weapon he could register as lethal.

Rock spent most of the night bragging about his heroics in World War II. He boasted about winning the Purple Heart. He was trying to charm the socks off of me.

He talked about catching mice with his bare hands. He had no need for a flyswatter, he led me to believe. He could squash a pesty insect with two hands clasped together. All living things were afraid of him, he insisted. Both great and small.

Especially Dobermans and humans, he said.

Most people either loved Rock Norton dearly, hated him fiercely or they were intuitively – instinctively - deathly afraid of him, he said. He chuckled at that one.

Tonight, I was none of the three.

I just wanted to *catch* Rock Norton.

Dead or alive.

And convict him of murder.

26

The next afternoon the telephone rang while I was making a huge pot of homemade chicken soup in my kitchen.

It was Rock Norton.

"Thank-you for having dinner with me last night, Pretty one," he said with a sweet lilt in his voice.

"Thank-*you,*" I told him. "It was great to meet you."

"I just wanted to call you and tell you how pretty you are in person," he said. "You're the kind of girl a man could fall in love with."

I almost dropped my wooden soup spoon into the boiling water. Trent told me Rock Norton would be falling in love with me.

I couldn't say anything. If I did I would have stuttered. I peeled raw carrots with a scraper and chopped celery on a cutting board. I decided to save the onions for later.

"Did you hear me Pretty One?" he asked.

Gulp.

"Yes, I heard you, Rock," I said. But my mind was elsewhere. I wasn't thinking of the evil face behind the voice talking to me, I was thinking of the kind face of our county Sheriff. I scraped a sweet potato with a paring knife and diced it on a cutting board while I meditated.

I knew I had to think of something else fast! A serial killer just told me he was in love with me!

I don't know why, but the Sheriff was the first thing that came to my mind. Probably because it was a pleasant thought. He was a striking, unforgettable man who towered well over six-feet-tall. He resembled Robert Redford, in a rugged sort of way, with the spice of Michael Douglas and Rock Hudson all rolled into one. He was good-looking and gentle – yet at the same time he was a hard-core police officer. He was a born leader – a general who would guide his people well.

I was too distracted by Rock's advances. I made an excuse and told him I had to get off the phone. I threw a few bullion cubes in my stock pot and wiped my hands on a dish towel. I realized that I had just had a divine revelation! I knew instinctively that I had to call our local Sheriff before it was too late!

If Rock was falling in love with me, then *killing me* was right around the corner. I needed help!

I had heard rumors that the Sheriff was the tallest in our county's history. It was said that, literally, his desk had to be enlarged when he took office - because he was so huge. His height reminded me of Abraham Lincoln. I couldn't help but compare the two – and I considered him to be just like Lincoln - one of the wisest and most powerful, honest men in this town.

I also knew that experience was on his side. The Sheriff was once a Lieutenant in charge of homicide at IPD when the LaSalle Street Murders run broke on that fateful December 1st morning. He was a cop - just like Lt. Ryker. Both of them were still cops who were working in law enforcement that bitterly cold afternoon. Just like Ryker, the Sheriff had actually walked through the blood-stained LaSalle Street house and saw the mutilated victims.

He knew the cast first hand.

Still in the middle of making my soup, I decided to be bold and *call* him.

Why not?

I turned the burner under my kettle down to low and marched

in the living room to meditate. I debated with myself about making the call. Since the Sheriff had a reputation for being unbelievably truthful, compassionate, understanding, generous, kind and a man of his word, I decided to find out if he was for real!

I pulled out my white pages and found the number for the Marion County Sheriff's department and dialed it. I boldly requested an appointment with him for the following Tuesday afternoon.

"Can I ask what this is regarding?" asked Terri, the Sheriff's secretary of 18 years.

"I can't say," I told her. I had reservations about who I could trust.

"But it is very important," I said.

When it came time for my appointment, I drove about 13 miles west on East Washington Street until I reached the corner of Alabama and Washington Streets downtown. The County Jail was just east and a bit south of Monument Circle. I parked on a semi-circle driveway in front of the cream-colored, five-story brick building. I gathered up my purse, a large stack of documents, legal folders, manila envelopes and a bag of cassette tapes. I slid my high heels onto the concrete and marched inside with integrity. I had justice to protect for this town! I had to solve a murder and save this city from danger!

I went into the Sheriff's huge, unassuming office, cradling dozens of the tapes I owned of Rock Norton and me talking on the phone together. I guarded them with my life and held them against my chest as though they were a newborn baby swaddled in a brown paper sack. Most of them were dated months back - way into the early summer when I first began tape recording Rock. The cassettes were of deadly, incriminating conversations. Conversations where Rock told me Robert Gierse was "a loser and a good-for nothing son of a b- - - - who deserved what he got."

Rock detailed many intimate details about Robert Gierse, Robert Hinson and James Barker. He even talked about (on tape) what Robert Gierse had to eat before he died. He described Bob's "fat wallet" that sat on the coffee table after he was murdered. Rock told me what the death house looked like – from the outside *and the inside.* . He described the blood-letting that went on that gruesome night – with picturesque detail. From the sound of his voice, I could tell he enjoyed the gory details!

My tapes were overwhelmingly compelling. If Lonnie Trader didn't care about them, then I had to convince someone to hear what they had to say!

That someone who listened was the Sheriff. He was the only one who cared.

Like a King on a throne, the Sheriff sat in an accomplished, oversized brown leather chair, facing me. He was almighty and powerful, yet he didn't act like royalty at all. He didn't exude one ounce of pride. In fact, he treated me like I was just as important as he was. He didn't avoid eye contact either. He stared at me the entire time I talked – which I'm certain was about a mile a minute.

I was so impressed that he was giving me – a nobody – a single mother from the Eastside of Indianapolis - time out of his busy day. He looked me through and through with these sensitive, very intense eyes. I was so nervous to have finally garnered his attention. After all, he *was* a cop.

"You *have* to listen to this," I said, beginning my presentation.

I couldn't tell if the Sheriff was looking at me suspiciously or if he thought I was crazy. There was no expression on his face but fairness.

"Please, Sheriff," I literally begged him. "Please. I know who committed the LaSalle Street Murders! Please listen to this tape. Just give me five minutes. You can hear it for yourself."

I carefully picked out one of the tapes and put it in my tape recorder. I was glad I brought it with me.

When I hit the "play" button – the Sheriff's eyebrows grew together with concern. I watched him listen to it with intensity.

"Turn it off," he said, after hearing one skinny black tape. His expression was of deep concern.

"My God!" he said with precision. "This guy is a nut!"

I sighed with relief.

He believed me.

And in five minutes, the Sheriff was doing something about it. He picked up the phone and called Lieutenant Mike Ryker.

He ordered a meeting right away.

"Something has got to be done," the Sheriff said, looking over at me from behind his desk while he talked on the phone to Lt. Ryker.

"And that means now!"

27

The very next morning, I learned the Sheriff was already behind the scenes taking action. To this day I do not know what steps he took, but I know he made things begin to move and shake in the police world. He and Mike Ryker were having conferences right and left. The Sheriff was a real police officer, not just a politician who only cared about election votes. He wasn't someone concerned with fame and fortune. He set to work catching a killer.

While I waited for something to happen, I continued to concentrate on my daily conversations with Rock Norton. I still called him every single morning, like clockwork. We always talked about Robert Gierse and the LaSalle Street Murders because that was his favorite topic. I always taped him and documented everything in my diary. I had been keeping a diary since I was in college - so journaling every word Rock and I said to each other was easy. Frequently Rock said completely incriminating things – fingering himself as Bob Gierse's killer. It was unbelievable, yet he never confessed completely.

I decided that a different plan was needed.

I thought that, if I met him in person again, he might confess. (Up until now every attempt we made at dinner was without tape recording devices. This was a good thing for my safety).

I called the Sheriff and told him my idea. I invited him to dinner with Rock Norton and I asked him if he would go along – undercover. He took me up on my suggestion, and offered to provide a body wire (hidden under my clothing so that Rock Norton wouldn't know I was tape recording him.) The Sheriff offered to observe our dinner with surveillance equipment.

"Hopefully I'll get a confession on tape," I assured the Sheriff.

I knew it was risky. Actually, it was downright dangerous. But I believed it was my only hope.

It had to be done. I had to meet Rock Norton once again.

I called Rock and arranged another dinner date. I was edging closer to him. Inch by inch.

28

October 1992

The black, 1986 Buick Grand National swerved into my driveway, the motor thundering to announce its arrival like a Harley Davidson motorcycle on a sunny Sunday afternoon.

Only it wasn't sunny, it wasn't Sunday and it wasn't a summer afternoon. It was a typically overcast evening in Indiana in October – sweater weather – and it was time to rock and roll.

I was still sitting at my kitchen table, polishing my nails with a shiny coat of candy apple red polish. My hair was clamped with steaming electric hot rollers and I wore a silk bathrobe that clung to my shoulders. It covered the goose bumps that ran up and down my arms when I heard Trent's footsteps on my front porch.

I looked at my watch as I walked barefoot to my front door. It was 5:15 p.m. He was early. I pulled the door open a notch and looked at Trent's face. I saw him take a look behind himself – quickly – before he caught a glimpse of me standing in the entryway, shivering.

"You ready Darling?" Trent asked, giving me a half-grin and a half-serious look.

"I am ready," I said, giving him a dry look as he watched me pull my hot rollers out, one by one. "I'll be out in 5 minutes. I'm waiting on the Sheriff to call when the police van is at Post Road."

"I'll be out in the car," he said, signaling for me to take my time. I knew that meant he needed another cigarette before the action began.

Trent knew I was nervous. Just like I was the first time I met him and wrote a story about him. Now, two years after I wrote the bounty hunting story about him, we were good friends. Every once in a while, I thought I might be developing a school-girl crush on him, but I figured he didn't feel the same about me, so I didn't dwell on it. I was happy to have him as a friend and tonight - Trent was acting as my body guard on one of the most dangerous stories I had ever encountered.

This time, I wasn't writing for *The Indianapolis News*.

I was doing something on my own free will. I was volunteering my services as a special agent for the police. I was going to dinner with a man I thought was a serial killer. I believed he was likely a sociopath who had been claiming lives throughout the United States for over two decades.

I was a rogue cop and a freelance private detective. I wanted to solve a murder.

Everything was so surreal. I couldn't believe I was actually trying to catch him and put him behind bars. I'd never done anything like this before in my life. But I had to admit – it was kind of fun.

The plan was this: I was going to try to get Rock to confess to the killings - on a tape recorder hidden under my dress.

Trent's job was to make sure I wasn't killed – and that I made it home safely to my son, David, by midnight.

After I closed my front door, I felt my stomach churn as I walked down the hallway to my bedroom to prepare.

"What do you wear to have dinner with a serial killer?" I asked myself out loud as I looked at the three dresses I had laid out for the evening. I finally chose a very sophisticated black chiffon cocktail dress because it would best conceal the electronic apparatus I was about to put on.

I suppose I felt a little guilty. I knew Rock was falling in love with me, and I was using his constant advances to date me as an opportunity to put him in jail. When I agreed to take him up on his repeated requests to take me out to dinner, I am certain he didn't expect me to wear a body wire – connected to the Marion County Sheriff's Department via remote transmission around my bra – when I said, "Okay, let's get together."

"I'm looking forward to seeing you tonight," Rock Norton had said when he confirmed our dinner date. He acknowledged that it was a business-meeting-only – so we could work on the book together, in person.

"You too," I had said in an honest way. Rock was looking forward to gazing into my blue eyes and I was looking forward to seeing the Sheriff put handcuffs on his wrists.

I knew I was being thrown into his arms for a *reason*. I wanted to catch him but I definitely didn't want him to catch *me*.

Trent was my backup. He was my safety net in case anything went wrong. After all, I would be alone with Rock Norton in the restaurant. Even though the Sheriff and a select few undercover deputies would be outside in a van, listening to every word we said, I felt better knowing someone was *inside* watching out for my safety in case Rock Norton tried to lure me outside.

Or in case anything went wrong.

29

I had just put on silk, jet-black pantyhose and shiny black pumps when I heard a quiet knock at the front door. I knew who it was before I opened it. There were two Marion County Sheriff's deputies and the Sheriff's daughter-in-law, Cindy Denver, standing in front of me.

Within minutes, the female cop had secured a tape recording device connected to a very long wire around my torso. I wore nothing but a multi-colored bikini bra and a black slip as she wrapped it around my stomach. She slid it underneath my arms and around my back. She secured it with what I thought was some sort of delicate tape.

"You're all set," she told me. "Good luck."

"Thanks," I told her, beginning to get really nervous. "This thing feels a little warm. Is it supposed to feel like that?"

"Yes," she said. "That's the battery."

"Where's your father-in-law at?" I asked.

"He's up at the restaurant," she said. "It's time to go."

As though I had rehearsed the routine 100 times, I methodically slipped on my dress and a coat and walked to my car – my blue, 1989 Honda Accord – and got in. I looked in the rear view mirror and watched Trent back his Buick Grand National into the street. Even though the windows were tinted, I knew he was nodding to me that everything would be okay.

When I finally reached the restaurant, Mickler's Steak house on East Washington Street, I saw the brown Sheriff's van in the parking lot. I walked over to it, as planned, and looked inside for a moment. The sheriff was sitting inside. He gave me a few last instructions.

"Try to get him to talk about the first time he was inside Robert Gierse's house," the sheriff said. "We know for a fact he wasn't in there after the murders or during our investigation. He said we let him inside but we didn't."

I nodded, feeling comforted to know that the Sheriff was near-by, guiding me with instructions.

"Don't go anywhere, you guys," I told him, as it sunk in that I was going to be at a remote restaurant in a secluded location – alone with a man I knew had slaughtered three men twenty years ago.

"Don't worry," the Sheriff said with little expression on his face. "If he kills you tonight, I promise to solve your murder."

The other deputies in the van laughed.

I looked over at him, knowing he was joking with me just to calm me down. These guys in the van were narcotics officers. They were used to undercover work. This was my first time.

"Thanks," I said dryly. "I appreciate that."

I turned away from them and walked inside the restaurant.

30

I stood in the lobby of Mickler's Steak house, anxiously waiting for Rock to arrive.

Everything was in place – ready for the anticipated Sting operation: The Sheriff and his deputies were outside in the northeast corner of the tree-lined parking lot, inside a brown Marion County Sheriff's van. My bodyguard, Trent Marsh, was already inside the restaurant, seated at a table by himself. He was waiting for the waitress to bring his iced tea and salad to him.

Out of the corner of my eye, completely fixed on ignoring him, I saw Trent, at a round table dressed with fine white linen, silverware and crystal. I saw him examine the menu. His eyes were ahead of him, reading, yet I knew he was observant of my every move. I was confident Trent would not let me out of his sight.

As I stared at a framed photo on a wall behind the cash register, I coughed out loud, letting the Sheriff know I was still connected to him via remote control. I felt myself growing more and more anxious with every minute that ticked past 6:30 p.m.

"Where *is* he?" I thought to myself. "It's not like Rock to be late. I suddenly wondered if Rock had known I was on to him. Maybe he knew instinctively I had set him up. Maybe he wasn't going to show up after all.

As I smiled at the hostess for the fourth time – giving her a reassuring nod that my dinner date was on his way – I heard the door open and footsteps quietly, yet firmly, walk up behind me. Rock had the amazing, stealth presence of a deer in the middle of a forest.

And I was the hunter.

"I'm late, Pretty One," Rock said out loud.

He was here. The time had come to look danger in the eye again – face to face.

I turned around to greet him. Quickly, but not too anxiously. He appeared a little bit more groomed today, more so than the first time I met him.

"That's okay," I said, smiling at him. "I understand you had to work."

"That damned Lou," he said with disgust. "I should know better than to get my employees from the Wheeler Mission. Harvey brought six engines to me at the last minute. I had to get the cars parked inside the garage before I left. Traffic was terrible getting here."

I was surprised Rock looked disheveled and slightly fatigued. He wore a blue mechanic's uniform and what looked to be a blue railroad conductor's hat. He evidently had worked in a dirty, dusty place all day long.

"You look lovely tonight, Pretty One," Rock said, his hardened eyes softening as he looked me over head to toe. He was not too obvious with his intentions.

"You are too gracious to take *me* out to dinner," I told him.

"I'm never too gracious for you, Pretty One," he said, motioning for our redheaded waitress to seat us. "I'd take you out to eat every day if you'd let me."

I was too nervous to eat, so I ordered a garden salad just to be polite. Rock ordered a T-bone steak, a baked potato and a Caesar's salad. He refreshed himself with a Coca-Cola with just a little bit of ice.

We chatted about the weather, Rock's work and my son, David, for a few minutes until I could take no more. I told Rock I had to use the restroom. The body wire I wore under my bra was getting hotter and hotter by the minute. My skin felt like it was on fire – as though a lighted match was touching it!

I walked deftly past Trent, who was pretending to be engrossed in his steak dinner. I glided by him nonchalantly, hoping to give him the message that things were not going as well as expected.

"I hope you guys are getting all of this," I said out loud, once I was in the safety zone of the women's restroom. I spoke to no one but the police officers listening to my remote-controlled voice next to my bra. "I know you're laughing – but *I am scared.* Okay? Scared," I said, extra loud for them to be certain not to miss what I was communicating. I wondered if they could hear how loud my heart was beating on this electronic thing. I felt like I was Jodie Foster all alone with Hannibal Lechter in the movie, Silence of the Lambs.

"This battery on my bare skin is hot," I said out loud. "And I mean HOT."

I patted a dab of ivory Maybeline face powder on my cheeks, added a fresh coat of strawberry-ice lipstick to my lips and fluffed my hair with my fingers. I glanced at myself one more time in the mirror before I went back to my seat. I hoped that no one else had been in the restroom to hear me talking to what appeared to be no one but myself.

When I returned to my seat, I decided to strike up a conversation with Rock about his childhood in Grubbs, Arkansas. The conversation – and Rock – became long and subdued.

He told me about a time when his father scared him to death as a child.

"Once upon a time," Rock said, beginning his story. He then told how he and his siblings were seated at the dinner table – a long wooden table in their farmhouse kitchen. Rock's mother put steaming hot mashed potatoes, a tender beef pot roast, a plate of buttered bread and homemade strawberry jam on the dinner table for everyone to eat. When she sat down to join them, the family cat jumped up on top of the table, right next to the food.

Rock's father, he explained, was angry with the cat!

In order to punish the cat, Rock's father quickly grabbed a

steak knife and stabbed the cat in the chest – impaling it – directly into the wooden table.

To Rock's horror, the cat was still alive, trapped to the table by the knife. The cat could not escape, and slowly bled to death right there on the dinner table, right next to the mashed potatoes.

Rock was forced to watch his own cat slowly bleed to death right in front of his very eyes. His father made him eat his dinner and watch the cat die at the same time.

Although the cat execution happened not too long after the depression – way out in the middle of a barren Arkansas cornfield – Rock Norton never forgot it.

I could tell by the faraway look in his eyes – he never would.

"I hated my father for that," Rock explained to me in a disgusted, angry voice. "And I hated him for how he used to beat my mother half to death."

It was all I could do to maintain my composure with Rock about his move to Indiana.

"My father beat me half-to-death with a chain out in the cornfield," Rock told me. "After that, I left and moved out on my own, even though I was only a young boy."

He explained that he had had enough of his father's abuse when he was 16-years-old. He said he packed his bags and moved out of the house and headed for Indianapolis one day. He said he never looked back.

I knew I needed to change the subject, so I asked Rock about something I knew made him happy. The Indianapolis 500.

"You were quite a hero out at the Indy 500, weren't you?" I asked him.

"Yes, I was," Rock said, smiling. That's all he needed. He took off with an overwhelming amount of pride. I think he was trying to re-invent himself when he met me.

Rock spent the next 20 minutes talking about his days as Chief Mechanic for the Indy 500 during the 1960's. His eyes and his entire face lit up when he talked about the Indy cars. I could tell this was a time of his life when he was very proud of himself.

Slowly, I turned the conversation to the topic of Rock and I both being neighbors, living on the East side of Indianapolis together. Then I finally eased into the topic of the LaSalle Street Murders. I told him I wanted to hear more about his ex-wife, Diane, and the man she fell in love with after their divorce.

"I'm looking into the secret files at B&B Microfilm," I told him. "What do you think was on that film?"

Rock was glad I asked his opinion.

"Whatever it was – it was top secret," he said. "It was information that was smarter than he was."

"You don't think he was too intelligent, do you?" I asked Rock. "Tell me more about Robert Gierse. "

I tried staring into Rock's pitiful, piercing eyes again. I looked at my tall glass of Sprite. I wondered if Rock had poisoned it while I was in the restroom. I couldn't bring myself to take another drink.

"Robert Gierse was a coward," Rock said simply. "I only met the son of a b- - - - once."

I looked up at Rock, trying not to notice his blatant anger towards Gierse. Was this wise of him to tell me his emotions? I scribbled down what he said in my notebook.

"Really?" I asked, coquettishly, trying to appear naïve to Rock.

"Yeah," Rock said, oblivious to the fact that I was dictating everything he said on paper. He didn't seem to care that I was documenting his innermost thoughts and emotions of hatred on paper.

"Tell me about the first time you ever met him," I coaxed Rock.

Rock was quick to respond. "Well, I was over at Diane's apartment one Saturday morning to pick up my children for the weekend," he explained. "When I got up to her apartment, there stood that lazy son of a b - - - - with his pants off, right there in Diane's kitchen."

"I didn't say a word to him – but that guy ran like a coward as soon as he saw me," Rock laughed out loud. "Can you believe he was actually afraid of me? The guy was just standing there, in his underwear. He grabbed his pants and ran out the door."

The more Rock Norton talked about Robert Gierse, the more I could tell he intensely hated the man who dated his ex-wife.

"Yep, Diane looked a little embarrassed, but I didn't let her know what I thought of her new beau," Rock said, lost in thought. "I really loved that woman. She was the greatest person I ever knew – male or female – in my entire life."

I looked at Rock. His passion was sincere.

"Can you think of anyone who would want to harm Robert Gierse?" I asked Rock. "Do you think he had death threats before he died?"

"Sure I do," he answered. "A lot of them. Robert Gierse was a loser from day one."

"What do you mean?" I asked, intent on keeping Rock on track.

"I mean, I watched that coward run from me and straight to his car, to that big fancy Cadillac of his that he had," Rock said with an explosive voice. "He couldn't get away from me fast enough."

Rock looked up at me with a piercing stare. When I looked up at him, he quickly looked away to the right, and then his eyes darted back down at his steak.

"That son of a b - - - - was afraid I was going to kill him," Rock said, reminiscing with a laugh.

I was spooked. At that instant, Rock's laugh sounded just like my father's laugh.

"Why would he be afraid that you would kill him?" I prodded Rock, conscious of the tape recording device around my bikini bra. I was hoping that the Sheriff could hear what what I was saying.

Rock grew silent.

"I don't know" he said. "The guy was supposed to be macho. Really tall, over six-feet. He weighed about 250 pounds. He could have taken anyone on that night."

"That night! What did Rock mean, that night! I thought we were talking about a Saturday morning! Was Rock talking about the night of November 30th, 1971 when Bob Gierse was probably murdered?"

"Shortly before his death, do you think Robert Gierse knew someone wanted to kill him?" I asked Rock.

"Yes, I do," Rock said, a thin smile crossing his face.

I felt my hand shake slightly as I wrote down his answer.

Unexpectedly, Rock changed the subject.

"So, what are you driving tonight?" Rock asked me.

"Did I see your car out there" he wanted to know.

I swallowed hard.

"I drove my Honda," I told him honestly.

"That little blue one?" he asked.

"Dear God," I thought. Now Rock has my license plate number. I glanced over at Trent. He was nearing completion of his steak. I wondered how much longer he was going to be able to dawdle over his food. The restaurant was barely crowded. There were about four or five other couples having dinner, and two other gentlemen were seated by themselves near Trent.

I was becoming more and more nervous. The reality that I was truly dining with a murderer was getting to me. Now that Rock was talking about my car, I became more worried. Floyd said Rock was a serial killer. I knew I wasn't going to be getting a confession out of him tonight. I knew I needed to get out of there before Rock decided to walk me out to my car – and make me one of his preys.

"You know, I think I need to be leaving," I said, trying to wrap up the conversation with bravery.

"It was really nice of you to come out of hibernation and have dinner with me again, Pretty One," Rock said. "I always enjoy your company."

"Oh, it was my pleasure," I told him. "But I really should be going now. I think you gave me some good information to use in my book."

"Is it still *our* book?" Rock asked.

For a moment, I almost forgot he was still the co-writer of my book.

"Yes, of course," I answered sheepishly.

"I enjoyed your company, Pretty One," Rock said, smiling with his lips parted. "We could get a lot more done if you'd go get your tooth brush and your pajamas and come over to my place."

I pretended he was joking and dismissed him casually.

"I don't live very far from you," he said. "I'm right at the corner of Ritter and Washington Streets. Do you know where that is?"

"Umm, yes I do," I said. I knew I had to think quickly. And I had to stay in Rock's good graces. "You're right behind the blood bank, aren't you?"

"You got it," he said. "You *are* pretty smart, aren't you Pretty One?"

I felt pretty stupid at the moment. God, why did I get myself into this?

"Really, Rock, I have to go," I said, dabbing at my lips with a paper napkin. "I had better go."

Rock seemed to be enjoying my uneasiness.

"What's wrong, pretty one?" he asked me.

"Well, umm, I really am worried about my son," I said. "He's not old enough to stay by himself, so I left him with a neighbor girl to look after him. And tonight's a school night, you know."

"I understand," Rock said, nodding. He could tell I was nervous. He seemed to be enjoying it.

I fumbled in my purse for my car keys. I snatched them with my thumb and forefinger and hopped up out of my seat. "Let me give you some money for dinner," I told him.

"No, no, I've got it," Rock said. "My treat."

"Well, thank-you," I said. "I really enjoyed meeting with you again. But I have *got* to get going."

I looked at my watch. It was ten minutes after eight.

The adrenaline inside me was indescribable. Fear was in my throat as I tried not to look to the left or to the right. I had to get out of the restaurant and the parking lot without Rock following me. Hopefully, Rock would be detained for a few minutes when he paid the bill. I knew I only had seconds to stay a step ahead of him.

I darted past Trent, trying to be unassuming at a slow pace. I tried not to look like I wanted to *run* out of the restaurant. But I did.

I could feel Trent watching my escape. I could only hope the Sheriff was listening to me.

The cold October air met my face with a blast. I slipped my black trench coat over my shoulders as I walked to my car.

I only glanced over my shoulders once to see if anyone was following me.

When I did, I noticed a dark-haired man coming out of the

restaurant to get into his car, but thankfully, it wasn't Rock Norton.

I slipped my car keys into my ignition. I prayed my car would start. I had seen too many movies where a victim fell prey to her killer because her car wouldn't start.

I looked in my rear view mirror and noticed the Sheriff's van was faithfully still there. I felt instantly relieved just to know the Sheriff was nearby.

Thankfully, my car started right away. I pulled the car right onto East Washington Street and then I turned right again on Post Road. At Post and 10th Street there was a small Italian restaurant. I turned left and headed west – to Harold's Steer Inn near Emerson Avenue. This was the "getaway" plan that Trent and I had arranged ahead of time.

My heart was racing.

I was so afraid Rock would be following me. The reality that he was a killer hit home tonight. For some reason, when we were on the telephone together, he seemed so harmless. But in person, he was fierce and frightful, in a Charles Manson sort of way.

Fortunately, I made it to my destination. I waited in the parking lot for about five minutes. I saw Trent pull up and come to a rolling stop next to me. I hopped out of my car and into the Grand National. We sped off, leaving my Honda parked at the restaurant.

"You did it Darling," Trent said as I got into his car. I could see his eyes were fastened to his rear view mirror. "Did you get anything good on tape?"

"I got some good stuff ," I told Trent, sighing with relief. "But no confession."

"I hate to tell you this, Darlin'" Trent said, still staring at his rear view mirror. I could see a flicker of headlights flash across the pupils of his eyes.

"What?" I asked him desperately.

"You got more than you bargained for tonight," he said.

"What do you mean?" I demanded, still breathing hard. I swatted at my back where the body wire was irritating me.

"Because, Darling' – you weren't the only one who had a

bodyguard in that restaurant tonight," Trent said.

"Huh?" I asked.

"Did you see that guy with a mustache, the one wearing a suit and tie who was seated across from me, reading his newspaper?" Trent asked.

"Yeah," I said, trying to remember the man with dark hair and an olive complexion.

"That was one of Rock Norton's boys," Trent said. "He didn't take his eyes off of you all night long. He didn't eat much, just sat there doing nothing but watching you and Norton together. Pretended to be reading his paper but he didn't do much reading."

I was silent.

"He was Mafia, Darling'" Trent said. "No doubt about it."

I knew Trent knew what he was talking about. Trent was known by the US Marshall's as somebody who could catch any escaped felon, wanted dead or alive. If Trent said the man watching me was a Mafia figure – I knew he was right.

"Oh God, Trent," I said. "No!"

"Oh yes," he said. "And do you want some more bad news?"

"Go ahead," I said, captured in the adrenaline of the moment. "What?"

"Well, don't be alarmed," Trent said, looking to his left in the mirror on his driver's door as he talked to me. "We're being followed right now."

"Followed?" I asked, frightened. I felt like I was in a movie. "Oh my God! Is it Rock?"

"Nope," Trent said. He was so calm. "Rock was driving a white Ford LTD tonight. Whoever is on our tail is driving a dark Green Marquis. He's been following us ever since you got into my car at the Steer Inn."

I closed my eyes and started praying.

"You had *better* pray," Trent said, as he accelerated his Grand National faster. "Make sure your seat belt is on because I'm going to have to lose them!"

31

October, 1992

The next morning, Trent and I talked about what happened over coffee at a Denny's restaurant.

I enjoyed a strong cup of Java, black, and Trent ate a large order of biscuits and gravy with his. While he was eating, he gave me a look that a big brother has when he's about to lecture his little sister.

"Who do you think followed us last night?" I asked him.

"I don't know," he said. "But whoever it is wanted you to know that they are on to you."

I looked up at Trent and waited for more. I knew his sermon would be lengthy and that he had an opinion about my relationship with Rock Norton. Somehow, I knew he wouldn't mince words.

"I expect Rock Norton knows more about you than you think he does," Trent said.

"I do know he is pretty sneaky," I told Trent.

"He may be sneaky, but remember, MURDER is his specialty," Trent warned me. "I'm certain he wants to make you his next victim. He's toying with you right now and you had better be careful. Last night was just a warning. Next time I may not be around to help you."

I had nothing to say to Trent's comment. My coffee suddenly lost its taste.

Trent picked up his cell phone and dialed his best friend. He was planning a trip to Mexico with his friends and his little brother. He looked over at me and said, "I think this might be a good time for you to go out of the country too."

I knew Trent was joking, so I rolled my eyes at him.

"I can't do that," I said.

"Maybe not," Trent said. "But it wouldn't hurt you to go out of town for a while. Let the old man, Rock Norton, try to forget about you. Seeing you in person may have made him hungry."

"Hungry for what?" I asked with naïve innocence.

"Hungry for blood," Trent said. "Yours."

I shuddered at the thought.

"How did you lose that guy last night?" I asked Trent, changing the subject. "Just in case I'm all alone on the highway – how do I do it?"

"Four right turns," he told me. "If you were watching me on I-465 last night – I made four right turns, very quickly – after I knew the guy was behind me. The key to losing anyone is four right turns. Plus you have to drive like a bat out of h - - -"."

I made a mental note of what he said in case it happened to me again. I remembered the headlights that were following us after we left the restaurant.

In a fog of darkness they appeared and in a fog of eeriness they disappeared.

"I'm going to be out of town for a while," Trent said, letting me know he was going to Los Angeles to chase a skip that was wanted for murder in Las Vegas. Later he would be meeting friends in Mexico. "Don't ever let your guard down. You have to be careful every time you leave the house from now on."

I nodded my head and waved good-bye to Trent. I knew that I had entered into another level of danger. If Rock Norton had a Mafia bodyguard sizing me up with a microscope during dinner – from head to toe – then the whole idea of capturing Rock Norton was now twice as dangerous.

When I talked to the Sheriff later in the day, he said they did not hear anything on the tape recording during last night's stake out that would incriminate Rock Norton. Our dinner date was a waste of time, for the most part. Unfortunately, all I did was wet Rock Norton's appetite for more….of me!

Now, I knew I had to maintain constant contact with Rock Norton or I would really be in danger. I had to keep pretending that I didn't think he was a murderer – even though deep down I knew he was.

32

I finished typing another chapter and turned off my computer. I stretched and peered out the bedroom window above my bed. It was a very clear, pitch dark night with a full moon. I couldn't help but notice the air had an eerie chill to it. I kicked my thermostat up a bit and kept busy tidying up my house. I helped my son prepare for a project at school the next day. I fell asleep watching television while it was still early.

Later on, shortly after the eleven o'clock news was over, my phone rang. Perhaps it was my imagination, but I thought the ringer on my telephone was softer than usual.

"It was good to see you yesterday," I told Rock when I heard his voice on the other end of the line. He had telephoned me to wish me good-night.

"Thank-you for buying my dinner yesterday," I said.

"Thank-you for meeting *me*, Pretty One," Rock told me. "You are more beautiful each time I see you."

For a brief moment, a wave of nausea swept over me.

I smiled sweetly, as though Rock could see me smiling back at him over the phone.

"Have a good day tomorrow," I told Rock. "I know you've got

a lot of important business coming into your shop."

"I do," he said. "Thank-you for caring about me. And you too – I hope you have a good day tomorrow getting into whatever trouble you like to get yourself into."

All of a sudden, I realized Rock's laugh was more than sinister. He was mocking me!

"Oh, my God!" I thought out loud. "HE KNOWS!" At that moment, I KNEW that I KNEW *he* knew I was on to him.

He knew I was aware he was the LaSalle Street killer!"

"Good night, Pretty One," Rock said nonchalantly. "I hope to see you again soon. Next time you'll have to stay longer and not run out on me."

"We'll see," I said, doubting I'd ever meet Rock Norton in person again. "Good-night."

"Good-night, Pretty One," he said.

It may not have been productive – but at least I did it. I had dinner with a serial killer. And I had him asking for more.

Now I knew I had to move on to bigger and better things. And *quickly*.

I had to out smart him.

33

Thanksgiving
1992

The turkey holiday came and went. No matter what I did, I still couldn't get Rock Norton to confess to me.

Nor could the Sheriff and I convince anyone at the Marion County Prosecutor's Office to arrest him.

I was getting tired of wrangling with him. I was fed up with being flirtatious with someone I didn't even like. I felt like I was trying to lasso a bull in a bullpen. So I set to work on a new angle. I figured there had to be *some* way to get him to confess to the murders. If I knew he was truly a murderer, then I knew I could do it. That's all I needed, I believed - the truth behind me.

I figured I had to get him in the right mood to confess. I began to go to the library and read up on serial killers. I rented horror movies and slasher documentaries. I even interviewed sociologists and psychologists. I prepared myself for the mental challenge. I wanted to get inside of Rock Norton's mind.

I decided to try to get his goat.

I told him the police were after him and they considered him a chief suspect in the LaSalle Street Murders.

That was the first time I ever heard Rock cuss. Then he sort of shrieked. I was a little frightened, but I knew he wasn't mad at me. I told him Floyd Chastain was the one that had incriminated him.

I told him Floyd had ratted to the cops and that he had set Rock up.

Rock was furious. His cage had been rattled. It was starting to work.

"That Chastain is a good-for nothing liar!" Rock screamed into the phone. He yelled so loud it actually hurt my ear.

"I've got to go, Pretty One," he said. "I've got business to take care of. Now I'm going to have to go out and get a damn attorney."

Rock didn't call me again for three days.

34

Shortly before Christmas, I received a phone call from Floyd Chastain again. We had been talking on a regular basis, usually every Saturday afternoon. He was always trying to come up with new leads to help me catch Rock Norton.

Floyd told me Rock had killed an elderly woman named Verna, and that he had bragged about killing a young girl named Connie. He said she was a teenage runaway and she lived in Mars Hill somewhere.

"He says he buried her in his basement or in the backyard behind his house," Floyd insisted.

"You should look into it," he said. "I don't know where – but if he's a serial killer I'll bet you'll find human remains in his backyard. There's a mini-barn out there somewhere. See if you can't get the police to dig it up and see what's underneath.

"You've got to be kidding," I told Floyd in awe.

"Ma'am, I am telling you – Rock Norton is extremely dangerous. He's killed lots of people – both men and women – in his lifetime. Be careful. He's a serial killer."

I couldn't shake off what Floyd had told me. I thought about it every time I went to bed and every time I woke up.

After wrapping Christmas presents one night, I felt extremely sleepy. I'd eaten a large dinner at Laughner's cafeteria –my favorite - fried chicken, mashed potatoes and green beans with bacon. A thick biscuit with buttered honey seemed to make me want to doze. The last time I looked at the clock, it was about 10 minutes after 10 p.m. I remembered hearing Floyd's words in my mind as I fell asleep.

"Be careful. He's a serial killer…

"A serial killer….

"A serial killer….

****

It was March, 1969. Connie Thomas was young – around 19-years-old and fresh in 1969. She had a pristine way about her, for a tomboy. She was an orphan. A plain but innocently -pretty girl who became a ward of the state of Indiana when her mother and father were killed in a terrible auto accident in Southern Indiana.

Connie was still in high school and had no one in the whole world.

Except Rock Norton.

He met her at the Twin Aire shopping center on the Southeast side of Indianapolis on a rainy Tuesday morning. Her tennis shoes were drenched and her brown hair was sticking in thick, wet ringlets to her face. She was standing next to a bus stop, fidgeting with her wet panty hose that was plastered to her skin when Rock pulled up in an unmarked police car. He asked her if she was lost.

Connie had such a vacant look on her sweet and dainty face that Rock couldn't help but feel sorry for her.

He let her in his sedan – and the rest was history.

Rock drove her to his home on the East side of Indianapolis. It was somewhere near a Truck Stop around 38th Street and Shadeland Avenue. He put her belongings in his basement, but he let Connie sleep in the spare bedroom he had downstairs – right next to the kitchen and an open wood-burning fireplace. He gave her the "special room" – it had deep blue rose and ivy wallpaper that gave it a homey, garden-type feeling. She even had her own, private shower. He wanted her to feel comfortable, cozy and secure.

Rock smiled when he noticed young Connie had fallen fast asleep after he fed her a bowl of steaming hot vegetable soup. He had prepared it the day before and even had homemade buttermilk biscuits and apple cobbler ready to warm her tummy.

She was exhausted, he knew. He saw she was clutching a teddy bear she had pulled out of her backpack when she drifted off.

He took the opportunity while she was sleeping to slip something from her belongings and slide it into his deep coat pocket. He knew she wouldn't miss anything today. Not as tired as she was.

He flipped the light off in her bedroom, tip-toed out and shut the door.

Walking slowly but methodically upstairs – Rock Norton fingered his souvenir for a moment before he took it out to examine it closer. He grinned as a bolt of lightning lit up the dreary, darkened hallway – and his army boots – that were leading him up to his second-story bedroom.

A loud clap of thunder seemed to shake the entire 3500- square foot Dutch Colonial home he had bought in 1962 and refurbished himself. He made the house just the way he liked it. Eighteen rooms and no two were alike.

Rock couldn't wait to add this prize from Connie's bureau to the collection he treasured.

It would look nice with the others he was keeping in the attic.

****

When I woke up I was in the middle of what sounded like a severe thunderstorm outside. I was petrified. It was December but we were having extremely unusual weather. It was incredibly warm and balmy outside when I turned in. I remembered someone on the evening news had mentioned it was possible we could have tornado warnings by midnight.

The house was pitch black and the windows were shaking it was storming so hard. I was trembling and sweating profusely. I couldn't tell if we had lost power or not. I looked up and out the window – it appeared the entire neighborhood was in a blackout. I felt dampness around my T-shirt and realized my clothes were drenched from sweat.

I jumped off the couch and ran to my back door to make sure it was locked. I double checked the deadbolt – twice - and even slid a large chest of drawers in front of the steel door.

My heart was still beating incredibly fast. It felt like I had been running a relay race. I was shaking so hard I started to cry.

I realized I just had my first nightmare about Rock Norton.

It was the first of many more that would plague me over the next few years.

35

Life was marching on. It was Christmas Day, 1992. I talked to Rock on the phone for several hours. We gossiped about eggnog, chocolate chip cookies and the presents we had given our respective families. From what I gathered, Rock had given several of his children elaborate gifts but he received nothing in return. This appeared to anger him – for he seemed to lose his temper quite easily after Christmas. I think it was the pressure of knowing the police were after him.

Time slipped through all of January and we finally made it to Valentines Day, 1993, with still no arrest and no confession in sight.

The LaSalle Street Murders had become my life. Nothing else could get my attention. I took care of my son and my house. There was no room for a social life. No time for romance or even the dream of it. I was very lonely at night.

Shortly after the cupid holiday, I talked to Rock in the middle of the afternoon. He was extremely bitter towards IPD Lieutenant Mike Ryker.

I couldn't understand why. Until I finally figured it out.

He was jealous!

"I am sensing that Mike Ryker has been flirting with you ever since you first met him," Rock said with venom in his voice. "That was on December 1st, wasn't it?"

"Oh brother, here we go again," I thought as I rolled my eyes to the ceiling. He's talking about his favorite day – December 1st – again. The anniversary of the LaSalle Street Murders always triggered a "tragedy" for Rock.

"What makes you think he did that?" I asked Rock. Of course Lt. Ryker never did anything out of line. But Rock was becoming obsessively jealous of him. It was starting to worry me.

"Because Lieutenant Ryker is a rat," Rock insisted.

"Oh?" I said nonchalantly. "I don't think he's a rat,"

"Yes, he is," Rock said. He was starting to argue with me. "And there's a simple solution for that."

"Yes?" I said, patiently giving him my attention. Rock thrived on that.

"For Lieutenant Loser (he always called him Lieutenant-Loser to make a degrading pun on the officer's last name) – he needs a sheep clamp," Rock said.

"A sheep clamp?" I asked.

I didn't understand.

"That's how they castrate sheep," he said.

"Oh, okay," I said, pretending not to hear Rock's disrespect for the police officer who wanted to arrest him.

"Did you know that damn Lieutenant Ryker spent the night with my ex-wife Diane the first night of the murders?" Rock asked.

I could tell he was so jealous he couldn't see straight.

"No, I didn't know that," I said. But I knew he was lying. I knew Ryker would never do anything like that. It was obvious that Rock *hated* Ryker.

Rock switched the conversation back immediately to Robert Gierse, Robert Hinson and Jimmy Barker's murder. And to Floyd.

"Do you know what my attorney says about Floyd Chastain?" Rock demanded.

"What?" I asked.

"He says Floyd killed these guys on LaSalle Street for money," Rock said.

"Hmm," I said. I didn't believe him.

Rock switched his train of thought again. "I lost my children over this murder case. Over this evil-minded man, Floyd. He would sacrifice anything for his own selfish desires," he said.

Rock seemed to be rambling. I think he was just tired and stressed out today.

"I was a green interment kid in France, during World War II," Rock said, seeming to enjoy the reflection of his past. But he pretended to be disgusted. "I met this French woman. She was a beautiful red head. She looked to be about in her 30's. I found out later that she was married."

"Well, when we got to a quiet place she started unbuttoning my pants," Rock said, describing the scene like it was yesterday.

I wondered where this conversation was headed. With Rock, his conversations usually didn't have to head anywhere. He often talked in fragments.

"I was only 19-years-old," Rock said. "I about whipped her head for doing that. Unbuttoning my pants like she did. That was sick! I don't like anyone to ask me to have sex with them! No, not this guy!"

I didn't even want to listen to what Rock was saying. It disgusted me.

"I don't think I've missed a thing," Rock said. "What do you think?"

"I think I have to go for now, Rock," I said. I quickly changed the subject.

I refused to engage in a conversation about his sexual conduct, past or present, even though the sociologist I interviewed at a local university, IUPUI, told me it was pertinent to the profile of a serial killer.

A serial killer is usually a sexual deviate – quite often a pedophile.

"I'll talk to you later," I said, putting rock in his place.

"Getting hot around the collar, eh Pretty One?" he asked. Then he laughed. "Call me tomorrow."

"Bye," I said.

"Bye-bye," he said.

36

February 17th, 1993

"Irvington Mortuary?" Rock said when he answered the phone.

When I called Rock for our morning chat, he was unusually sinister. He sounded a little bit like a werewolf, I thought.

Sometimes I hated his sick sense of humor.

"What are you doing?" I asked him, nonchalantly, trying to strike up our regular morning conversation. I ignored his funeral parlor joke. The Irvington Mortuary was right around the corner from his house. How tacky!

"I am having fresh strawberries and bagels," I offered, repeating myself. "What are *you* doing this morning?"

"Oh, me, I'm just looking at heads," he said, laughing out loud.

He *knew* I knew he was a murderer.

He thought it was funny.

I could say nothing. "What kind of heads?" I immediately thought.

"Human heads?" I asked.

Rock laughed even harder.

"I'm just doing a little bit of work," he said in a different tone of voice. "It's the head of a *car*, Pretty One."

"That's nice," I said.

"Have I ever told you about a man named Spoons?" Rock asked, immediately changing the subject. There was a creepy, creaking sound coming from the other end of the phone. He sounded like he was opening up a coffin as we talked.

"No," I told him. "You haven't."

"He's dead," Rock said. "You need to try to solve *his* murder just like you're trying to solve the LaSalle Street Murders."

"Oh," is all I said. I didn't always respond to his comments. He was used to it by now. I think he was just glad to have a listening ear, even if I didn't always interject.

We soon ended our conversation.

But within 50 minutes, Rock had dialed my number back up again. He seemed nervous and needy. He seemed to *have* to talk to me.

On some days, I just sat around, waiting for his call. I killed the time watching some game shows on television or cleaning my house. I was beginning to be able to tell when he needed to talk to me. I always waited for his call. I was usually right on time. We were beginning to know each other.

I talked to him three times within an eight hour period that day. I could tell he was really keyed up. I wondered what he had been up to all night.

"Spoons is from Knoxville, Tennessee," Rock told me, out of the blue, for no reason.

"Who *is* this guy Spoons?" I asked. I wanted to know.

"He's dead," Rock told me.

"Who killed him?" I asked.

"You'll find out soon enough," Rock said.

I didn't know what to do with this clue, but I knew it would have to wait. I documented it in one of my diaries and kept it in my dresser drawer. I covered it up with an ivory camisole and a pink slip. I threw a sweatshirt over it to make sure no one would see it if my house were broken into.

"Zach is a very mean German Shepard," Rock said. Again, he was changing the subject. I wondered if he might be on some type of medication. I felt like he wanted to communicate that he had serious protection at his house.

"Is he trying to intimidate me? I wondered.

About four hours later, the phone rang again.

"I've got to make a run to Arkansas," Rock said. He didn't explain himself.

"Oh?" was all I said.

"But I'll call you when I get back, Pretty One," he added. "I should be gone about eight days."

"That's fine, Rock," I said, assuring him that he could leave town safely. I knew he was becoming very attached to me, calling me to check in and all.

"Have a good trip," I said.

"I'll miss you, Pretty One," he said before he hung up.

"You too Rock," I said as the phone clicked a few times and went dead. Actually, I was glad to have the break away from him.

There was nothing but a buzzing dial tone ringing in my ears.

"What is up with him today?" I wondered out loud. "He is acting so peculiar."

37

THE GIRL WITH THE RED SWEATER

Eight days later

I woke before dawn with another horrible nightmare. I dreamed that I was at Robert Gierse's funeral. I was standing in front of his casket and saw that he wasn't really dead.
He was just asleep - thrashing around inside his casket. He looked like he was fighting someone. I felt sorry for him and I was calling out to him in my dream.

"Bob, Bob!" I cried out. "It's okay! Keep fighting him! Keep fighting back! You can make it! Don't give up! Don't die!"

The dream really shook me up. I was trembling and shaking, just like I did after every nightmare. My hands were quivering. I wanted to quit this case with everything I had! I didn't like it or enjoy it anymore. But it was too late! I'd already been thrown into the arms of a serial killer and I couldn't' stop now. I fought the urge to call Rock Norton and tell him I knew he killed Robert Gierse and I had proof!

As soon as I was fully awake and to my senses, I realized it would be a very stupid thing to do. I distracted myself by getting up and making a homemade coffee cake. I used fresh sour cream, buttermilk, brown sugar and pecans. Cooking seemed to take my mind off of murder. I loved to bake.

I waited until 5:30 a.m. to call Rock. I knew he would be home and he would be awake.

"I talked to Lieutenant Ryker while you were gone," I told Rock when he answered the phone. He sounded wide awake. I didn't even bother with hello.

"So what else is new?" Rock said dryly.

"Nothing," I said.

"You wouldn't tell me if there was," Rock said.

He changed the subject.

"Did you miss me, Pretty One?" he asked me point-blank.

"No," I said, more than firmly.

Rock knew I always turned down his advances, but that didn't stop him from making them.

"I missed you," he said.

"Did you get all your business taken care of in Arkansas?" I asked.

"Yes," he said. "I uncovered some strong evidence that will clear my name if the stupid police should ever arrest me."

"Wow," I said. "That's great."

"You'd better believe it's great," he said." It's damn great."

"I also found out where there's a dead body buried," Rock said, volunteering information to me.

I couldn't tell if he was teasing me or being serious.

"I know for a fact that there is a dead body – the body of a young woman – buried on the Southside of Indianapolis," Rock said. "Somewhere near a Maple tree and an elementary school. There is a flagpole nearby."

"What?" I asked.

Rock loved my frightened responses.

"What's her name?" I practically shouted at Rock.

"Her name is Connie," Rock said with a haunted voice. "But from now on, we will call her, `The girl with the Red Sweater.'"

I knew by the sound of Rock's voice, I couldn't take much more of this dangerous game. I believed now, more than ever, Rock was indeed a serial killer. He was starting to taunt me about more than the LaSalle Street Murder victims.

I prayed for something to happen – soon – so I could get out of this nightmare. Alive.

38

"When the officer got there – he found a lady in distress," the police officer said.

It was one of the best leads we'd ever had on the case, except for the day I found Rock Norton.

I got the call at 10 a.m. on a Monday morning. I was doing laundry. The Sheriff let me know a new witness turned up. I dropped everything to listen to him. Boy was it *hot*.

He said her name was Joyce. For some reason, that name sounded really familiar to me.

It seems there was an attempted break-in at her house over the weekend. She thought someone was trying to kill her – and she called the police.

The Sheriff said when they got there, they realized she wanted to talk about more than a robbery. The woman was distressed. She was hysterical. Frightened out of her mind.

She wanted to talk about murder. Murder on LaSalle Street. Twenty-one years ago.

This is what happened:

There were pry marks and fresh wood shavings at the front door. The woman inside, Joyce, was scared to death.

Until he got the call to the older, two-story wooden home just south of 21st Street and Franklin Avenue on the near Eastside, Officer Tony Vincent had been enjoying a slow night at work.

The 12-year Indianapolis Police Department veteran felt the run was going to be unusual the second he heard it come over the two-way radio he held in his hand.

Vincent was a tall, handsome, dark-haired Italian-looking police officer. He had a deep-rooted intuition other cops admired. Tonight was no different. He was more than skeptical as he patrolled the city. When he pulled into the driveway of Joyce's property, he knew it was a serious run. As he took his first foot-steps inside the aging house across the street from a Mom and Pop's pizza shop, he was cloaked in suspicion and intrigue.

He was not prepared for what he saw.

The lady inside resembled a ghost.

She was petite, blond and worn with age. She looked to be about 56-years-old, not a day younger. She sat at the kitchen table, in front him, chain smoking Camel cigarettes.

Vincent had a difficult time communicating with the woman. She was doing little more than staring into space.

"You just don't know," said the brittle woman with dark circles under her eyes. She gave him a pleading look. "You just don't know."

Vincent didn't know what to think. He wondered if she might have been drinking.

"You just don't know," she said to him again.

Officer Vincent stood in her living room, draped with room darkening curtains and nostalgic paraphernalia. He repeatedly tried to interrogate Joyce about the break-in at hand. She couldn't seem to hear the cop questioning her. Instead, her mind was a million miles away.

Suddenly, she blurted out a slur of words that Officer Vincent at first thought he misunderstood.

"THE BLOOD! THE BLOOD!" she cried out in an eerie, monotone, almost trance-like voice.

"THE BLOOD! IT WAS EVERYWHERE!"

Joyce kept repeating it, staring past Officer Vincent. Her eyes were fixed on the wall behind him, her stare penetrating the drywall as though she were looking straight through the police officer's body.

"I've never seen anything like it in my life," Officer Vincent said with a shiver as he described his interview with Joyce. "My spine turned to Jell-O."

Instead of telling Officer Vincent how her home was broken into on this cool March night, Joyce told him about how – 22 years ago – she had been LaSalle Street Murder victim Robert Hinson's date on November 30th, 1971.

Back then, she had the body of a model. She was voluptuous and sexy and had ivory skin that was as soft as a baby's bottom. She wore white, knee-high go-go boots, an expensive blue miniskirt and a soft sweater on her date with Bobby Hinson that night. The two had been out partying at local clubs when Bobby had run out of money. Hinson drove over to the house he shared with Robert Gierse on LaSalle Street at around 9:30 p.m. to get some cash.

He left the car running – with Joyce sitting inside to keep warm – while he ran inside to borrow a few bucks from his roommate, Robert Gierse. He pulled her into his arms and held her close. He told her that he loved her. He gave her a quick peck on the cheek and said a quick, "Back in a second."

Hinson would never return.

He would never come out to the car to get Joyce.

But Rock Norton would.

After about 30 minutes of waiting, Joyce heard her car door being thrust open. She felt a strong gust of December wind hit her in the face. She turned to see the ghoulish face of Rock Norton, standing in front of her like a salivating lion.

He forced her out of the car. He dragged her, pulling her by the hair and the arm into the house. She was screaming for mercy all the way.

Once inside, Joyce sensed death immediately. The house smelled like dead flies and perfume. She witnessed a gruesome murder scene – the brutal murder and throat-slitting of her lover - that would devastate her life forever.

She would never be the same.

Vincent was in near shock.

He immediately put a call in to IPD Lieutenant Mike Ryker - even though it was close to midnight. He couldn't wait to tell him what had just happened.

He couldn't wait to tell him what Joyce had just confessed to.

It was the biggest break - in the LaSalle Street Murders – ever.

Within minutes of Vincent's call, Ryker had called the Marion County Sheriff.

They were both astounded. From the intimate things she said, they knew Joyce was telling the truth. They both agreed her statements matched evidence they had gathered in 1971.

Unfortunately, it only took a couple of days for Joyce's story to make it all the way to the top of the Marion County Prosecutor's Office.

Lonnie Trader listened to everything.

She examined it all with a fine tooth comb.

Once again, with a cavalier wave of her tiny hand, she dismissed everything.

She didn't want to hear what Joyce had to say about the LaSalle Street Murders. Even though Joyce was an eyewitness to the slayings – Trader had no desire to use her testimony.

 In fact, she had no desire in even talking to Officer Vincent. She didn't want to hear what he had to say.

She wasn't interested.

And she still didn't want to arrest Rock Norton for murder.

Period.

39

Spring, 1993

I couldn't wait to tell Rock Norton all about Joyce. As soon as Officer Tony Vincent told me about the incident, I was busting with excitement. The Sheriff said he knew this would be all we would need to arrest Rock Norton.

But he was wrong.

The people with the arrest-making powers said, "NO!"

And they didn't have to tell why.

No just means no.

I had to see what Rock had to say about it.

He was really ticked off.

"What a liar!" he screeched when I told him what she said.

I expected this type of response from him.

"I'm going to have to find that broad and shut her up," Rock said with venom. "I'll find that Joyce-woman and I'll set her straight. Permanently."

I wondered what he was going to do.

I worried that he was going to go kill her.

I knew she wasn't safe.

40

March, 1993

After another eyewitness came forward, I thought there would have been an immediate arrest.

But after two solid weeks, THE PROSECUTORS were still stalling their feet.

No matter how much Lt. Mike Ryker and the Sheriff tried to convince the DA that Joyce's testimony put together the missing links of a 20-year-old puzzle, they *still* refused to issue a warrant for Rock's arrest.

Why?

They wouldn't give out answers.

Silence was the only thing they issued.

And what was even worse, they decided to fire Mike Ryker.

They called him in and stripped him of all authority to ever investigate the LaSalle Street Murders ever again.

I began to feel sick at my stomach. I knew something fishy was going on.

I just couldn't figure out what it was.

I learned more when I interviewed Indianapolis Police

Department Deputy Chief Jim Holder. *This is what he told me:*

It was late. The Indianapolis Police Department Deputy Chief said he was coming back to headquarters very late one night when his beeper started going off.

He looked down at the number and realized it was the PROSE-CUTOR'S OFFICE.

"They wanted me right away," Holder said.

"When I got there, THE PROSECUTOR himself and Lonnie Trader were there," Holder explained.

They stood in front of Holder like they were the German Gestapo.

Holder – shaking his head with disgust - continued his story with displeasure.

"And the PROSEUCUTOR said, "Jim, I need a real favor. We're re-investigating the LaSalle Street Murders and we've got a little problem."

Jim Holder looked at them both with curiosity.

"And then THE PROSECUTOR asked me if I would exercise my authority and keep Mike Ryker out of the case forever," Holder said.

"Permanently." He said.

"So I did what they asked and I never heard another word about it," he said.

"Until the Sheriff asked me to look at some new evidence," he said.

AND THEN THE PROSECUTOR ORDERED A NEW DETECTIVE TO REPLACE LIEUTENANT RYKER.

His name was Detective Jon Padget .

41

Detective Jon Padget came to us in the form of an angel. He may have had whiskers, balding silver hair and a sizeable middle-aged spread, but I know he was sent straight from Heaven. He was the best thing that ever happened to the LaSalle Street Murders in a long, long time.

I had to find out what the IPD Police Chief had to say about the decision to bring him in on the case.

"I trust Jim Holder. His judgment is sound. Absolutely," Police Chief James Wood said when I confronted him with the news. Wood was a large, stately black man who had the presence of a US President. If he said he trusted Jim Holder assigning Jon Padget to the case – then I knew it was a good thing. We were on our way to victory.

"I've done everything I can to help the prosecutor," Wood told me with finality. "I gave him an investigator. Jon Padget was one of the best there ever was at IPD. I've extended myself as far as I can."

I could tell he was done.

He wanted to stay out of it.

It didn't take Jon Padget long to re-investigate the case. He sized it up and stirred it around - like a scientist inventing a potion or the first dose of penicillin. He looked into Rock Norton's past with a fine tooth comb.

He eventually came up with a verdict:

"Rock Norton left behind evidence like *"blood in the snow"* he stated.

His diagnosis?

ROCK NORTON MURDERED ROBERT GIERSE.

No doubt about it, he said.

He even said he believed Rock Norton was *a serial killer.*

Accordingly, he prepared a lengthy warrant for Rock's arrest. It didn't take him long, even though his report was several pages long. He hand-delivered it to the powers that be.

Guess what?

Once again, the PROSECUTOR'S OFFICE wasn't interested. They wouldn't hear of it.

They threw out Jon Padget 's probable cause affidavit – (which is a fancy word for arrest warrant) and discarded it like a dirty, sticky wrapper from a stale candy bar!

Rock Norton would NOT be arrested, the prosecutors said, and they didn't care what award-winning cop prepared the warrant.

They weren't interested!

I chewed on my fingernails until I reached Jim Holder for a comment. He was very concerned that, after Jon Padget 's recommendation of Rock Norton's arrest, no warrants were issued.

"I read Jon Padget 's probable cause thoroughly," said Holder, who was also IPD's former legal advisor. He was a man who knew what he was talking about.

"It was sufficient to issue arrest warrants."

"What's the problem?" I asked with disbelief. "Why wouldn't they go out and handcuff the old guy?"

"I think the problem was pure egos," Holder said. He spoke with disciplined, matter-of-fact determination. "I think THE PROSECUTOR has respect for Lonnie Trader and she (and some other grand jury investigators) have convinced him there's nothing you can do on the case.

"THE PROSECUTOR has always stated he has an open mind on this," Holder said. "And I think he believed that. But I don't really think he did. I'm afraid with the election coming up, this is a done deal."

He made it clear - there will be no arrest on the LaSalle Street Murders.

Carol Sissom, age 2.

Carol Sissom wanted to be a writer when she was a little girl.

Carol Sissom's mother often gave her daughter advice on how to solve a murder.

Carol Sissom grew up on the east side of Indianapolis. She had two sisters, a mother and a father who worked in auto body repair.

Carol Sissom unknowingly grew up near the LaSalle Street killer.

Carol Sissom was a single mother with no police training when she solved a triple murder. Here with son, David.

Bounty hunter, Trent Marsh, was Carol Sissom's bodyguard on some of her most dangerous investigations.

Carol Sissom, 1992, went undercover in 1993 to catch a man she thought was a serial killer. She helped police make the only arrest in the case in the history of the Indianapolis Police Department.

Marsh, known to be one of the best bounty hunters in the U.S., traveled to Florida to help Sissom uncover crucial evidence.

Robert Gierse lived in Chicago and St. Louis before he moved to Indianapolis.

Bob Gierse and his brother, Ted.

Bob Gierse lived in Chicago before he was killed.

Bob Gierse and his mother.

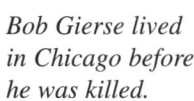

Robert Gierse's wife, before he was murdered.

James Barker was a best friend of Gierse and Hinson. It was said he was at the wrong place at the wrong time.

Barker served in the U.S. Army before he was murdered.

Robert Hinson, the third victim of the LaSalle Street murders, was very good friends with both Gierse and Barker.

*The home where the three men were murdered.
It was later remodeled.*

*Carol Sissom went to dinner with an alleged serial killer on a regular basis in
order to solve a triple murder. The suspect told her he had fallen in love with
her before he was arrested.*

Floyd Chastain, as a toddler. He later confessed he had to kill Bob Hinson in order to save his own life.

NUVO Magazine

Sketched floor plan of the Death House on LaSalle Street.

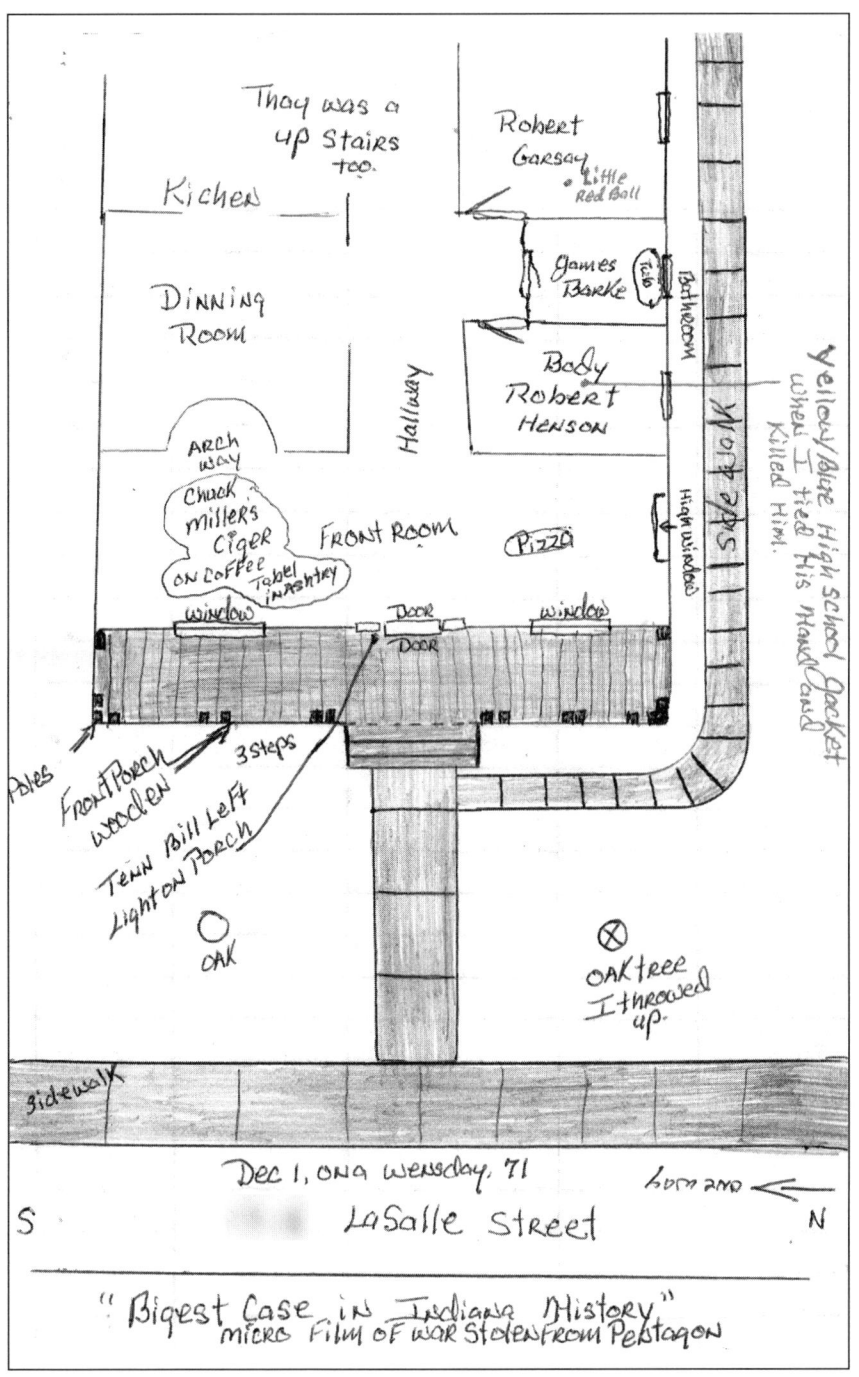

NOV. 1971 John Tairhorse, He was shot to Death over the mirco Film of war, that His Buddys Had. Body was Carried in the Trunk of the 1964 Blue Hardtop Chevy 327, 300 Horse 4 speed 770 mus.

Dark Blue 2 Door 64 Chevy

Trunk Full Blood

Dumped the Body →

EAgle Creek

Gave us the Car to cut up... That Chevy AND I cut up, at my GRARGE 3100 moorsville Rd. Motor went to Robert. Parts to "Sid Junk yard" on 67, By my GRARGE. "Dog House Doors seats."

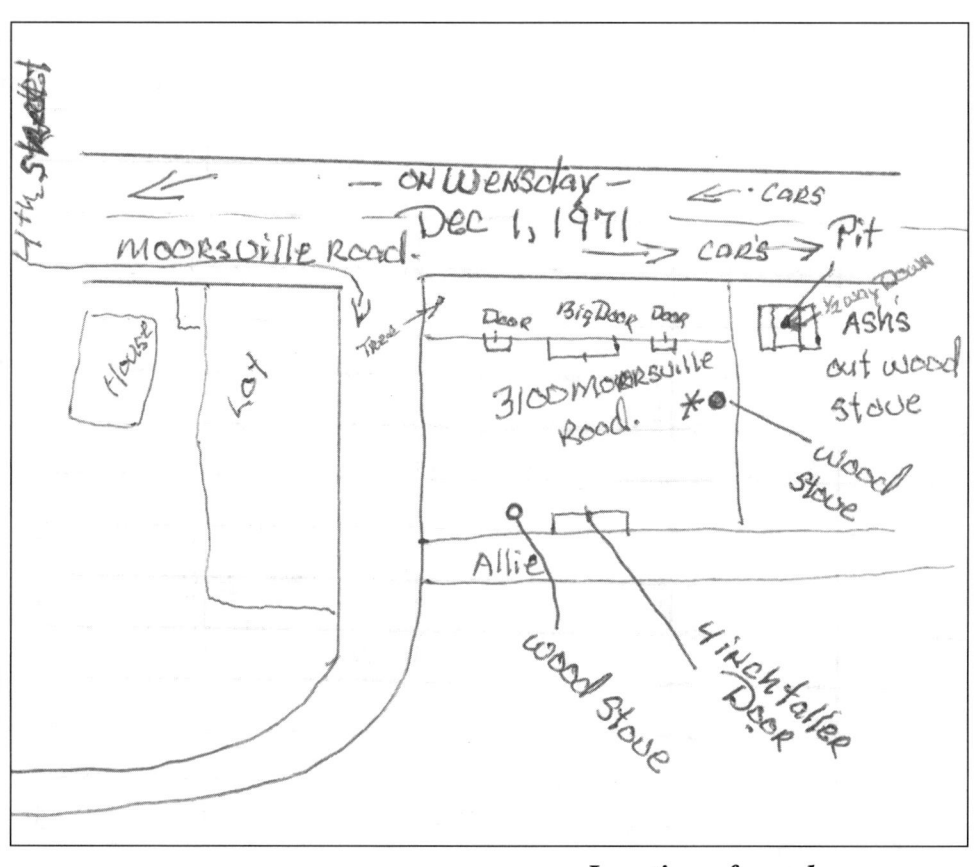

Location of murder weapon.

Murder of Bobby Lee Atkinson.

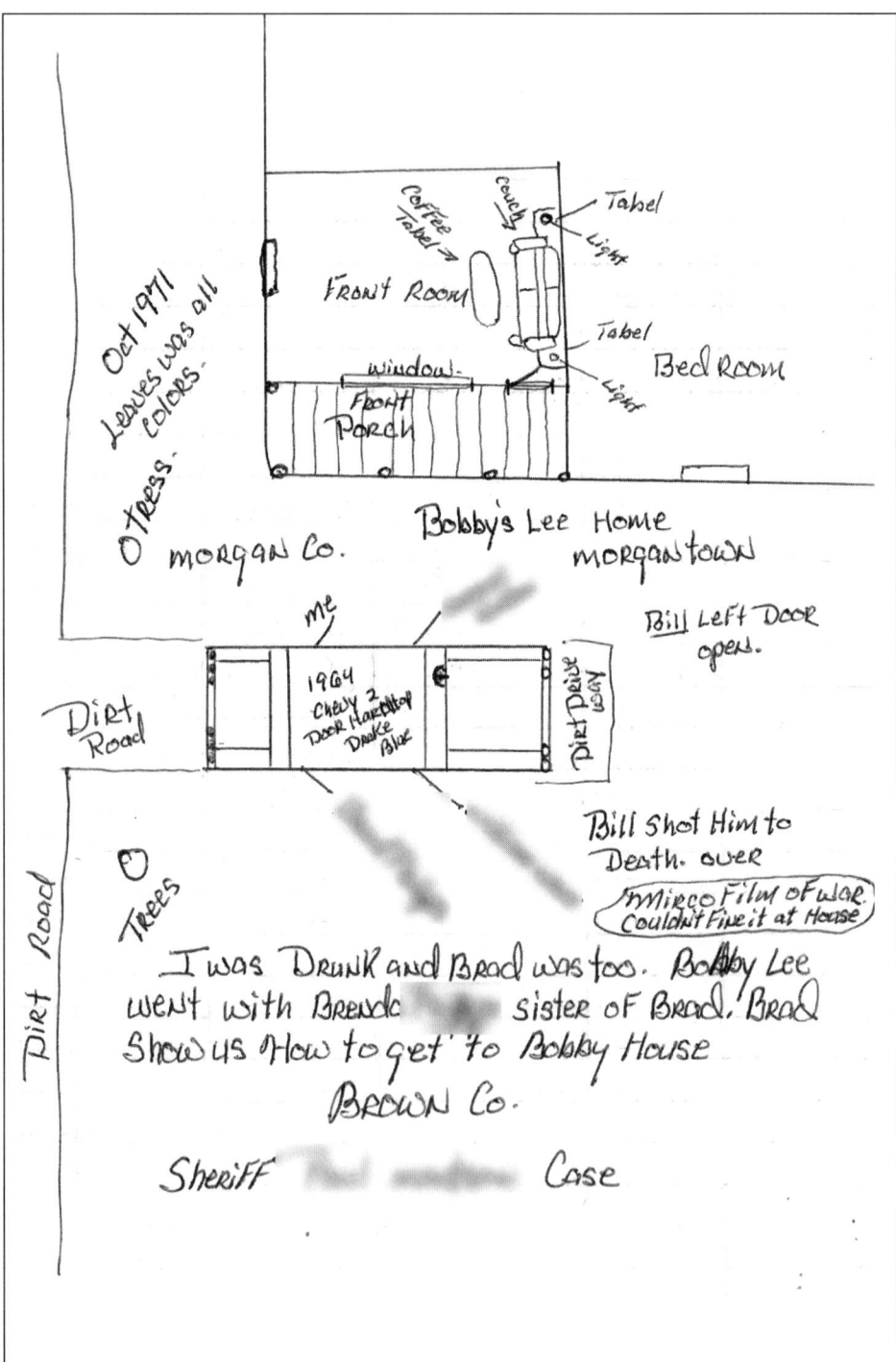

Oct 1971
Leaves was all
colors.

O trees.

Coffee Table →

couch

Front Room

window

Front Porch

Table
Light

Table
Light

Bed Room

Bobby's Lee Home
Morgantown

O morgan co.

me

1964 Chevy 2
Door Hardtop
Drake Blue

Dirt Road

O TREES

Dirt Road

Bill Left Door open.

Dirt Drive way

Bill shot Him to
Death. over
(mirco Film of war.
couldn't Fine it at House)

I was Drunk and Brad was too. Bobby Lee
went with Brenda ▓▓ sister of Brad. Brad
show us How to get to Bobby House
Brown Co.

Sheriff ▓▓▓ Case

Murder of Connie Thomas took place here.

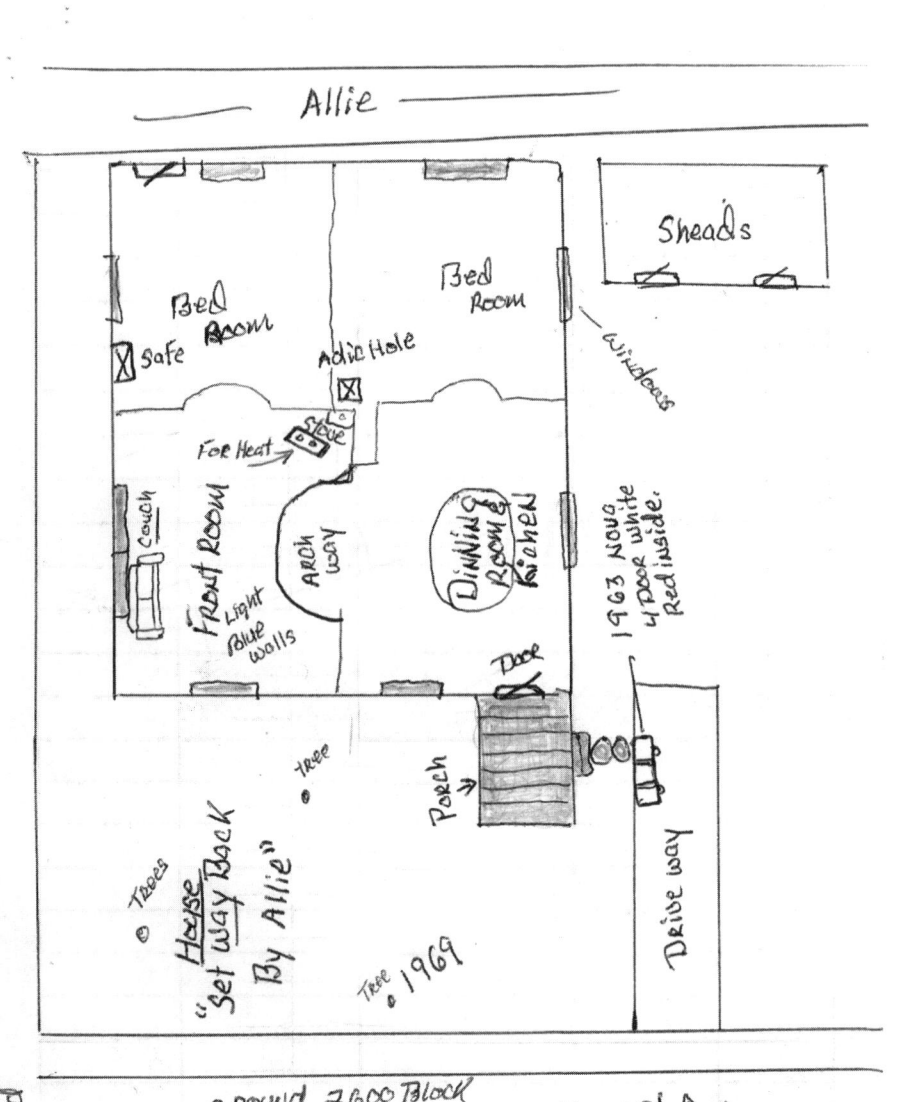

Car similar to one Connie Thomas owned.

windoes

Van 1974 Chevy Long Bed(so VAN).

Packing House in 1975 July 30 wensday

Tenn Bill. Hoffa & Driver me.

a skip Host

Big Door

Door

Welder Room

Where I welded 2 Tops on Boards Black white Stope.

Door

I Beam on FLOOR 12"

Botterns 2 Block 1 Green 1 Red.

Bottens for skip Host

small ←

Going code

Back →

Going ↓

Back ↓

turned on the writer Ground them up.

Both men one at a time

I put Barrel under this end By Drone

Light Green Grinder

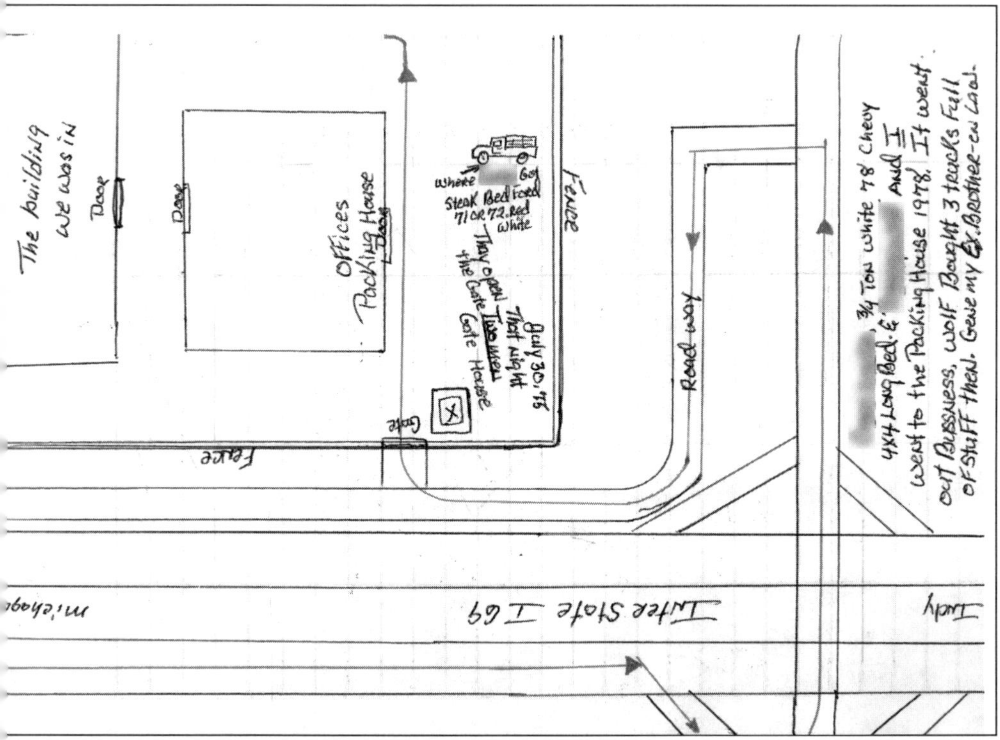

The building we was in

Door

Door

Offices

Packing House Door

where I Got Steak Bed Fixed 71 OR 72 Red White

Fence

They open That night the Gate Two men Gate House

July 30, 75

Gate ☒

Fence

Road way

¾ Ton white 78 Chevy 4x4 Long Bed E And I went to the Packing House 1978. It went out Buissness. Wolf Bought 3 trucks Full of stuff then. Gave my Ex Brother-en Law.

Michegan

Inter State I 69

Judy

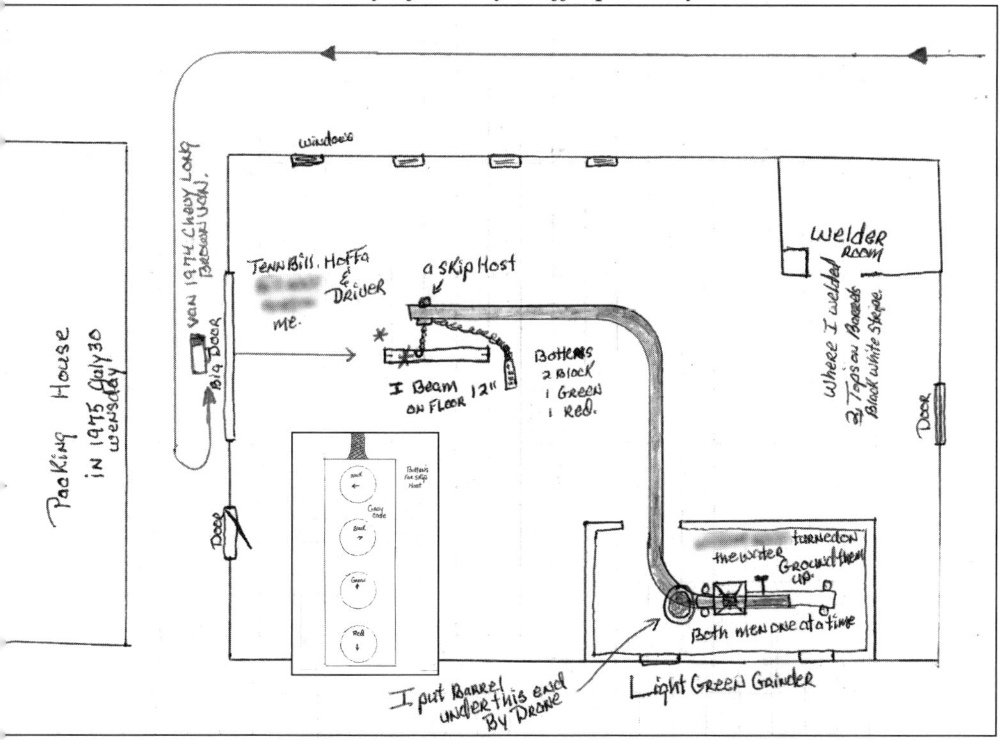

THE LASALLE STREET MURDERS

Let's call it
Who dun it!

The bizarre, true story of the relationship between a news reporter and a notorious serial killer.

by
Carol Schultz

This book cover was designed by Carol (Schultz) Sissom and the LaSalle Street killer.

Murder case's court debut has a touch of Hollywood

By George McLaren
STAFF WRITER

The LaSalle Street murder case opened in court Thursday and played like a movie script:

Missing evidence. Lying witnesses. Greedy investigators. Compromised police files. Conflicts among detectives.

And a $1 million deal for the story rights.

Defendant _____ 70, faces three counts of murder in the 1971 slayings of three men at an Eastside residence.

Paula E. Lopossa to release him on bond pending trial. The details of the case came out during witness testimony in a hearing on the matter.

Defense attorney Richard Kammen is trying to show that the prosecutor's case is weak and that bond is appropriate.

"This murder was a tragedy," Mr. Kammen said afterward. "There's no question about that. That _____ should be prosecuted on this type of evidence is equally a tragedy."

See MURDER Page 2

LEADING ROLE: Writer Carol Schultz has been investigating the case on her own since 1992.
Staff Photo

Article from The Indianapolis Star

THURSDAY
DAILY JOURNAL

JOHNSON COUNTY, INDIANA

CENTS

Writer breaks LaSalle Stree...

EDITOR'S NOTE — This is the first installment of a two-part series on the LaSalle Street murders. On Friday, reporter Scott Hall describes how key figures changed their lives and broken their faith in the legal system.

By Scott Hall
DAILY JOURNAL STAFF WRITER

Carol Schultz story sounds like a Hollywood thriller: A petite young woman with the native killer...

SPECIAL REPORT

when he is finally arrested, she finds herself once in the story's true. Incredible as it is, the story is true, and neither could...

THE 25-YEAR ...

Dec. 1, 1971 — The bodies of James Barker... and Robert Hinson are found beaten and bou... brothers slashed in a house on Indianapolis east side.

March 1991 — Free-lance writer Carol Schultz beg... investigating the murders for a newspaper story and la... decided to write a book on the case.

July 1992 — Indianapolis resident _____ coming to have psychic abilities, begins helping Schultz with her research.

September 1992 — A Florida prison inmate implicates _____ in the slayings. Schultz notifies Marion County prosecutors, who are reluctant to pursue the case.

July 1996 — A grand jury indicts _____, who is arrested and charged with the three murders.

March 22, 1996 — The grand jury begins to review evidence and interview witnesses.

Article from The Franklin Daily Journal

42

SHOCKING NEWS

Saturday morning

Floyd called me just before dawn and confessed to more involvement in the LaSalle Street Murders.

Even though there was no arrest pending, things were still moving swiftly. It was as if the case were a piece of driftwood floating down a river.

It was shortly after 6 a.m. and my face was melting into my pink pillowcase like a stick of hot butter. I was surrounded by down feathers and a cushiony softness that lured me back to sleep even though I heard my telephone ringing incessantly. I was having a pleasant dream about something – inevitably something besides murder and mayhem.

Darn it!

Floyd's repeated collect calls from the prison jolted me awake. I reached over and picked it up with a sleepy voice.

Floyd needed to talk. He said he'd been praying all night and it was urgent he confess to something.

I rubbed my eyes awake and listened to what he had to say. I thrust my feet on the floor and padded to the kitchen for a cold glass of orange juice. I sipped it slowly while I listened to him confess.

Floyd admitted he did more than drive the getaway car on December 1st, 1971. He said Rock Norton made him stand outside and be the lookout man.

He said he watched Rock kill Robert Gierse and a man by the name of Tennessee Bill Howard slit James Barker's throat. Afterwards, Floyd said Tennessee Bill and Rock came after him. Rock handed him a knife.

It was still dripping with blood. Human blood.

He said Rock told him he had to cut Robert Hinson's throat or the knife would be used on him.

"It was kill or be killed," Floyd explained.

What did he do?

Floyd said he obeyed Rock Norton's orders.

He said he slit Bobby Hinson's throat.

And then he went outside and threw up, he said.

I cried out loud when I heard it. I wept for Bobby Hinson.

Floyd was overflowing. He continued because he wanted to talk about Rock's other serial killings. He rattled off at least 10 other names of victims he was certain Rock Norton had murdered. One of them included an ex-wife named Norma. Another was a man by the name of Al Reynolds. Another was a woman named Verna. Another was Barbara....

Floyd told me he believes there is a body buried in Rock Norton's backyard.

He said it is the body of a young girl who was only 19-years-old when Rock Norton murdered her, he said.

"Her name is Connie," Floyd said. His voice echoed, like a train conductor calling out names for passengers.

The prison operator cut off our call and I was left hanging.

43

A week later

It was a gray and cloudy Tuesday.

I moaned and rolled over while I was still in bed. I stared at my phone before I touched it. I pulled the receiver up to my ear and listened for a dial tone. I looked outside as I dialed. The skies were a usual Indiana gray and I felt like the earth was moving faster than usual. It had to be. I was living in a nightmare.

I called Rock and his phone was disconnected. I instantly sensed danger. I worried because I *knew* something was up. Something was wrong. Very wrong.

"Oh Jesus," I said, and pulled a tissue to my nose. After all this agony, Rock couldn't just disappear on me.

I made a few more calls around town and found out that he was really gone! Lock stock and barrel! Rock's phone number at his shop was also disconnected. All of the lines going into his place of business and even the spare number he had given me were dead.

I started to panic. I called the Indianapolis Power and Light Company and gave them Rock's address. I checked on his electric bill. A representative told me his lights would be disconnected within 24 hours.

I speed dialed and called Citizen's Gas. A friendly woman told me Rock's gas service was in the process of being disconnected too!

I couldn't figure out what was going on! I was afraid Rock had skipped town!

Later that night, Floyd called me around 7:30 p.m. It was just after dark. I told him what happened and he said he thought Rock might be loading up to move out of the country.

He told me if Rock really was gone – I needed to have the police dig for dead bodies in Rock's back yard. He said he believed there might be more than one dead body buried in his basement.

He said Rock had a bad habit of killing young girls!

What was going on?

I knew instinctively Rock was running scared!

"Were the police scared too?" I wondered.

44

Monday morning

I woke up and decided to take my story to the media.

Publicity was the protection I needed right now.

I called NUVO Newsweekly, whose modern offices were located in Broad Ripple, Indiana. It was a quaint, cute little town with a canal and lots of sidewalk boutiques, coffee shops and a health food store next to the fire department. I talked to the editor, Scott Hall. He was a young, boyish editor with dark hair, a pretty wife and new baby. He seemed to sincerely believe what I was saying about Rock Norton. He was more impressed with my guts. He said if I wrote a good story, he would publish it.

Just before noon, I called Rock on his mobile phone.

I had to find him and tell him what I did.

"Where have you been?" I literally yelled at him.

"I had to take a little break from society," Rock explained.

"Don't ever do that to me again!" I said. I surprised myself. I sounded like I was scolding my child.

Then I told him about NUVO and the story I was going to write for them.

"That's very good news, Pretty One," Rock told me. His voice sounded a little moody. "Get all the publicity you can get. This is the story of a life time."

"I know, Rock," I said.

"You *are* going to win the Pulitzer Prize, Pretty One," he said. "And I'm going to help you do it. Now that you and I have joined forces – our book will get national attention."

I sighed. I wondered how long I could keep up this game.

Rock sensed my anxiety.

"Are you worried about me, Pretty One?" he whispered.

I conceded.

"Yes," I said.

"Are you afraid I'm going to jail?" he asked.

"Yes," I whispered back.

Were Rock and I becoming attached to each other?

"The police are going to find my fingerprints were inside that house," Rock said. "I just know it."

"Why?" I asked.

"Because I was in there *after* the murders," he said. "Remember? The police let me in to have a look because I told them I knew those bums were international spies. Well, they're going to start saying I was in there *before* the murders. They're going to say they found my fingerprints on a bottle of beer. Just watch and see. My ESP is telling me this is going to happen."

I couldn't say anything. All I could do was document it in my diary.

Rock said he wanted me to know why he had the electricity disconnected at his shop.

"Why?" I asked.

"I'm getting close to 70-years-old, Pretty One," he told me. "The threat of me going to jail for murder is getting very near. I will probably die in jail. I have to liquidate everything now. "

I could tell there was heavy stress in his voice.

He explained further. "I have two places of business now. One garage is just too full of . . . debris . . . and clutter . . . " he said, his voice trailing off. "I have to downsize."

He said moving from one shop to another had put him under

146

a lot of emotions.

"I didn't like parting with some very important things," he said.

"I'm sorry, Rock," I said.

I couldn't explain it, but I felt strangely sorry for Rock tonight.

I think he felt sorry for me, too.

"I'm worried about you too, Pretty One," he told me. "I want to help you get all of the credit for the book you are writing, Pretty One.

I was dumbfounded.

"What do you mean, Rock?" I asked.

"I don't want any credit at all," he said. "I'm going to help you solve these murders, but I want *you* to get all the credit."

"Thank-you, Rock," I said. "But don't worry about me."

"I have a lead you need to follow up on," he said.

"What's that?" I asked.

"That Robert Gierse," he said. "He reported a burglary right before the murders."

"What?" I said.

"Look into it, Pretty One," he said. I know he could hear me scribbling on the other end of the phone.

"And another thing," he said.

"That Floyd Chastain. He's a dangerous criminal. Beware of him. He killed Bob Hinson for money."

I wrote everything down as fast as I could.

Rock changed the subject.

"What are you going to name your book?" he asked me. There it was again. The same question. For the hundredth time.

He seemed so sincere. I was irritated that he asked me the same question at least once a week. It was a joke he seemed to enjoy.

"I have the perfect title for your book," Rock insisted again. He knew very well that we had discussed this on several different occasions.

He blurted out the words again.

"Let's Call It Whodunit," he said.

"What do you mean?" I asked him again, as though he had never suggested the same title before. I kept hoping he would say something incriminating against himself again.

"Just that," he snorted. "It's more than a Whodunit you know!"

I stood corrected and hung up the phone.

He wants me to catch him! I realized.

He's making fun of me. And trying to help me all at the same time! He's making fun of the fact that I know he's a serial killer! I can't catch him and he knows it!

45

Spring, 1993

The most horrible thing happened tonight!

I ran out of milk, eggs and Pepsi for my son, so I went to the grocery store at 7:30 p.m. It was warm out and I was in a hurry, so I just wore what I had on. I grabbed my car keys and hopped in my Honda. It was such a short trip I even left my front door unlocked.

I sped down to Cub Foods, which was at the corner of Washington Street and Shortridge Avenue, about three miles away. I was inside, looking for my son's favorite brand of sour cream potato chips when I turned the corner near the milk and butter refrigeration section. When I looked up I saw an old man with a gray and weathered face staring at me.

It was Rock Norton! His eyes were dancing above me!

Eek!

I immediately looked down at myself. I had on a comfortable – yet skimpy - pair of white jean shorts and a pretty pink top made of silk that was cut around my cleavage with white lace. I looked at my feet – I had slipped on a pair of white leather sandals and I carried a blue beach bag for a purse. I was feminine and dainty and I knew Rock Norton liked it. I suddenly felt like a beauty contestant strolling down the runway for his review.

Rock Norton was looking at me like I was a mouse that had slipped out of its cage.

I literally shrieked under my breath. I turned on my heels and ran to my car, leaving my groceries in the cart behind me. I thought I was going to pee my pants.

I was so scared I just sat in the front seat of my sedan, shivering. I closed my eyes and prayed, begging God for mercy. My heart was racing so fast I thought I was going to pass out. My hands were trembling so much I couldn't even steady the key into the ignition. I felt like I was in the middle of a horror movie. I locked all the doors and made sure the windows were rolled up.

I was terrified!

After about 20 minutes, I was able to gain my composure and drive home. I tip-toed inside and kept the lights off and sat on my couch in the dark. The only light inside was the digital clock on my VCR. I grabbed my Bible and clutched it to my chest.

Two hours later my telephone rang. I knew it was him.

"Hello?" I said, pretending to be occupied with a television program. I was still sitting in my living room, in the dark.

"Hello, Pretty One," Rock said when I answered the telephone.

I tried to sound calm.

"Hi Rock," I said. I gripped the phone.

"I saw you at Cub Foods tonight," he said.

I nodded. I knew he couldn't hear me shake.

"Those were some very pretty white shorts you had on," he said.

I suddenly felt very choked up.

Fear was my middle name.

"I – I – I didn't see you," I lied to Rock.

I could hear chuckling on the other end of the phone.

"Well, I could certainly see *you*," he said. "You have a very nice set of legs, Pretty One."

I was so nervous I made an excuse - like my house was on fire or something - and I hung up the phone.

I ran to my front door and shook the door handle furiously. I had to make sure it was locked, again. I crumbled to the floor and sat there, sobbing. I wished I had never started investigating the LaSalle Street Murders. I wished I hadn't turned into an amateur private detective.

I fell asleep crying.

I stayed in the same spot, huddled in my own tears until dawn broke through the curtains.

46

The next morning, I got a call from the Sheriff. It was a beautiful day and the birds were singing. It felt like the morning after a tornado in Indiana. The sun was shining and I felt positive. The sound of the Sheriff's reassuring voice made me feel safe.

"That Floyd positively identified Joyce tonight," he told me. He said Floyd admitted to seeing the woman inside the death house.

He told the Sheriff that Joyce was Number #5 in the lineup of pictures that the police had laid out before him.

Even though the Prosecutors had no intention of making an arrest, the Sheriff had no intention of giving up.

"Floyd said Joyce was a very young girl the night of the LaSalle Street Murders," the Sheriff relayed to me. "She had no idea what was going on when Rock Norton pulled her inside that house."

"That is so incredible " I told the Sheriff. "But where do we go from here?"

"I don't know," the Sheriff told me. "But I know that crazy Rock Norton did it. Our only problem is getting the Prosecutor to make an arrest."

"Sheriff," I said out loud.

"I'm starting to get scared," I said.

"I know," he said. "You're starting to do some pretty dangerous things, with that nut Norton falling in love with you. You're setting yourself up, you know."

"It's too late now," I told him. "I can't go back. I can only go forward."

"I tell you what I'm going to do," he said. "Would it make you feel better if I parked one of my sheriff's cars out in the front of your house? That way if Norton drives by your house he will think there's a cop inside?"

I was instantly relieved.

"YES!" I said without hesitation.

"Would you really do that?" I asked. "That would make me feel better, Sheriff."

Within four hours there was a tan Sheriff's cruiser parked in front of my house. It was locked. As far as Rock Norton was concerned, it was mine. For the time being.

The only requirement the Sheriff asked of me was that I move the squad car once a day. He suggested I park it facing in different directions to make sure Rock would think I was either married to a cop - or I was one.

We knew he would be driving by.

But we didn't know when.

We didn't want him to know I was alone.

47

I was stunned to see there was a media frenzy when the news about the re-investigation of the LaSalle Street Murders leaked out. It reached all three networks at the same time. The first breaking story hit at 6 p.m.

I knew the reporter who tastefully produced it, but I could only guess who leaked it to him. Regardless, when the media got full wind of what was going on it was crazy. The first and most dramatic piece aired on WISH-TV 8. It ruined Rock Norton's dinner and gave him quite a bit of heartburn.

News Anchors aired excellent footage of the Sheriff and Mike Ryker going to Florida to interview Floyd Chastain. They detailed information about how Chastain knew Rock Norton and that he was an official suspect. They told the city everything we already knew. It was good.

Rock called me as soon as the lead story aired. He sounded like he was choking on a piece of chicken.

Boy was he upset!

He said he is going to sue the city of Indianapolis for accusing him of murder.

"I am losing my mind, Pretty One," he said.

"No you're not, Rock," I said. I reminded him he had to help me solve the case and win the Pulitzer Prize. "Hang in there. You're going to make it."

I watched the rest of the CBS show and prayed to God some more.

Life was really getting scary. I felt extremely nervous.

After the show was over, my telephone rang.

It was my bounty hunter friend, Trent.

"I just saw the show on TV. You need to get a gun, NOW, Darling'" he advised me. "If I saw the show on CBS you know Rock Norton did. He *has* to know you're onto him by now. Things are getting too dangerous for you and your boy. Don't leave your house after dark. Call me if you need me."

48

A freakish Spring Day
1993

I learned Rock Norton definitely had a need to rescue women!

Indiana was known for abrupt weather changes. It was frigidly cold on an unusual Friday morning. The wind chill factors were making records as they nipped at my bones. Unfortunately, the deep freeze caused me to lose water in all areas of my house. The bathroom and the kitchen faucets didn't even have a merciful reserve drop to slide down my sinks. I couldn't flush toilets, do laundry or cook. My son complained that he couldn't take a bath. I sent him to his grandmother's house to shower.

I was miserable.

At 6 a.m. I called Rock. It was my usual time. I told him all about it. Since we always talked about everything anyway, why not tell him?

Sometimes, when you talk to a serial killer every day - you just run out of things to talk about and you share life experiences. It seemed like I'd known Rock for an entire lifetime.

He was very worried about me.

"Pretty One," he said. "I'll come over and thaw out your pipes. Just you and me rubbing ourselves together should do the trick."

"Oh, for God's sakes," I moaned at Rock. I thought he was joking. But when I called him back – later that evening – Rock told me he went out and bought a blow torch to unfreeze my pipes!

This totally freaked me out! Like I would really let him come over to my house to use his blowtorch on my pipes.

But it was nice of him anyway, I told him.

We both knew he *knew* where I lived. So why pretend anymore?

Rescuing people, especially women in distress – must be one of his favorite ways to capture people.

And all of his preys.

Animal or human.

I knew I was about to become one of Rock's helpless victims. If I had invited him into my house to repair the water, I would have been a murder victim, I am certain. I vowed to wait for hell to freeze over before I ever let Rock Norton come over to my house. Let alone come over to thaw out the pipes under my kitchen sink.

I decided to get out my blow dryer and do it myself.

My life was rich in suspense.

49

Rock said he wants to put up a $1,000.00 reward to find out where Floyd Chastain was the night of December 1st, 1971.

March 4th, 1993

Rock Norton told me the dead men on LaSalle Street borrowed $100,000 dollars of Mafia money and they didn't pay it back.

Robert Gierse bought a new car with the money, Rock said.

He woke me up at 5 a.m. to tell me this.

I didn't know what to think.

"That was a lot of money back in 1971," I told him. "Why would they borrow so much money from the mob?"

Rock was super-charged.

"That's for you to figure out," he said. He was full of enthusiasm and he sounded pretty feisty. "The only clue I'll give you is they borrowed it the same year they died. 1971. Look up Gierse's car registration and find out when he bought that shiny Cadillac of his."

Rock said there was a very well-known person at the Indianapolis 500 involved in the LaSalle Street Murders. It was someone that no one would ever suspect.

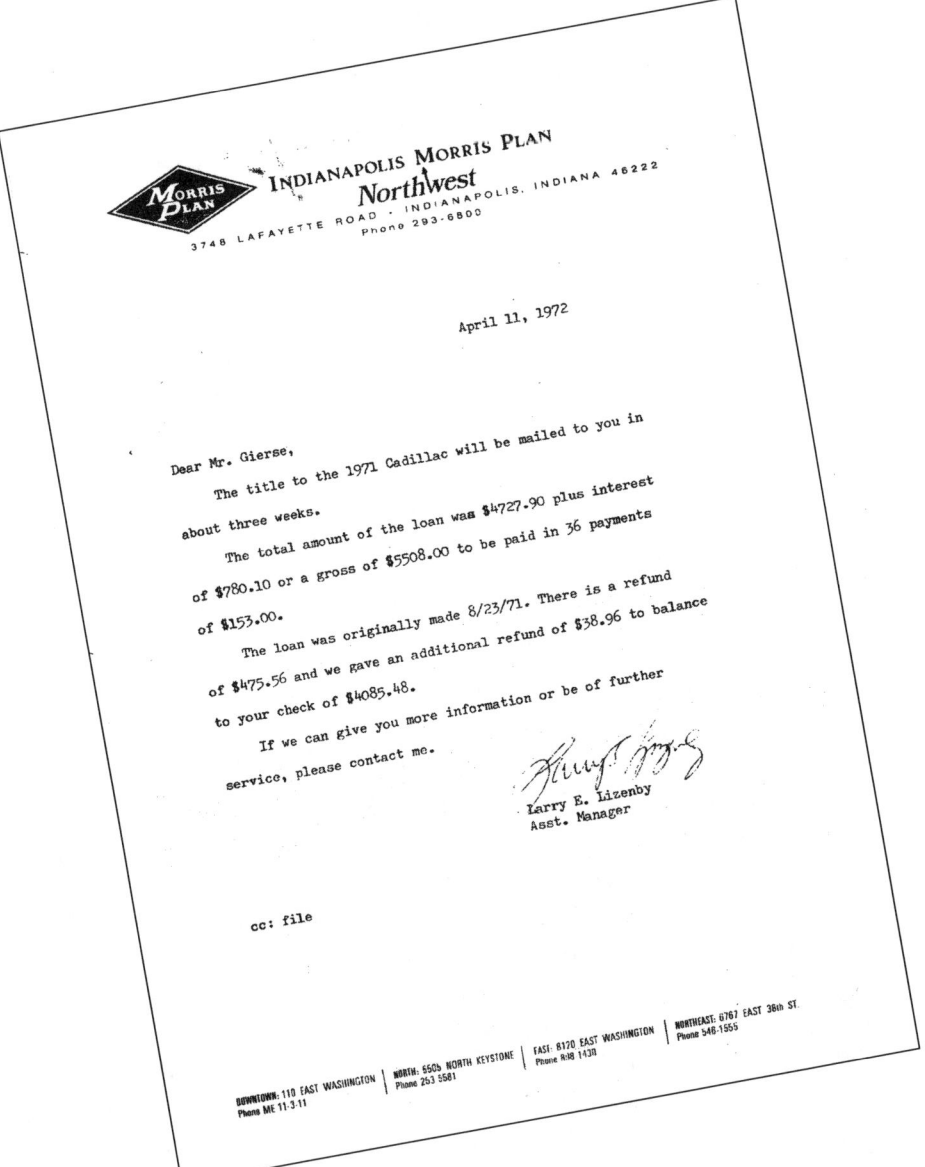

INDIANAPOLIS MORRIS PLAN
Northwest
3748 LAFAYETTE ROAD · INDIANAPOLIS, INDIANA 46222
Phone 293-6800

April 11, 1972

Dear Mr. Gierse,

The title to the 1971 Cadillac will be mailed to you in about three weeks.

The total amount of the loan was $4727.90 plus interest of $780.10 or a gross of $5508.00 to be paid in 36 payments of $153.00.

The loan was originally made 8/23/71. There is a refund of $475.56 and we gave an additional refund of $38.96 to balance to your check of $4085.48.

If we can give you more information or be of further service, please contact me.

Larry E. Lizenby
Asst. Manager

cc: file

DOWNTOWN: 110 EAST WASHINGTON Phone ME 11-3-11 | NORTH: 5505 NORTH KEYSTONE Phone 253-5581 | EAST: 8120 EAST WASHINGTON Phone 898-1430 | NORTHEAST: 6767 EAST 38th ST. Phone 546-1555

50

March 4th, 1993

Rock was obsessing over his ex-wife, Diane Norton, again this morning.

He was always proud to be her armor— even after their divorce.

"I beat the sh——- out of some guy in the early 1980's after I caught him in bed with my wife," he said.

"What for?" I asked.

"He was hiding," Rock reported.

"My little son said, `Dad! He's hiding in the toilet!'" Rock said, reliving the experience like it was yesterday.

"Ha ha ha," Rock said. He was enjoying the memory.

"So I got the guy out of the john," Rock said. "I said, Marty, sit down! I want to talk to you. Before he could I took him out the back door and whipped his head real good. I whipped that man to death," Rock said with glee. I could tell he was in a place of enjoyment. "The guy was bleeding all over the place."

"You get strong on things like that," Rock told me.

I maintained my silence as I listened in horror.

"I beat him up and he was bleeding all over the place. The old man with a broken arm beat him up. It was a pleasure to beat up my ex-wife's ex lover!

I am in awe that Lonnie Trader refuses to allow this man to be arrested! He is savage!

51

March 28th, 1993

Rock Norton wanted to brag about being 67-years-old.

"Happy Birthday, Rock," I told him over the telephone. It was the day after and he was in a jolly mood.

"I had a dream about you on my birthday," Rock said to me. I had never heard him giggle before.

"What was your dream?" I asked him nonchalantly, daydreaming about the Sheriff putting handcuffs on him and leading him to jail as a surprise party.

"I'd rather not say," Rock said. His voice trailed off. He immediately made a sudden personality change. His voice deepened and he sounded extremely mellow. I wondered if he suffered from clinical depression.

"But we were *together,*" he whispered.

I didn't reward him for making such a bold statement. I stayed silent.

He continued his poetic passion. He didn't seem to care I wasn't talking back to him. It scared me.

Rock sounded more than low. He was extremely melancholy. I looked around my house to make sure the windows were locked. For the first time, I actually thought I should get a gun. I made a mental note to call a gun store later in the day.

"Pretty One, I wish you were over here," Rock said before he hung up the phone. "I'd snuggle you up under the covers and tell you how important you are to me!"

I shook my head and clenched the phone.

"Snuggle? With a serial killer?" I thought to myself. "I think I'm going to throw up!"

I sat at the other end of the phone, my mouth hanging open.

Rock finally said the words I had been dreading.

"I am falling in love with you, Pretty One," he said.

It was the kiss of death for me. A serial killer had fallen in love with me.

I felt the tears streaming down my face. This was no way to live.

I had a vision of Rock Norton, standing in front of me with a knife, laughing.

52

THE HOLIDAYS
1993

The months were turning into years and we were all getting discouraged.

Another Halloween, Thanksgiving and Christmas all went by with still no confession from Rock Norton.

The Sheriff, Lieutenant Ryker, Detective Jon Padget and I – we all seemed to keep each other encouraged, but sometimes it was difficult. It was the most dangerous period of my life - because I was thrown into the arms of a serial killer and he was in love with me. I was the one living life on the edge.

I prayed often for God to protect me and my son.

Shortly after Christmas, I left my correspondent's job at *The Indianapolis News*. It was tough, but a decision I had to make.

Mark Ridolfi, my editor, sat across from me and stared at me with these kind, baby blue eyes. I knew he hated telling me what he had to tell me.

"You've crossed the line, Carol," he said. Helping the police had compromised my ethics as a journalist.

"Wearing a wire and doing undercover work for the cops is just *not* something a reporter should be doing," he said. Even though I was a two-time Eugene Pullium Scholarship winner and a First Place Thomas R. Keating Feature Writing Award winner, I knew I had to hang up my badge as a reporter.

Even though I had been a reporter for most of my life, I knew I had to give it all up to catch a killer – no matter what it cost me.

When I reached up to give Mark a hug I saw a tiny tear in his eye as he hugged me good-bye.

"You're a good reporter, Carol," Mark said. "Good luck."

I smiled at him and looked away before I burst out crying. I was wearing blue jeans, an oxford shirt and a black trench coat. I wrapped it around me for warmth and security as I took the elevator down from the second floor. I walked out of the red brick building at 307 North Pennsylvania Avenue for the last time.

I left *The Indianapolis News* with regrets, wishing I was a cop.

53

December 31st, 1993

New Years Eve was the perfect time to be vulnerable.

I carried my heart on my sleeve most of the day, wishing I had someone – anyone – to spend the evening and the sub-zero temperatures with. Howling winds that dipped into nearly 20-below wind chill factors blasted at my windows, giving me little motivation to venture outside on this particular holiday. I decided to seclude myself in the barriers of my home, nurturing my post-Christmas blues with great hopes of a promising New Year – 1994 – looming ahead.

Shortly after 4 p.m. I waved good-bye to my 13-year-old son, David, who tossed a carefree wave at me and a casual "See ya Mom," as he ran out the door and jumped into a car with his best friends Kyle and Brandon and Brandon's mother, Sherry. They were off to youth group festivities at Heather Hills Baptist Church – only a few miles away.

I feigned a hearty smile at them from the picture window as they drove off, happy that my baby was going to have a good time with his buddies and a sleep over with a good Christian family.

Trying to ignore my loneliness, I turned and padded to the kitchen in my favorite red velour bathrobe. I lit an Evergreen Christmas Tree candle in the darkened kitchen and grabbed a half-pound bag of Ruffles Potato chips from the counter. I fished in the refrigerator for a container of French Onion Dip. I fetched a half quart of low fat cottage cheese and headed down the unlit hallway to my bedroom to watch reruns of "Designing Women" on television. The only light in the house was the bulb from my 19-inch Samsung TV.

After reading a stack of Redbook, Good Housekeeping and Glamour magazines, I exhausted the movie I rented from Blockbusters the day before. Even though I enjoyed it, I was still restless. It seemed everyone I knew was out having fun on this festive night. Everyone but me – a lonely single mother who was spending most of her life trying to solve a triple homicide. A woman who rarely had a boyfriend and who seemed to have no life but the adrenaline of crime-solving she was addicted to. A woman whose best friends were homicide cops, hostage negotiators, FBI agents, private detectives, bounty hunters, narcotics officers and bail bondsmen. And an occaisional convicted murderer.

By 7:30 p.m. a hot bath, talking to a few girlfriends on the phone and even typing a poem on my computer whittled away more time. But I was growing more bored with every minute.

At 8 p.m. I couldn't resist the urge. I'd already talked to him once – just before 6 a.m. I had documented my daily phone call with Rock Norton on tape and in my diary. But now, used to his voice in my ear from the opposite end of my telephone receiver, I decided to call him just to see what he was up to. Why not?

"Hello?" he said, answering the phone on the third ring.

"What are you doing?" I asked Rock Norton, inflecting a lilt in my voice to sound joyful and upbeat.

"I am soaking my feet," he said with sarcasm. "It was a rough day at work with all of them losers. What are you doing?"

"Nothing. Absolutely nothing. It's New Years' Eve and I am bored stiff," I told Rock. I fished under my bed for my tape recorder and pulled it next to me as I spoke. I glanced around the room and looked for an outlet to plug it into the wall.

"Why don't you have a date with the blind man tonight?" Rock asked. I could hear him swishing his feet around in something. I imagined his thick feet immersed in a large tub full of hot water and Epsom salt.

"I am not dating a blind man, Rock," I told him, referring to a blind date I had with someone in 1992. "It didn't work out and you know that."

"Well, you should be out on a date with someone," Rock said dryly. "Blind man or not, you should not be sitting home alone, like me."

"That's why I called," I told Rock honestly. I slid a blank tape in my recorder and plugged it in behind my computer. On the average, I garnered about 5 hours of tape recordings of Rock Norton each week. I figured tonight would be more background information for my book. Or it might just be the night he confessed to me on tape. If I could ever coax him into the right frame of mind to expose his past.

"I figured you might be sitting home alone, tonight," I told Rock.

"I am," he said. "There is no woman alive out there who wants to spend time with me. So be it. There are plenty of other fish in the sea."

I said nothing in response to his prophetic statement.

"So what do you want to talk about?" he asked, waiting for me to respond. I could hear him switch off his television set that was blaring in the background. I knew I had his full attention.

"I don't know, what do you want to talk about?" I asked him. I looked over to make sure my tape recorder was running correctly.

"About you coming over here with your toothbrush and your pajamas?" Rock asked. I could almost hear him raise his eyebrows.

"No, silly," I said in a joking voice. I quickly changed the subject.

"How about something else. Something besides Robert Gierse or Robert Hinson or Detective Ryker," I said.

"Those three people are about as worthless as you can get. Do you want to talk about how you're going to win the Pulitzer Prize for writing your book and for helping me get that lazy Sheriff off my back?"

"Hmmm," I asked Rock, leaning back against my bed and fiddling with my socks with my toes.

"That Barney-Fife Sheriff wants me to go downtown on Wednesday and take a polygraph test," Rock said with a snort.

"He wants me to volunteer and take it for the sole reason because he *asked* me to," Rock added.

"What does your attorney say about that?" I asked him.

"He told me to tell the Sheriff where he can go with his polygraph test," Rock said. "But I am going to think about it. It might be the right thing to do."

"What do you think I should do?" Rock asked me.

"I think you should do whatever your heart leads you to do," I told Rock.

"I think I am having chest pains thinking about it," Rock told me.

"It would probably benefit you to go ahead and take it," I told him. "Especially since you say you are innocent."

"You're *damn* right I'm innocent," Rock said. "And that damned Sheriff will never prove otherwise.

"I saw a lot of death in World War II," Rock continued. "I saw human death like no one else has ever seen. In the war. But I have never murdered anyone."

I was silent. I thought about reaching for my notebook and pen, but I didn't feel like it. Just for tonight I didn't feel like being on duty. I doubted tonight would be the night Rock Norton would break down and confess to the LaSalle Street Murders."

"That's what we can talk about," I told Rock, content that my night wasn't going to waste.

"What?" I asked.

"The war," I said. "We can talk about the time you won the Purple Heart. Tell me one of your favorite war stories.

"I love to hear your stories," I said, building up his self-esteem.

I felt like I could literally hear Rock shaking his head.

"Not tonight," he said. "It brings back too many bad memories."

I respected his wishes. "How about Arkansas?" I suggested. "Let's talk about good memories. Ones in Arkansas where you grew up and where you lived as a little boy."

"I have no good memories as a little boy," Rock said with purpose. "I left Arkansas when I was only 16-years-old. I left home and moved to Indianapolis all by myself to get away from my father. I got a job right away and I've been on my own ever since."

"You have got to be kidding," I told Rock. "You were practically a child."

"A child?" Rock said. "I was a child alright. My dad beat me half to death out in the cornfields of Arkansas. I knew it was either kill him or be killed. I had a heavy decision to make."

There was a long pause in our conversation. I remained silent.

"So I left Arkansas. Permanently. At only 16-years-old. With no money and nothing but the shirt on my back."

Rock said, "I didn't even look back."

All of a sudden, my bedroom got chillier and chillier.

I had always wondered if Rock Norton had murdered his father.

54

New Years' Eve
December 31st, 1993

I had to break the silence.

Rock was listening to me breathe as we both debated on what to talk about next. I didn't like the intimacy our quietness together conveyed to him.

"I know!" I almost chirped. "Let's talk about your most favorite New Years Eve ever! What is the best New Years' Eve you have ever spent in your entire life?"

"Tonight," Rock said with a teasing inflection. "It may be over the telephone – but at least I'm spending it with you."

Rock's statement frightened me, but I moved on with our conversation with momentum. I ignored his advance. I briefly thought of Jodi Foster in the movie, "The Silence of The Lambs" and wondered how she endured such a relationship with Hannibal Lechter, played by Anthony Hopkins.

"Okay," I said, quickly changing the subject. "How about let's talk about your children? What's your greatest New Years' you've ever spent with your children?"

Rock grew quieter and my bedroom grew even colder.

"It was the New Years' Eve after Robert Gierse was murdered," Rock told me. I could tell he was meditating, so I held back.

"That was your best New Years' Eve?" I asked Rock quietly.

I couldn't believe he was saying this. "Was it your best New Years' because Gierse was dead? I wanted to ask. But I didn't tempt him. I said nothing. I waited for him to talk. He seemed lost in deep thought.

"It was the last New Years' Eve I ever spent with my child that died," Rock said. "I told you that I had a baby that died, didn't I?"

I was shocked, "No, Rock," I said. "You never told me that."

"It was by my wife, Norma," he explained. "One morning, she got up and went in to look at the baby. He was in his crib, face down. He wasn't breathing.

"She screamed," Rock continued, repeating the scene. "I looked at him and knew immediately. The baby was dead."

"Oh, Rock, "I apologized. "I am so sorry. I can't believe you went thought that pain. What happened?"

"Well, they don't know," he said. "I expect it was that Sudden Infant Death Syndrome. When I went in there and looked at him, there was a little spot of blood on the sheet in front of his mouth. He had died in the night, I think."

I wanted to weep for Rock, just visualizing the death of his son, a tiny little baby and his wooden crib.

"What was his name?" I asked, interrupting his mesmerization.

"John," Rock said. "Just like John the Baptist."

I had to change the subject. The night was becoming too depressing, too heavy. I wasn't in the mood for death and horror tonight. It was a holiday and I didn't want to have to interpret everything Rock said.

"Death is painful, Rock," I told him. "I'm sorry."

"It's a part of life," Rock insisted. "Everyone dies sometime."

I nodded in agreement and thought of the Bible verse, "It's appointed unto man once to die," but I said nothing.

Suddenly, Rock flipped the conversation over like a pancake on a griddle.

"I'm reading a good book right now," Rock wanted me to know.

"What is it?" I asked, relieved that he was the one that changed the subject.

"It's about Hitler," Rock said.

I could feel him smiling, waiting for my response.

"Hitler?" I said out loud.

"Yes," Rock said in a peculiar voice. "He was a very misunderstood human being."

I raised my eyebrows, but waited for Rock to continue.

"Hitler was a serial killer, you know," he said.

"I would say that, yes," I said.

"It's an interesting book," Rock said. I felt like he was teasing me in an obscure way. I knew he was serious about Hitler, but he was trying to push a button with me. I wasn't going to let him.

"Umm-mm"," I said sarcastically. I didn't care if it made him mad.

"You should read it," Rock said. "You will learn a lot about the deep inner-thinking of the man."

"Okay, Rock," I said, making a mental note of my assignment from him. He was giving me a clue. He liked this game. It was another one of my daily tips to help me solve the LaSalle Street Murders. I knew I had to pursue it. But I didn't feel like pursuing him tonight. I was getting pretty sleepy. And besides, the clock was just about to strike midnight.

"I think I'm going to hang up now," I told Rock with sincerity. "I wish you a very happy New Years. I cannot believe we spent almost three hours together on the telephone tonight."

"I know," he said. "I wish I had a glass of champagne. I'd offer you a toast right now."

"All I have to toast with is a can of Sprite," I said.

"All I have to toast with is a glass of Kool-Aid," Rock said back to me. I heard him laugh.

"Okay," Rock said as my bedroom clock ticked mysteriously into Midnight. It was now officially the year of 1994.

"I am giving you a toast, Pretty One," Rock said. I imagined his Kool-Aid glass being lifted towards the ceiling.

I waited.

"I hope that this year your book becomes a bestseller and that you win the Pulitzer Prize for solving the LaSalle Street Murders," Rock said with utmost sincerity.

His flattery was thick. Almost buttery. He definitely knew how to charm a woman so that it worked. To his advantage. He knew how to make a woman vulnerable in his presence.

"Thank-you, Rock," I said, lifting my Sprite can into the air towards the phone. "And I hope that this year all of your dreams come true – and that the truth about the LaSalle Street Murders really does come out."

"Good night Pretty One," Rock said. I could tell he was tired yet grateful that he hadn't spent New Years Eve alone, after all.

"Good night, Rock," I said.

Although my New Years Eve had been bizarre, I was glad that I hadn't spent it crying myself to sleep and feeling sorry for myself that I didn't have a date. I meditated on the fact that, literally, I had just spent New Years Eve with a man I believed was a serial killer.

I sat on the edge of my bed for a few minutes and prayed silently to myself. Afterwards, I got up and walked down the hall to turn up the thermostat. The house was colder than a morgue. Everything was so pitch black that I stumbled along the way. I couldn't believe how chilly everything had become.

In the distance, I heard a magnificent celebration of fireworks cracking and popping. After the artillery quieted down, I thought I heard an eerie rattle at the back of the house. My adrenaline quickened and so did my pulse. I padded to the kitchen in my bare feet. To my amazement, the ceiling light had burnt out. I was still in the dark. The chilly house seemed to get even darker.

I glanced at the digital lights flickering on top of my Kenmore kitchen stove. It was almost 12:30 a.m.

There it was again. This time the noise rattled my nerves more than a little. I felt goose bumps up and down my entire body. I suddenly felt anxious. What was it?

I couldn't help but wonder if Rock hadn't decided to drive over. I knew he knew where I lived. Maybe he knew the Sheriff had given me a decoy police car out front. Even though Rock and I didn't talk about it, I knew he had plenty of time to drive over here after we hung up the phone.

But did he have enough motivation? Was it time to meet me face to face again? Were his game pieces all in a row? Was tonight the night?

I peeked out of all of the windows in my kitchen and living room. I saw nothing but more darkness. I made sure every door and window was locked before I turned and walked back down the blackened hallway, penetrated with nothing but my silhouette making shadows on the wall.

There appeared to be a full moon bringing in the New Year.

I knew I had to shake off the eerie, almost spooky feeling I had. I climbed into bed and barricaded myself with quilts and covers.

"Dear God," I said out loud for anyone listening to hear. "Please protect me and my son tonight. Keep us safe."

As I started to drift off, I heard the rattle again. The sound was coming from somewhere near the back of the house. I didn't have the energy to get up and investigate again. My eyes grew too heavy to open. I could fight it no more. I felt myself being overcome with sleep.

I rested soundly in the fact that Rock wanted me alive.

At least for right now.

55

January, 1994

Rock was excited that we spent New Years' Eve together last night.

It may have been on the telephone, but he was happy we were together.

I suggested we share New Years' resolutions together.

"I want to lose weight this year," I said. "At least 15 pounds."

"Hmmm," Rock said. "I could put you on a diet that would help you lose weight."

I declined to comment on his sexual innuendo.

"What is *your* New Years' resolution this year?" I asked Rock.

"To get that detective – Dick Tracy-wannabe off my back," Rock grumbled.

I giggled to myself, making sure Rock didn't hear me. He had such funny nicknames for all of the cops who were after him. He called Sheriff Barney Fife. He dubbed Lt. Ryker as Dumbo and Detective Jon Padget was Dick Tracy.

"Do you know that damn Sheriff wants me to take *another* lie detector test?" Rock demanded. I listened to him grow furious.

"I'm sorry," I told Rock, trying not to sound plastic. "You can always tell him NO. You don't have to do it."

"Yeah, he'll probably arrest me if I don't do it, Pretty One," he said. "Don't you know anything about cops? They are all dirty. Dirty to the bone. Every single one of them."

"Oh?" I said.

He changed the subject.

"Do you know how to get rid of fingerprints?" Rock asked me.

"No," I said.

"Put them in the microwave," Rock said.

"What?" I asked. "You put your fingers in the microwave and turn it on?"

"No, Pretty One," Rock said, sounding frustrated with me. "If you have, say a gun or a knife that you don't want your finger-prints on, you just put the knife in the microwave and turn it on for a few minutes and it will totally erase your fingerprints."

"Wow. Thank-you, Rock," I said. "I'm glad I learned that in case I ever need to eliminate my fingerprints from anything."

"You never know when you might need that information," Rock said. "I have a lot of little tips like that to help you out."

56

April 2nd, 1994
1994

Rock hinted that he was the one that murdered Verna today.

When I woke up, just after 6 a.m., Rock called me and we read the morning paper together.

"This is so cozy," Rock said over the telephone. "I wish we were in bed together reading the paper."

I ignored his comment. He continued, as usual. He was reading an article about The LaSalle Street Murders and himself. He seemed to enjoy it.

"I'm very unhappy with the police department," said James Barker's mother, who lives in Clarksburg, West Virginia.

"My son deserved better than this," Endress said in the newspaper article.

"Well, lady, you had a bad son," Rock Norton said after he read Mrs. Barker's comment out loud.

What he said made me want to cry. I had talked to Endress on several occaisions and I knew how deeply she loved her only son who was murdered at a young age. Rock was so cold and heartless.

"That Ryker's probably got something new up his sleeve," Rock said.

"Probably," I agreed with him.

"Well, do you want to get the "BIG P" or not?" he asked me.

"Big P?" I asked him.

"Big P. THE PULITZER PRIZE, Pretty One," he said. "Wake up."

I was startled for a second.

"Ummm, yes, Rock," I said. "Of course I do."

"Well, he he he," Rock said, laughing. "Ryker and the Sheriff screwed up this case 21 years ago. Now they are screwing it up again."

I remained silent.

"They weren't good cops back then or they would've caught me way back then," Rock said.

WHAT? I couldn't believe what Rock just said.

Spring came and went. There was still no confession from Rock Norton.

57

THE VIDOCQ SOCIETY CAME TO HELP US

**Summer
1994**

**I hadn't seen the bodies, but I got a chance to see their bloody
clothes and smell the dried blood on them, over twenty years
later.**

"It was nauseating, Trent," I said, explaining to him how Mike
Ryker had invited me to the evidence and property room to get a
whiff of Robert Gierse and Robert Hinson's clothing. I saw that
they were dark and putrid and the vapor reeked of must, death and
horror.

"It's a shame this murder didn't happen today," Trent offered.
"There is so much new technology today. I bet a good evidence
man could crack this case just by examining those bloody clothes.
Maybe the killers left behind a few fibers or hairs that would

incriminate him."

That afternoon I meditated on what Trent had to say. I decided to do something about it.

I consulted my friend at Unsolved Mysteries, Katherine Kavich, who wanted me to keep her updated on my investigation. I told her about being able to view the victims' bloody clothing and that I thought the right forensic expert might be able to solve the case with them.

She suggested I contact an organization of homicide investigators based in Philadelphia, called *The Vidocq Society.*

"They are an elite group of homicide experts – the best of the best in the world," Katherine said, insisting I give them a call. "I'll bet they will be able to help you out."

I left a message on the Philadelphia-based telephone number. The next morning a man by the name of Fred Bornhofen returned my call. I shared with him all of our difficulties in getting our Prosecutor to arrest Rock Norton. I told him that, even though politics appeared to be playing an important role in the LaSalle Street Murders investigation, our local Sheriff was still determined to help out.

"What do you think is your biggest problem?" Bornhofen, an international security expert asked me.

"Obstruction of Justice," I told him. I shared everything, and pleaded with him to come out to Indiana and bring justice to investigate a case that was stumbling on its way to the courtroom.

I didn't have to say any more.

The case was sent to the Vidocq's founder and director, Frank Friel, who was the first New York City cop to review our entire case.

"I determined the case has strong viability," Friel said.

I was elated, but not surprised.

"There are serious concerns establishing Floyd Chastain's credibility, but it is usable with independent corroboration, produced by virtue of what he's told the Sheriff," Friel said.

"A fresh approach can produce new leads, and Vidocq has the manpower and resources to have a strong impact on the case," Friel told me.

On July 13th, Friel sent Vidocq member Fred Bornhofen to Indianapolis to coordinate the case. Bornhofen, famous for solving a $15 million dollar oil fraud case in Texas and Oklahoma, intensely reviewed the evidence with the Sheriff.

I picked him up at the airport and we had dinner downtown.

"At first I thought it was just another hopeless 22-year-old case," said Bornhofen, who also lectures for the FBI on terrorism.

"But I discovered the Sheriff was very knowledgeable and the prosecutor hadn't spent the time to review everything and had possibly come to an erroneous conclusion.

"And I discovered the witnesses, if properly presented to a grand jury, would force them to collect more information," Bornhofen said.

Bornhofen returned to Philadelphia to plead the tremendous cost to Vidocq's board members.

Though cautiously skeptical – Vidocq accepts only four out of hundreds of cases presented each year – they voted unanimously to help us.

I thanked God for this one.

"I thought the case was weak at first, but after much research I knew it was very solvable," said William Fleisher, Vidocq's commissioner and a supervisory special agent for US Customs.

"This case has very usable witnesses," Fleisher said.

"It would be nice to have a cardinal or a priest as a witness," he said.

"After all, Floyd was in prison for murder and Joyce is an alcoholic, according to the police. They are questionable witnesses.

"But you just don't find them involved in these cases," Fleisher told me.

"Usually, your witnesses have credibility problems, including previous lies they've made," Fleisher said.

"A guy in prison is gonna lie – so what?" said Fleisher, a former FBI agent who specialized in Boston, Detroit and New York's organized-crime units.

"THAT DOESN'T MEAN THAT A LIAR CAN'T BE TELLING THE TRUTH," he said.

"And whores can be raped. This is why the finder of facts, the juror – has to weigh the credibility of the witnesses."

And determine the truth.

If we could just get the case in front of a jury, I knew they would see the truth.

58

August 1994

Robert Gierse did work for the Pentagon in Washington, D.C.

It was during a period of his life when he was a microfilm expert.

"I got a call from Bob when our father died," Ted Gierse said with a matter-of-fact attitude on the telephone during one of our countless interviews. He didn't seem surprised when he learned his brother was at our nations' capitol.

"I asked him where he was," Ted recollected. "And he told me he was in Washington. He said he was doing some microfilm work at the Pentagon."

I knew from extensive interviews that Bob Gierse was supposed to be the leader of the Gierse, Hinson and Barker trio. Gierse was said to have a photographic memory.
I closed my eyes and meditated.

I wondered if Robert Gierse had seen something at the White House that he shouldn't have when he was there.

I wonder how much a plane ticket to Washington D.C. will cost me.

59

I'm not the only one who thinks there may be an obstruction of justice in the Marion County Prosecutor's Office.

Bill Fleisher, co-founder of the Vidocq Society, tried to comfort me.

"Prosecutors don't like to take a chance on a trial unless they have an air shut case," he said.

The Vidocq Society co-founder Bill Fleisher says this is likely true with the LaSalle case.

"But even if a man is acquitted, at least he's brought to the bar of justice," Fleisher says.

"The law doesn't say you arrest someone because you believe you can convict them. That's not our system. Our system says you're innocent until proven guilty.

"And that's *not* the prosecutor's job – nor the policeman's, nor the judge's," says Fleisher.

"I think the system – not to mention the public – gets cheated by an overabundance of caution on behalf of prosecutors who won't take a case for fear of losing," Fleisher said.

Fred Bornhofen said he can't comment on the investigation, but admits the female witness – Joyce – has passed a polygraph and Dr. Halbert Fillinger, a noted pathologist who teaches at the Texas Rangers Academy and the Suret (French FBI) has analyzed the case.

More important, he sent the Sheriff the expertise of a master forensic hypnotist and a world-renowned psychologist.

Oscar Vance, Chief Detective of the Montgomery (Pennsylvania) District Attorney's Office, came to Indianapolis for an in-depth case study.

Vance then hypnotized the female witness – Joyce.

The hypnotism produced "unbelievable" results.

"There are a lot of myths about hypnotism," said Vance, executive director of the International Association of Forensic Hypnosis (IAFH).

"It's not psychic or mystical. It's purely an investigative tool," Vance, a former investigator for the disciplinary board of Pennsylvania's Supreme Court said.

"Witness recall is used to reconstruct events exactly as they happened," he said. "It can be vital to re-establish conversation, facial feature or to identify cars and license plate numbers.

"There is no age or time barrier. If it's recorded in the memory you can retrieve it," Vance said.

According to Indiana law, the pre-hypnosis and post-hypnosis interviews are admissible in court. The actual hypnosis-induction is used to help the investigator corroborate and prove the case.

"I can see why the prosecutor felt the case was not organized at first," said Vance. He said the female witness's recall was "very productive."

"The Sheriff has two very good witnesses," said Vance. "Floyd and Joyce."

Patrick Brady, President of the IFAH, said Vance's techniques are innovative and progressive.

"Vance not only used his vast homicide experience, but he's one of the best there is," said Brady, former director of the Boston Police Department's hypnosis unit.

"Forensic hypnosis is the purest, most sophisticated form of interviewing in law enforcement," Brady said.

Brady, ruled a courtroom expert on hypnotism, said, "We're

behind the Sheriff out here. I'd be happy to fly out to explain hypnotism to a jury."

But will Indianapolis ever give him a chance?

On August 19th, the Sheriff flew to Michigan to meet Vidocq's co-founder, Richard Walter, an international forensic psychologist who profiled the case.

Profiling homicides and serial killers became famous in the movie "Silence of The Lambs," but Walter pointed out it does not peg a specific person.

"We're referring to a group and a type which then shapes the investigation," said Walter, who made time for the Sheriff while profiling a serial killer for England's Scotland Yard.

Walter's world-renowned expertise is in great demand. He has profiled thousands of homicides, specializing in serial killers.

Recently named to Great Britain's Board of Medicine, he has helped solve murders in China, Australia and many other countries. He is the author of many journals and writings.

"The (LaSalle) trail was relatively easy because the perpetrator was so specific," said Walter. "He was saying, 'I'm tough. I'm smarter than you.' There was great lust for power."

Walter said the killer or killers made many mistakes, including leaving too much information at the scene. "I learn a lot by the organization of the crime, such as if you clean up your crime scene tools and take them with you. Also, by the type of violence done, and what wasn't done.

Floyd insists that the murder weapon – a long sharp butcher knife – was taken from the LaSalle death house after butchering the men's throats, and thrown in a pit somewhere on the property at 3100 South Millersville Road, Indianapolis, in an area called Mars Hill.

"This was not a subtle case," Walter said. "(He) was leaving horror and drama – other-wise he would've cleaned up the crime scene or taken the bodies with him."

"There is an unspoken emotional flow that percolates and remains consistent," Walter said. "Every variable in this case is highly meaningful."

"Based on levels of behavior, emotionality and other things he can't mention," Walter said he believes the Sheriff's "on target."

60

SEPTEMBER, 1994

I never gave up trying to get Rock arrested.

The cops and I – the Sheriff, Ryker, Padget, Campbell - we were a lonely team. We felt like we were fighting a losing battle. Yet I still continued to talk to Rock every single day on the phone – even though it didn't seem to be working.

With the help of Frank Friel, Fred Bornhofen, Richard Walter, Oscar Vance and the other national experts from the Vidocq Society – a new fresh arena of lieutenants were brought to the case.

Fred Bornhofen kept me encouraged on a daily basis. He always had a positive word to say – an intelligent bit of new information that always kept me going. He was a professional who knew my relationship with a serial killer was serious.

In September, Fred invited me to the Vidocq Society's annual awards dinner in Philadelphia. There I would be able to meet all of the faces I had been talking to for so long. I was impressed with this society of homicide experts – and I quickly accepted. I made extensive plans to attend the black tie event. I invited my sister,

188

my son, David and my bodyguard, Trent to go to Philadelphia with us.

The most exciting part of the event – I learned from Fred Bornhofen – was that I would get to meet Actor Steven Seagal at the dinner. I was shocked to learn he was a fellow Vidocq Society member.

"Steven Seagal?" I asked Fred with disbelief. "I didn't know he was a member of this elite group of homicide experts."

"Steven Seagal is the best," Fred told me with assurance. "Haven't you watched any of his movies? He's the real McCoy. Those movies aren't all acting, you know."

The thought of Steven Seagal helping me solve the LaSalle Street Murders immediately crossed my mind. If he was a fellow Vidocq Member, then anything was possible.

Although I had already seen Seagal's incredible movie, UNDER SEIGE, I had to admit I hadn't seen them all. I went out and rented as many of them as I could find in my favorite video store. I watched them all.

I couldn't wait for the black tie awards dinner in Philadelphia.

61

"STEVEN SEAGAL"

October, 1994

9 p.m.

After I returned the rental car I could finally relax.

The emerald green, 1994 Pontiac Bonneville I rented from Enterprise Leasing on East Washington Street had given me more than a luxurious taxi-cab ride from Indianapolis to Philadelphia, round trip. Yet there was still this terrible aching in the middle of my back that spread down through my legs and the bottoms of my feet.

I kicked a pile of rust-colored autumn leaves that collected in front of my back door, let myself into my house and headed straight for the bathroom, kicking my shoes off as I walked. I couldn't wait to undress and step into a ceramic tub full of tepid water, light a couple of cinnamon-apple candles and think about the past weekend that was – without a doubt – one of the most interesting weekends in my entire life.

Steven Seagal.

The name alone should be enough to send any female, star-chasing, Hollywood-dazed fan daydreaming. But to me the two words meant one thing: Hope.

With my eyes closed and my head finally tilted against the back of the tub, I smiled as I remembered the wadded up Kleenex I had safely tucked in an envelope on top of my kitchen table. It was my keepsake from a weekend to remember.

Everything was perfect on Saturday night. From the $450 black sequin evening gown I wore – cut around my waist with shimmering nylon netting, trimmed top to bottom with black shiny pearls – to the matching strapless satin sandals I bought and even the pearl earrings studded with miniature diamonds I had dangling from my ears.

I felt like no less than a movie star myself when I stepped out of the limousine to go inside the Evanston-Hughes mansion just before 7 p.m.

The black tie event, honoring some of the most elite homicide experts in the world, was held in a secluded cul-de-sac in the woods overlooking the Delaware River – just a helicopter ride away from downtown Philadelphia. This year, I was more than a guest at the invitation-only affair. Having just been inducted into the VIDOCQ SOCIETY myself, I was honored to now be a part of a prestigious family that was honoring one of their own – the striking Hollywood actor and ambassador for crime fighting himself – Steven Seagal.

Greeted at the door by an FBI agent and a DEA special forces investigator, I was handed a crystal glass full of champagne, a frosted strawberry and a single red rose. Lights flashed all around me as I was captured on film by a cameraman standing in the foyer.

After dodging a camera crew from the television show 48 Hours, I first searched for my confidant, world-renown serial-killer expert and profiler Richard Walter. I knew the psychologist and special agent for the police in Lansing Michigan would be available for interviews at the awards ceremony. I was anxious to finally put a face to the voice I had talked to on the telephone for so long. A voice that had patiently and strategically taught me how to handle a bizarre, intimate relationship with an alleged serial killer for the past two years.

After a dinner of venison, violin music and intriguing conversation consumed my night, I could hardly believe the event had come to an end when it did. There were so many cameramen and special police agents crowded around Steven Seagal, I never in my wildest dreams would have believed he would have talked to me that night.

But he did.

After he received the esteemed bronze medal of honor for 'OUTSTANDING CONTRIBUTION TO LAW ENFORCEMENT IN THE UNITED STATES", Seagal mingled with the crowd. One conversation led to another and finally we were literally standing next to each other. I introduced myself.

"I heard about your case," Seagal said to me point blank.

I tried not to stare into his eyes.

"It looks like your prosecutor is your fly in the ointment," Seagal said.

I shivered to know that the one and only Steven Seagal knew about my case. About the LaSalle Street Murders in the small Midwestern town that I doubted he had ever been to. Yet with amazing intuition, Seagal knew what I suspected was holding my case up.

Neither one of us even whispered the word corruption.

Without a moment's hesitation, I shared with the veteran actor my struggles in trying to get police to issue an arrest warrant for a man I believed to be a serial killer. It took me less than ten minutes to tell Seagal my story of how I had been relentlessly trying to solve the greatest murder mystery in Indiana for years.

With my hands, I illustrated my frustrations with The Marion County Prosecutor. Steven Seagal seemed to compassionately understand my endeavors. Not only did the star volunteer top-secret advice, he amazingly offered to help me with my plight to solve the LaSalle Street Murders.

"I'll do anything I can to help you," Seagal said, giving me his personal secretary's phone number in Los Angeles.

I scribbled the number quickly in my notebook.

"Send me a package next week with as much information about the case as you can," Seagal said. "And call me next week."

I stared down at my right hand with Steven Seagal's handprint-embedded tissue crumbled in my palm – forever as far as I was concerned. I knew that Seagal had made a lasting impression on my life. Not because he was famous, but because he offered to help me solve my murder case.

I watched with a mother's pride as my teenage son, David – incredibly handsome in a black vested tuxedo, took pictures with Seagal for our family scrapbook.

On the nearly 700-mile drive back to Indianapolis, in the dark with David snoozing in the backseat of the Pontiac for most of the ride home, I meditated on my trip. I knew that with Seagal's prestige and his status with the police, help was on the way for me.

On Monday morning, I knew I had to send that package to Los Angeles. I had to make that call to Seagal's office.

Time was of the essence.

For every day that a serial killer is free – innocent lives are in danger.

Carol Sissom and Vidocq Society founder, Frank Friel.

Carol Sissom with actor, Steven Seagal, who offered to help with the LaSalle Street murders. Seagal won the prestigious Bronze Medal of Honor in 1994. Carol "Schultz" Sissom won the same award in 1995.

Actor Steven Seagal with Carol Sissom's son, David Schultz. David now lives in Hollywood and is a professional actor.

Carol Sissom won a national award and a Bronze Medal of Honor for "Outstanding Contribution to Law Enforcement" for helping solve the LaSalle Street murders. Actor Steven Seagal received the same medal the year before, in 1994.

62

"THE FLY IN THE OINTMENT"
MONDAY MORNING

October 18th, 1994

I spied a large manila envelope in my mailbox.

Glancing at a stack of envelopes and a blue-lettered Missing Children's advertisement, I tugged at the yellow folder. It was tucked in between them. In the corner, I read that it was from the National Federation of Press Women.

After opening it, my mouth fell open.

"FIRST PLACE" it read.

I turned it upside down and looked at it like it was a new invention. I couldn't believe my eyes.

The article I had written for the controversial newsmagazine, NUVO, had just won a first place award from The National Federation of Press Women.

I was more than elated. My public pledge to solve the most celebrated murder case in the history of Indianapolis forged on – now with more fuel than ever. With a national award under my belt – and a famous Hollywood actor behind me – I believed I could now convince someone – anyone – to arrest Rock Norton.

Admittedly, Rock Norton had likely murdered many people during his lifetime. Solving Rock's mysterious maze of killings throughout his amazing life was difficult enough. But it was the local prosecutor in Indianapolis who refused to arrest Rock that confused me.

I just couldn't figure out why.

I chewed on my fingernails and read my own story, over and over again.

MY AWARD WINNING STORY

On December 1st, 1971, three businessmen were slaughtered in their home on North LaSalle Street. Robert Gierse, Robert Hinson and James Barker were bound, beaten, gagged and had their throats slit ear to ear. News of the crime made headlines for weeks – reaching world-wide outlets that claimed it was the biggest thing since Charles Manson.

Indeed, it was a murder investigation that read like a soap opera from the day the bodies were found: The young men had their own microfilming business, copying top secret records with Pentagon, CIA and Mafia ties.

And they were playboys who left hundreds of scorned lovers.

Overwhelmed with thousands of leads, police could never solve their biggest case.

Indiana's greatest unsolved mystery is no longer a "WHO-DUNIT", but about why prosecutors won't make an arrest...

This is the award winning article I wrote – exposing why I think the Marion County Prosecutor's Office obstructed justice in the LaSalle Street Murders. According to the Sheriff, Lt. Ryker and Detective Jon Padget, there is no reason Rock Norton should not have been arrested. Every time attempt was made – The Prosecutor over ruled with an iron hand. He undid whatever the detectives and the police officers started.

WHY?

The following article won a national award:

Indianapolis has been waiting over 22 years to hear what happened in the tiny bungalow on LaSalle Street on that cold and gruesome night.

On April llth, 1994, an Indianapolis Police Department homicide detective – Jon Padget – answered that question.

Padget was assigned to the LaSalle Street Murders in 1993 – after the Sheriff repeatedly requested an arrest for Rock Norton. Finally, after removing Mike Ryker from working on the case, they assigned someone with a new, fresh insight.

Their only mistake – they didn't plan on him making an arrest.

I believe they never intended on him issuing an arrest warrant for Rock Norton. This is what he did in April, 1994.

Five months later, on September 16th, 1994, just five months later – the Marion County Prosecutor's Office made sure that no one – including many still-frightened Eastside residents – ever hears Jon Padget's explanation for what happened on that fateful, gruesome night.

There has been a bitter disagreement between detectives and prosecutors which surpasses the quarter-of-a-century old question of "WHODUNIT" in Indiana's greatest unsolved mystery.

Now – the REAL mystery is about WHY prosecutors REFUSE to make an arrest? Why do they refuse to take action on a veteran homicide cop's findings.

In April, after several months of investigating Rock Norton, Jon Padget delivered a 24-page probable cause affidavit to prosecutors.

In his arrest warrant, he demanded two arrest warrants for the LaSalle Street Murders.

Five months later, Jon Padget said he picked up the morning newspaper to find out that his request for two arrest warrants were denied.

Jon Padget said he was told he had "over-stepped" his bounds in the case.

Marion County Deputy Prosecutor John Commons said the case was not prosecutable.

Investigators are prepared to challenge John Commons and the legal and ethical judgments of the Marion County Prosecutor's Office in this instance...

I folded the newspaper up and tossed it across the marble counter of my country kitchen. I could read no more of my own story. It grieved me to know my case had been tossed from police to prosecutors like a volleyball over a beach net ever since Floyd confessed to me on September 1st, 1992.

63

I found out that the LaSalle Street Murders was linked to the White House.
Could this be why the Prosecutors wouldn't make an arrest?

March, 1995

THE MEETING

"Floyd?"

"Yes, Carol, - um – I mean, Miss Schultz," replied the voice on the other end of the telephone.

Floyd still struggled with my real name after I told him the truth. I let him know I was not Betty Thompson, but really Carol Schultz.

"Floyd, I want you to tell me about this meeting regarding the LaSalle Street Murders. It was about – when was it?" I asked pointedly into the telephone receiver as I pushed two fingers down on the orange PLAY button on my tape recorder.

"It was *after* the murders on LaSalle Street," Floyd answered me as though he were a guest on the television show "60 Minutes."

"When?" I asked him.

"It was early in the morning. It was probably about 1 a.m. when I got there and it didn't end until 3 or 4 a.m."

"Can you remember what day of the week it was?" I asked.

"I've been trying to remember, but I don't remember that," Floyd apologized.

"It was right before Chuck Miller got killed."

"Was it after the murders or before?" I prodded.

"No, it was right after the murders," he insisted.

"The same night?" I asked.

"No," Floyd said. "It was a couple of nights after the murders."

"Okay. Okay. Just tell me the story from the very beginning," I told Floyd with the assurance of a doctor handing a patient a lollipop."

"Well, I was at the house on Collier Road – my Mom and Dad's house. I lived behind them in an apartment. Tennessee Bill come by and picked me up in a Peterbilt 18-Wheeler. We left there and we dropped off a load in Louisville – there's a stop over there where the Sears Auto Parts store used to be. And then we left there and went to Bowling Green, Kentucky. We picked up a load and came back down and went to Bud's Truck Stop just inside of Marion County on I-465. But then Tennessee Bill looked at me and said, **"No, we're going over here to this meeting."**

Then he got on the telephone there and he called some guys and they come by and picked me and Tennessee Bill up in a 1970-1971 Cadillac Fleetwood Brougham. It was gray with a black vinyl top. Inside it had a thing on the back seat that you pull out. Flip it up and you can rest your feet on it. It was a BIG OLE limousine."

"Who was driving it?" I interrupted Floyd.

"A guy who was about 265 pounds. He was black-headed. He had brown eyes. His hair was about down to his shoulders. And the guy in the back, he had long brown hair down 'bout to where his belt would be. He was wearing glasses. He weighed 140, 155 pounds maybe," Floyd continued.

"Do you remember their names?" I asked him.

"No, I don't remember their names," he answered.

"That's okay, Floyd," I assured him.

"And from there Tennessee Bill got in. He was riding shotgun and I rode in the back seat right behind Tennessee Bill. They took us up through town and wound up at Tommy's Starlight Palladium on Michigan Avenue."

"What did the lounge look like?" I asked.

"Well, it was lit up and all like it was a restaurant. We went up there and we pulled up right next to Chuck Miller's 754-flatbed truck. That bed was about 18-foot long. We went on inside. Chuck Miller was there, Tennessee Bill, The Expert was there, Johnny Wilson Dough was there, a couple of other guys I don't know their names they wuz there. And there was this guy there named Jimmy Riddle, who was there.

"And then there was this blond waitress with big knockers who wuz there," he said.

"They pushed all the tables together. This guy, I don't know his name, he was the Chief Lawyer for the Teamsters – he was there."

I was speechless for nearly five seconds.

"How do you know he was the Chief Lawyer for the Teamsters?" I asked Floyd, nearly stuttering.

"Because he wuz talking lawyer business in the middle of the meeting," Floyd explained without hesitation.

He was the Teamster's lawyer and he looked just like William Bracy – the big White House guy."

"How do you know this other guy's name was Jimmy Riddle?" I asked.

"Well, he didn't say his name was Jimmy Hoffa," Floyd explained. "On the way back in the car I rode shotgun, next to Tennessee Bill. On the dashboard there was a gold plate that said James Riddle. It had two little rivets in it like stars with screws in it to hold the plate onto the dash. It was his car."

"And so, anyway, there at the lounge there's all these discussions – about trucks and different things. And this guy Bracy had this briefcase with him, which was a fold-out type. The kind you push and it pops open and all- like a woman's purse. And James Riddle was looking at the pictures of the trucks and he was discussing things about them."

"What pictures of WHAT trucks?" I interrupted Floyd.

"Semis," Floyd said simply.

"It was in his briefcase," I asked.

"Yeah," Floyd said. "He wuz showing him some pictures of the new-type semis and all 'cause the man's been in prison and he's getting out. And he's getting him *out* of prison."

"How did you know he was getting out of prison?" I asked.

"Because he said he was," Floyd said simply. "He said he was from Brazil, Indiana. I remember that part. He also had white socks on; had a pinstripe suit on. He took his suit jacket off and I could see he was wearing a white shirt and he was drinking coffee. He kept telling this lawyer guy, `Now, make sure you get me out.'"

"He was in prison out of state, but he came all the way down here for the meeting. I don't know how he did it, but I guess he got furloughs 'cause I took furloughs when I was in the FEDS. But, anyway, when they was discussing that and different things, this guy I think his name was Vinnie, he said something to him but I don't remember what. Wasn't nothing to amount to a hill of beans."

"Then, later on, he got mad because I interrupted him and he told me to go and sit by myself," Floyd said.

"Where were you sitting?" I couldn't help but ask.

"Well, I was sitting pretty close to him. But he told me to go and sit by myself because I interrupted him and he – boy – he went off."

"Why did you interrupt him?" I asked.

"Because I wanted to know about the Cadillac going back to the house where them boys was murdered," Floyd said.

"Because I know Tennessee Bill drove it away," Floyd remembered.

"Tennessee Bill drove it away?" I questioned him.

"Sure did," Floyd insisted.

"Where did he take it?" I asked him.

"I don't know," he said.

"Why did he take it?" I demanded. I could feel my heart racing.

"I don't know," Floyd said. I could hear him shrugging his shoulders. "Probably because I left some microfilm in the Cadillac."

"I don't understand," I told Floyd.

"Carol, I mean, Miss Schultz," Floyd explained, frustrated with me. "Chuck Miller got in his 1960 blue El Camino and he drove it away and Tennessee Bill drove the Cadillac away. And Johnny Wilson Dough put the Cadillac back at the murder scene. And so they wuz talking about that. And Tennessee Bill was there. He was drinking water, and they was discussing everything.

"Then Jimmy Riddle said to the guy that looked just like William Bracy, "Go out with him and get the stuff out of the trunk (of the Fleetwood Brougham). And then he told him, "Tell your wife to keep praying for me and saying her Rosary.""

"Who said this?" I asked quickly.

"Jimmy Riddle!" Floyd said. "He said, 'Tell your wife, Heloise, to keep praying for me and saying the Rosary.' And so then he shook hands; and I thought it was kind of funny because he had this flowery shirt on with short sleeves and it was cold outside."

"Yeah?" I asked. "Was it snowing that night?"

"Just a tiny bit," he said.

"But was it cold?" I drilled him.

"Very cold," he answered.

Suddenly, my telephone line went dead. I wanted to panic, but I knew that the prison telephone system only allows for ten-minute telephone calls. It interrupts all calls at precisely ten-minute intervals.

I waited, paced the floor, and wished that I could call Floyd back. Finally, the telephone rang again. I grabbed it quickly.

"This is the MCI operator. I have a call from a Florida prisoner. Will you accept the charges from a Floyd?" inquired a nasal female voice.

"Yes!" I nearly screamed.

"It's me, Miss Schultz," Floyd sounded as nervous as I was.

"Where were we?" he asked.

"We were talking about the man leaving," I said.

"Yeah," Floyd recalled. "Now they're going to get this guy Riddle out of prison and this guy that's supposed to take everything back to the White House and the President to get him out.

"He said that he would get him out of prison. So he *had* to be on furlough at the time that he was there. See, 'cause once you're in the Feds, you can get a 10-day furlough with no problem for good behavior."

"Floyd, do you remember what you had to eat that morning?" I asked, trying to confuse him by changing his train of thought.

"Who, me?" Floyd asked.

"Yes," I answered.

"I had, yeah, I remember! It was smoked ham, you know, and I had two BLT's after that. So it was ham and egg sandwiches and then I ate two BLT's. Tennessee Bill got mad at me 'cause he had to break a hundred dollar bill to pay for the dinner."

"So you did nothing but eat for three hours?" I asked in bewilderment.

"Well, I ate and listened to them and the waitress kept coming over and everything. She was a nice little lady. But she kept waiting on their table 'cause they shoved all the tables together and they was all talking."

"Okay," I told Floyd.

"But this meeting lasted until about 4 o'clock in the morning. They was all still there then," he said.

"Go back to the man that you thought was Bracy. Describe him more to me, Floyd. What color of eyes did he have? What color was his shirt?" I demanded.

"Well, the shirt was kind of flowery blue and it had some yellow in it like a Florida shirt, you know how you wear Florida shirts?" Floyd asked me.

"Yes," I said.

"It was just like that. But he had a pair of suit pants, and he had a pair of penny loafers on. I do remember that. And he was dark-headed."

"How long was his hair?" I asked.

"He had a regular nice haircut. You know, the State of Florida, when they give you an original haircut, it was about that size. You know, so you're real presentable to the public. A public haircut. But his hair wasn't long.

"They was two long-haired guys there with him. They was carrying weapons I imagine because they acted like they was body guards or something," Floyd recalled as though he were re-living the meeting."

"Now get back to this guy you think was William Bracy. The same William Bracy that was President Nixon's right hand man at the time," I said.

"How were his mannerisms? Did he have glasses or a mustache or anything remarkable?" I asked Floyd.

"Yeah, he had glasses in his pocket, but you could tell they had been on his face because he had two indentations on his nose where they had been riding, you know. I'd say he was about 45 or 50 years old then," Floyd told me.

"How big was the room you were in?" I asked, my mind racing with questions.

"The room wasn't really that big," Floyd said. "There was a lot of people in there, but they sat away from us. They kind of kept us by ourselves."

"What other people were in there?" I wondered.

"Well, they was waiting on other people, you know. They was talking in the lounge and finally they shut the door just to let Bracy in there by himself," Floyd said.

"You mean the bar was open?" I asked.

"Yeah," Floyd said.

"Back to William Bracy . I mean, ex-white House Aide William Bracy, Floyd. WHY DO YOU THINK IT WAS HIM?" I asked.

"That is a pretty big accusation," I said, nearly scolding Floyd.

"Because I've seen his pictures. And when I seen these pictures, I remembered him." Floyd defended himself.

"How many years passed by from the time you saw him to the time you saw his picture?" I asked Floyd.

"I imagine it's been 20 years," Floyd said.

"Floyd, how could you know somebody's face twenty years later?" I asked him.

"Well, how did I identify that lady with the Oldsmobile

Cutlas? They called her Joyce" Floyd said with a trace of arrogance.

Indeed, Floyd *had* identified a woman named Joyce who had appeared in Rock Norton's garage over 20 years later. Even the top forensic specialists at the Indianapolis Police Department admitted that Floyd had a photographic memory. The Marion County Sheriff called his memory "incredible."

"Really, Floyd?" I asked him point-blank. "Are you are telling the truth, Floyd – God is listening to you right now!

"On a scale of one to one hundred, how sure are you that the man you saw at that meeting in Indianapolis 20 years ago was William Bracy? I asked.

"I am one thousand percent sure it was William Bracy," Floyd said. **"1,000 percent sure."**

I said nothing, but just enveloped the silence and the impact of Floyd's accusations.

"Okay, back to James Riddle," I said, cross-examining Floyd. "How do you know that was him?"

"Because I got pictures of him and I sent them to this guy at the prison and he got back to me and told me the guy was James Riddle. No doubt about it," Floyd said.

I was exhausted. It was hard for me to disprove Floyd's bullet proof memory.

"Well, if he was wearing a pinstriped suit, what color was it?" I asked.

"Same color as mine. Dark charcoal with a dark stripe in it. I just bought mine right before I come to prison," Floyd said. "And he had a white shirt, loosened up and he had, you know, them things on the cufflinks. They was cat eyes. I remember that too, because I had a pair like them one time."

"So what did William Bracy and James Riddle have to drink?" I asked.

"Riddle was drinking coffee, that's all he was drinking. Bracy, I don't know what he was drinking, but I do remember they were passing this national union jacket around and he was showing it to Johnny Wilson Dough. It was a white jacket with the union symbol thing on it.

"I can tell you who has a picture of it," Floyd said.

"Who?" I asked.

"Them two detectives from the Indianapolis Police Department who hate me so bad," Floyd said.

"You mean Sgt. Brian and Lt. Pink?" I asked.

Instantly, I recalled Floyd telling me that Sgt. Brian and Lt. Pink had promised to prove that Floyd was a lunatic.

"Yep, them two," Floyd said quietly. "They got a picture of Johnny Wilson Dough wearing the same jacket he had on the night of the triple murders. They showed it to me when I was down at Little Rock. They're the detectives who brought me a Pepsi and chocolate candy. They interrogated me, got really mean real fast and then made me sign a piece of paper recanting everything.

"Carol Schultz," Floyd said firmly. "Remember, they said if I didn't recant the whole story my 70-year-old Mama would have an accident real soon?"

I let my head fall in the palms of my hands. I remembered very well the day that Floyd called me crying, saying two detectives from the police department had visited him and threatened him, telling him he had to recant his entire LaSalle Street confession.

"How long was William Bracy at this meeting, Floyd?" I asked.

"About an hour," Floyd said.

"What did he do for this whole hour?" I asked.

"He listened, then he showed James Riddle some papers and told him to sign here and sign there," he said.

"Who signed what?" I asked. I had to know.

"James Riddle signed all of the papers that Mr. Bracy handed him," Floyd explained.

"How many papers," I prodded.

"About four," he answered.

"What did the papers say," I asked.

"I don't know what they said. They had me on the other side of the room," Floyd said.

"Where were these papers before Riddle signed them?" I asked.

I didn't let Floyd take another breath before I fired another question at him.

"Were they talking about the LaSalle Street Murders while they were signing these papers?" I asked.

"Oh, yeah," Floyd said. "William Bracy asked if them boys on LaSalle Street was dead because he said he had to pick up the microfilm. And Johnny Wilson Dough told him he made sure they were dead after he took the Cadillac. So they were discussing that and then Bracy gave the papers to Riddle to sign."

"And then the long-haired guy took him outside to the car to get the MICROFILM and he left," Floyd said.

"What else?" I asked instinctively.

"James Riddle said he was glad everything was taken care of so he could get out of prison," Floyd said.

"But why?" I pleaded with Floyd. "Why did the LaSalle Street boys have to DIE to get Riddle out of prison?"

"I don't know, Carol," Floyd's enthusiasm ebbed for a moment. "Something about some microfilm, and I guess it's from the Pentagon and all that stuff."

"What was on the microfilm, Floyd?" I asked.

"I don't know," Floyd said sadly. "Rock Norton knows."

"Do you really think he knows?" I asked with disbelief.

"Yeah, 'cause he took the machines home with him and the other film," Floyd explained.

"How many cans of MICROFILM did you take out of the house that night?" I asked.

"I didn't take any. Tennessee Bill did. I imagine there was 30 cans, though. Little cans. On each one of the things he carried out two, so I would say 60 cans. And how ever many films is in one of those little cans."

"Where were they?" I asked.

"I don't know. Tennessee Bill knew where they was though. He carried them out of the house. Of course, that was after Rock Norton was in there looking through everything. Chuck Miller was walking around too. He went through *everything*."

"What room did the microfilm come out of?" I asked. I tried to picture the death house on LaSalle Street.

"I don't know. Tennessee Bill carried it out and put it in the trunk of the Cadillac."

"He came out of the house?" I wondered.

"Tennessee Bill carried it out of the house on LaSalle Street. He carried in the blue typewriter and went back in and then come back out with some microfilm."

"What were you doing at the house?" I asked Floyd.

"I was waiting out front," Floyd said. He didn't deny his involvement.

"I was their getaway driver. Plus, then that's when they told me to cut the man's throat. Said they'd slit my throat if I didn't slit the boy (Robert Hinson's throat)."

"YOU KILLED HIM FLOYD!" I wailed. "WHY DID YOU KILL HIM?!"

"Yes, ma'am," Floyd was remorse. He repeated the same story he had told me earlier. "Tennessee Bill Howard told me to cut the man's throat and Rock Norton said, "KILL HIM! Rock told me if I didn't slit his throat he would slit my throat."

"And that's what I did," Floyd said quietly. "I slit his throat. He made a lot of gurgling sounds when he was dying."

I was overwhelmed. My mind was spinning. I thought I was going to faint, but the adrenaline of my mission to find the truth on LaSalle Street fueled me to continue questioning Floyd.

"Floyd, are you positive that was William Bracy at the meeting?" I asked again.

"Yes ma'am. 'Cause they kept talking lawyer-talk. He was saying he was the Chief lawyer for this national union and everything else."

"When he left and went outside, did he have a winter coat on?" I wanted to know.

"Yes, he did put a coat on. But it was one of them, what they call – not a car coat – it was a long trench coat," Floyd revealed.

"Bracy?" I asked.

"Yep," he said.

"What color was it?" I asked.

"It was gray with brown and black in it, you know, made in the material," Floyd said.

"So he was wearing a trench coat in the middle of the winter?" I asked.

"Yep, but he had a flowered shirt on," Floyd reminded me.

"Did he have a dark or light complexion?" I asked.

"He was just like he'd been out in the sun or something," Floyd said. It seemed strange. "It was like he'd been jogging. He had more sun on him than I had and that was in the winter time."

"How did you get back home?" I asked.

"We went back to the Cadillac Brougham, and the man driving was the same chauffeur that took us there and drove us back," Floyd said. "I sat in the middle of the front seat. On the dashboard was this little plate that said James Riddle on it.

"The driver – he drove us back to Tennessee Bill Howard's truck. Then me and Tennessee Bill got in the rig and all and fired it up; released the air brakes, and I went back to my house."

"Oh, my God," was all I could say.

"That's when Tennessee Bill told me he had to kill Chuck Miller by cutting his brake lines," Floyd remembered. "It wasn't too long after that when Chuck Miller ran into a train over on Kentucky Avenue."

"Was the meeting still going on when you left, Floyd?" I asked.

"Yes, ma'am," Floyd replied.

"Did James Riddle look tired?" I asked.

"Yeah, he was tired because he said he had to go back to wherever he came from. He kept drinking a lot of coffee," Floyd said.

"What about William Bracy?" I asked.

"He had done left by that time," Floyd said.

"Did you know how he got there" I wondered.

"Yeah, he left in this little car that was parked beside the Cadillac," Floyd revealed.

"What did it look like?" I was curious.

"I seen it real good when we pulled up," Floyd said.

"It was one of them Fords."

"What year?" I asked.

"Let's see," Floyd hesitated.

"About a 1970. It was one of them ones you rented at the air-

Charles Miller Succumbs Following Traffic Accident

Charles E. Miller, 41, 4423 Mann Road, died in Marion County General Hospital at 2:10 a.m. yesterday, almost 24 hours after the pickup truck he was driving struck a tank car on the Penn Central Railroad sidetrack at Tibbs Avenue and Raymond Street.

Police said Miller was driving south on Tibbs Avenue when his truck veered off the pavement, striking a utility pole and then the railroad car.

THE DEATH, 10th in weekend traffic in the state, boosted this year's Marion County traffic death to 105, compared with 106 at this time last year.

A resident of Indianapolis for 35 years, he was a lathe operator at Titan Electric Company.

He was a native of Liberty, Ky., and an Army veteran of the Korean War.

SERVICES WILL be held at 1 p.m. Wednesday in Farley West Morris Street Funeral Home. Burial will be in Mount Pleasant Cemetery.

The Indianapolis Star

port over there. It was a rental from Avis, I think," he said.

"How do you know it was a rental car?" I asked him.

"Because it had a rental tag on it. I don't remember what it had. I just remember tag numbers from years ago," he said.

"Where was the tag at?" I asked.

"It was kind of a license plate and you got a tag they put on," he explained.

"Where was it parked?" I asked again.

"It was parked right beside the Cadillac when we pulled up. That's the one they got into and left in," he said.

"What Cadillac?" I asked.

"The guy in the Cadillac got the film out of the trunk," Floyd insisted. "Then they got in the car and left. The man left and another guy came back in to chauffeur, then we left about two hours later."

"Floyd, I'm thoroughly confused," I said. "You pull up in this Cadillac limousine and you see a white rental car there. Was there a Cadillac there too?"

"No," Floyd laughed at me. "The Cadillac that we drove in, that's the one they got the film out of the trunk from."

"How do you know?" I demanded.

"Because I watched the man go out and get it!" Floyd said.

"You watched him?" I asked.

"Yeah," Floyd admitted. "He put it in the car of this guy who looked just like the guy from the White House – William Bracy's car. And then he left."

"Are you sure he put it in the white car?" I asked Floyd.

"I'm positive," he said. "He put it in the backseat. He opened the back door and put it in there. The big guy did."

"What big guy?" I asked.

"The Chauffeur guy," Floyd said. "And then Bracy just drove off."

Suddenly, a female telephone operator interrupted us.

"Your time limit is about to expire," she said as I nearly jumped out of my seat.

"That's enough for today, Floyd," I told him.

Suddenly, for no reason, I felt like someone was watching me. I turned off the tape recorder. I wondered if my own telephone was bugged. I could take no more.

"I have to go now," Floyd," I said.

"I have just one more question. This guy James Riddle. Who in the heck was he?"

"James Riddle?" Floyd almost laughed. "That was his first and middle name. I didn't find out his last name until almost twenty years later when I saw his picture in the prison library and my friend Bud West told me his last name.

"Riddle's last name was Hoffa," Floyd said. "His full name was James Riddle Hoffa."

I couldn't believe my ears! **JAMES HOFFA!**

I could feel my stomach starting to churn. My mind immediately flashed to a restaurant on the Westside of Indianapolis. I had interviewed the owner once. Roger Hoffa. He was Jimmy Hoffa's first cousin.

"**OH MY GOD**," I thought to myself.

Floyd said he had been at a meeting with the one and only **Jimmy Hoffa** – five years before the infamous leader of a national union had disappeared.

All I could say was, "Call me next Saturday, Floyd."

"Okay, Miss Schultz," Floyd said, leaving me with a warning. "Don't be afraid to expose this story. The truth has to come out. God will protect you and your little boy."

64

WAS JIMMY HOFFA REALLY THERE?

I found out that President Nixon's former Aide, William Bracy, was still alive, after all these years.

Bracy is founder of one of the largest prison ministries in the world, I learned.

After spending time in prison for Watergate, well after the President's impeachment, Bracy has extensively publicized the fact he gave his life to Jesus Christ – and that he has become a "born again" believer.

He founded an organization titled "Better Life", which is now based on the East Coast. It is one of the largest ministries in the world. Bracy and his ministry are dedicated to helping inmates cope with life through the hope of God.

Bracy is dedicated to writing Christian books and preaching the Gospel of Jesus Christ.

I wondered – did this include keeping his past life a secret?

I attempted to talk to Bracy several times, but he would not grant me an interview, although I attempted to reach him through countless avenues. I even contacted a literary agent in Orange, California, who knew Bracy and one of his ghost writers. Bracy, who has penned several novels since his White House era, refused to respond to the agent's attempts to get an answer on my behalf.

I desperately tried to contact Bracy.

Bracy refused to talk to me.

While I commend Bracy for his plight to preach the gospel and help others, I expect him to answer the many questions I had about the LaSalle Street Murders – and his alleged involvement.

Was he keeping a dark secret about Jimmy Hoffa?

I didn't know.

Shortly after Floyd's statements, I made plans to interview Bracy in person in Tennessee when he was speaking at a College commencement ceremony. That weekend, I received notice that there could be a threat to my life if I made the trip. That same afternoon, I found a man with long dark-hair sitting in a sedan in my driveway, watching my home. He talked on a cell phone as he watched my property and the back door of my house for quite some time. He was no one that I or my family knew. He was not the gas man, the cable man, the electric man, a mail man, milk man or any other type of utility or service man. He drove an unmarked car. I sensed immediate danger when I saw this man watching my house and sitting in my driveway. I discreetly took down his license plate number and the next week traced it to a vacant apartment on Main Street in Greenwood, Indiana. I later had an unconfirmed report that my telephone was bugged.

65

WHO IS TELLING THE TRUTH?

THREE MONTHS LATER

AUGUST, 1995
NASHVILLE, TENNESSEE

Leaning over to smooth out a wrinkle in my silk pantyhose, I glanced out of the large plate glass windows of the 36th floor of the Bullet Building. It was 99 degrees outside, and the haze and humidity over the magnificent countryside was so thick it looked like it was raining. I straightened up and gave the receptionist my name.

"Carol Schultz to see Mr. James F. Neal," I said firmly.

"Do you have an appointment?" asked the short, dark-haired receptionist in a thick southern drawl. She had shiny cherry dimples and didn't look a minute over 18-years-old. She spoke as though she hadn't traveled past the Eastern Tennessee Mountains a day in her life.

"Yes, I do," I said proudly. I couldn't believe that I had garnered an interview with one of the greatest former Watergate Prosecutors in our country's history.

It didn't matter that the interview request was for only five minutes.

It didn't matter that I had just driven seven hours on my birthday just to meet this man – a masterpiece of a human being engraved in our country's history books.

What mattered was that I was carrying a tape recording in my purse that could be the key to one of the greatest secrets in American history.

The receptionist – I couldn't help but mentally nickname her Dolly – spoke into the intercom and then looked up at me and smiled.

"Have a seat," Dolly said sweetly.

I sat down in a leather chair in the waiting room and fidgeted nervously. I still couldn't believe I was actually here. I still couldn't believe that he was willing to talk to ME, Carol Schultz, a freelance writer from Indianapolis, Indiana.

I couldn't believe that a man who had devoted his career to putting away the former national union President, James Riddle Hoffa better known as Jimmy Hoffa, was going to give me, a no name, a single mother from Indianapolis, Indiana, the time of day!

Less than an hour later, Carolyn Hazel Rigs, Neal's secretary, finally appeared and ushered me into Neal's office. She was one of the most graceful women I'd ever met in my life. I felt like Princess Grace was leading me down the hall.

I stared in awe when I stepped inside his office.

There, right on the wall above my head was a picture of Neal shaking hands with John F. Kennedy. And right next to it, a framed letter to him from Dean.

"Jimmy, no matter what the consequences in one's life, I will be forever grateful to you," the inscription read.

And next to it, a photograph of Neal with the producers of the television show, The Twighlight Zone. Neal had tried the famed helicopter crash case revolving around the series – which made national headlines.

I anxiously sat down while Neal grinned and looked down at me.

James F. Neal was shorter than I had imagined. He was in his sixties; he had salt and pepper hair and the frame of an elderly gentleman. Yet he still had the demeanor of a 30-year-old. And his scruffy gray and white beard belittled his intelligence – he spoke just like one of the most brilliant men in the world.

Stoic yet humble, Neal appeared very proud of his framed black and white photographs. He motioned to a picture of himself, standing next to the judge's chambers at the **Jimmy Hoffa** trial.

"**Jimmy Hoffa** was the biggest headache of my life," Neal told me, shaking his head. "I'll never forget those days."

I stood up and took the tape recording of Floyd out of my black leather purse. I reached in my satchel and pulled out a long, brown tape recorder. I laid them both on Neal's desk in front of him. I felt like a game show hostess getting ready to demonstrate a product for sale.

The room was as silent as a church before Easter services. I put the tape in the recorder and clicked the lid shut, without losing contact with Neal's eyes. I could tell he was watching me very carefully. I could tell he was impressed. I couldn't lose his attention.

And then I said simply, " I drove all this way, just to get five minutes with you and ask you one question."

Neal stared at me, appearing to look right through my very soul, amazed yet amused with my boldness.

"Please, listen to this conversation, and please, put my mind at ease. Please..." I said for the third time, taking a deep breath.

"Tell me that this conversation is just the figment of a lunatic prisoner's imagination," I said.

I pushed my index finger down on the PLAY button and Floyd's voice filled the room. Floyd detailed a very "secret" meeting at a bar in Indianapolis shortly after the LaSalle Street Murders. On this tape he described an eyewitness account of William Bracy and Jimmy Hoffa's alleged participation in this meeting, as well as their role in the most famous unsolved murder case in the history of Indianapolis. The tape revealed an overwhelming link between the deaths of the three microfilm businessmen on LaSalle Street – including one slain victim who had once worked for the Pentagon) and the release of Jimmy Hoffa from prison by former President Nixon.

Jimmy Hoffa was released from prison in December, 1971 – only a few weeks after the LaSalle Street Murders!

The tape quickly became monotone to me. I had heard this conversation nearly 1,000 times. I knew it by heart.

I intently watched Neal's face. Within seconds his smile quickly disappeared. Wrinkles surfaced on his forehead and his lips grew serious. The more Floyd spoke the more Neal frowned.

Suddenly, he twirled around in his chair and looked at the wall so that I couldn't watch him as he concentrated.

As Floyd continued describing Jimmy Hoffa and other details about the White house Aid William Bracy, I was unable to see Neal's expression.

I felt my heart skip a beat with anticipation.

Then, just as suddenly, Neal twirled around with a quick squeak of his swivel chair. He chewed on his left pinkie and grabbed a yellow legal pad. He scrambled for an ink pen and wrote several things down as he listened to my tape.

I started shaking. Was this famous man mad at me for wasting his time?

Neal tapped his pen across the legal pad and then looked up at me.

"Turn it off," he said. "I've heard enough."

I was disappointed. "But we haven't even reached the good part yet," I thought to myself.

I obeyed him and stood up – silently yet respectfully – in front of Neal.

"I'm sorry," he said with displeasure. His eyes seemed to be retracing an important era of his life.

I couldn't hold eye contact with him. I looked away, down at my purse and at the floor. I was embarrassed. I was certain I had just made a very important man angry with me. I was ready to run out the door and race to my hotel room to cry.

And then Neal spoke. Firmly and with precision.

"I cannot tell you that this is the figment of a lunatic prisoner's imagination," he said. **"There's too much on that tape that is true. Too much for the prisoner to have made it up."**

I felt like I was in the middle of a horror movie. Not the "Friday the 13th" kind of horror flick where you eat popcorn, but the "Marilyn Monroe gets murdered" type of horror story. Like the Pelican Brief. Like…? I suddenly wished I was back in Indianapolis, comforted by my surroundings and the neighborhood rooster who always woke me up at dawn.

Neal scribbled a name on a piece of paper. He handed it to me.

"But I'm really not the man you need to talk to," Neal told me.

I looked down at the name on the piece of paper in awe. I felt like I was holding the key to Fort Knox.

In bold letters it read: MIKE EPSTEIN.

"Mike Epstein?" I said out loud.

"Yes," Neal said. "Contact him immediately. He's the only man who can help you."

"Where is he?" I asked. "How do I find him?"

"I don't know," Neal said. "We've lost contact throughout the years. He worked for the US Department of Justice, Criminal Division, in the 1960's."

I heard he retired and was living in the Virginia Mountains somewhere," Neal told me.

I looked at Mr. James F. Neal. As much as I had wanted him to tell me that Floyd's detailed description of Jimmy Hoffa and his involvement with several Watergate spies was a fabrication, I knew in my gut this would be his answer.

I knew that the truth behind the LaSalle Street Murder was in the palm of my hands – and I knew that I had a long, dangerous road ahead of me. My suspicions that someone – someone possibly in the White House in the late 1960's and early 1970's – had paid Rock Norton to carry out the LaSalle Street Murders appeared to be true.

"And get the book on Jimmy Hoffa," Neal told me as he gave me a hug and sent me down the hall. "It's a shame the author died recently. That man really could have helped you. He knew more about Jimmy Hoffa than anyone – even me."

I hesitated at the door.

"Where do you think the microfilm went that was taken out of the house?" I asked.

"I know it either went back to the White House or it was destroyed," he said.

"What do you think was on the microfilm that was taken out of the LaSalle Street death house?" I asked.

Neal frowned again. "Illegal campaign contributions?" Neal suggested. "That's the only thing that I think it could have been."

Neal suggested that Jimmy Hoffa was making illegal campaign contributions to the President's election campaign.

Maybe the LaSalle Street boys found out about it.

I smiled, looking up at Neal. "Thank-you," I said.

"Let me know what you find out," he said, looking directly into my eyes. Somehow I knew that Neal knew I wouldn't stop until I found out the truth.

I walked out of Neal's office and down the hall with incredible strength. One of the most important men in the country believed in me. When I entered the glass elevators I pushed the fluourescent yellow button for the first floor and leaned my head against the door. I couldn't believe that this great man had devoted one hour – not five minutes as promised – to helping me.

And I couldn't believe what I knew was ahead of me.

How was I going to find this former investigator for the US DEPARTMENT OF JUSTICE? How was I going to find this man who had dedicated his heart, mind and soul to the mysterious relationship between Jimmy Hoffa, President Nixon (and his Watergate henchmen) for much of his career?

Suddenly I envisioned this former prosecutor, inevitably a white-haired, articulate older man, fishing at a beautiful, sun-splashed lake in the middle of the Virginia Mountains. I could see him sitting in a royal blue sailboat, hundreds of miles from Capitol Hill, relaxing, perhaps smoking a pipe full of sweet tobacco and drinking a glass of expensive Scotch. I could see that he now had not a care in the world – but inside his brain he harbored secrets about the White House and Jimmy Hoffa that no one else in the world knew about.

And I knew that I was the woman that could possibly hold the key to those secrets. The key that – once matched with this man's knowledge – could unlock those secrets and solve one of this country's greatest mysteries.

As the elevator landed on the first floor, I stepped out into the incredible, humid atmosphere in the heart of Nashville, Tennessee. The sun was so intense I was nearly blinded by its brilliance. I closed my eyes for just a moment.

I knew that the brilliance was coming not from the sun, but from the sun's source. I felt the incredible presence of God envelope my body.

Somehow, I had finally stopped asking the question, "Why me, God?"

I knew that I had to simply accept the fact that I was chosen to solve these murders and write a book about them. No one at the Indianapolis Police Department had ever dared to believe what I believed – let alone delve so deep into this realm of the case. There were only a handful of veteran police officers back home that believed in me – the Sheriff, Padget, Ryker and the Private Detective Don Campbell. But even these veteran homicide investigators doubted the White House link to the murders. Without their support I never would have convinced the Marion County Grand Jury that the Indianapolis 500 veteran mechanic, Rock Norton, committed the LaSalle Street Murders. Without their help and encouragement I never could have maintained an undercover relationship with a man I believed to be a sinister serial killer who had claimed lives all over the United States for decades.

I took a deep breath and opened my eyes.

Suddenly I envisioned the large brown envelope from the US DEPARTMENT OF CORRECTIONS that I had hidden away in my underwear drawer back in Indianapolis.

Inside the envelope was a letter from the warden of Lewisburg Prison, where Jimmy Hoffa was once imprisoned. Even though I had received his package over a month ago, I had never opened it. **I knew that it contained top-secret information about former prison inmate Jimmy Hoffa.**

I believed it would confirm my suspicions that Jimmy Hoffa did indeed take a little "trip" to Indianapolis in the middle of the night – for a very special meeting to orchestrate his release from prison – during his incarceration at Lewisburg.

I couldn't wait to open this envelope, but I knew I had to open

Former Teamster's President James Hoffa leaves the Lewisberg, Penn., peniten-
tiary on Dec. 23, 1971 after having his sentence commuted by President
Richard Nixon. (AP Photo)
This was only two weeks after the Lasalle Street murders.

Equipped with HUAC aide William Wheeler, formal blue suit, and a new briefcase, Congressman Richard Nixon brings the coveted microfilm to Foley Square, December 13th, 1948: he's about to make his historic intervention with the Hiss grand jury. Wide World Photos

Author Carol Sissom received information from a LaSalle Street Murders witness who said he believed President Richard Nixon could have had knowledge about the microfilm that was taken out of the LaSalle Street Murders death house. The same witness testified that he saw microfilm taken from the LaSalle Street Murder victims' home (after the murders were committed) and later given to a Nixon White House representative. This photo is not proof of what the witness said - it only illustrates the irony of the fact Nixon was no stranger to microfilm in 1971 - as he was captured by an AP photographer carrying microfilm with his own hands when he was a Congressman - in December 1948.

it in the presence of a trusted law enforcement agent –someone who could oversee the proper chain of custody regarding its contents.

"Jimmy Hoffa," I said, whispering the famous deceased union member's name out loud. "Were you in Indianapolis three days after the LaSalle Street Murders?"

"Did someone let you out of jail that night to perform union business 800 miles away from your jail cell?" I asked out loud.

"Who was the man sitting next to you at Tommy's Starlight Palladium at 3 a.m?" I continued.

"And why was this man seen putting microfilm into a rental car registered to the Secret Service?"

Suddenly I heard a car horn and opened my eyes. I could see green and white signs in front of me pointing to Nashville, Tennessee's world-famous Music Row. I suddenly felt a shiver run through me, in spite of the day's intense heat.

After all, it was my birthday. And I knew that some how, some way, God willing, I would find the answers to these questions.

And I knew that I had to find Mr. Mike Epstein.

66

After my trip to Nashville

Rock Norton had a sneaky way of startling me.

He liked to interrupt my sleep. He thought it was funny.

This time – it was a phone call that really frightened me.

Rock Norton dialed my telephone number at 6 a.m. and let it ring off the hook until I woke up.

"What?" I asked, still sleepy. "It's still night-time."

"No, it's not, Pretty One," he barked, disgruntled. "The sun IS up. Open those pretty little eyes of yours and get up."

He sounded like he'd been up all night. Like he hadn't slept a wink.

"I think those boys copied something that they shouldn't have," Rock Norton said.

Ironically, I had been reading through a file of information right before I went to bed. It was information I had received in the afternoon mail.

It was from the **WHITE HOUSE.**

I was lucky enough to obtain a copy of William Bracy's daily itinerary and calendar for the month of December, 1971.

I was exhausting the Legislative Archives in Washington, D.C.

David Pointer, an executive assistant, was phenomenal at helping me locate documents.

I tapped into the most lucrative gold mine when he helped me delve into THE WATERGATE SPECIAL PROSECUTION FORCE RECORDS.

To my astonishment, the famous William Bracy's calendar for December 4th and 5th, 1971 was available for my review!

All I had to do was pay for the copies and I received them in amazing fashion.

William Bracy had absolutely no White House or Washington, D.C. commitments for the night Floyd said he was in Indianapolis for a special, "middle-of-the-night" meeting regarding the LaSalle Street murders.

I could find no official or personal alibi for his whereabouts the night of the LaSalle Street Murders – Teamsters meeting!

I learned, William Bracy's calendar showed that he was in Florida.

This perfectly corroborated the fact that Floyd said former White house Aide William Bracy was wearing a "Florida"-type T-shirt in the dead of winter in Indianapolis that night.

Floyd had thought it strange someone would be in snow-laden, sub-zero, freezing Indianapolis –wearing summer clothing.

But I didn't stop there.

What I found on the phone was even more amazing.

I called every single car rental company in Indianapolis, tracing all vehicles rented in the city on December 4th, 1971.

The same night Floyd said a "meeting" occurred at Tommy's Starlight Palladium – where Jimmy Hoffa and William Bracy were in attendance – discussing LaSalle Street Murders business.

I found more proof that Brady was there!

I found a car rental company that had incredibly accurate record-keeping still in their archives. They had records dating back to December 1, 1971!

It was strange – and a stroke of luck – because most car rental companies didn't have records that went that far back.

But luck was on my side.

This company told me their records indicated they had rented a car to someone from the **SECRET SERVICE** on that same night. **THE SECRET SERVICE RENTED A CAR IN INDI-ANAPOLIS THE SAME NIGHT THAT FLOYD SAID HE SAW SOMEONE FROM THE SECRET SERVICE AT TOMMY'S STARLIGHT PALLADIUM!**

All of a sudden I felt like I was Julia Roberts in the movie, The Pelican Brief.

The only emotion I could give Rock was a nod of my head as he continued to talk to me on the telephone.

"What do you think those three boys copied that they shouldn't have" I asked Rock Norton.

"I'll give you a clue," Rock said with precision. "It will be up to you to figure it out."

"A clue?" I repeated his statement. I was floored.

"It had better be a good clue this early in the morning," I joked.

"Your clue is this," Rock Norton said, drawing it out so that he could tease me with it.

"747," he said.

"747?" I asked.

"Yes," he said. "Seven. Four. Seven."

I quickly wrote it down on the palm of my hand.

"There's your clue," he said. "The LaSalle Street boys copied something they shouldn't have and your clue is 747."

"Thank-you," was all I could say. I was humble with gratitude for his gift of information.

"Now figure it out, Pretty One," Rock Norton told me. "I have to go to work. But get on the stick. I want to see you win that Pulitzer Prize."

"Oh my God," I told Rock. "I can't believe you're telling me this."

Rock Norton laughed again.

"What is so funny?" I asked him.

"Now you're going to have to think of another title for your book," Rock said.

"I'm afraid to ask," I said, dryly.

"Now you're going to have to call it "***WHO REALLY DUNIT.***"

Rock Norton was still laughing when I hung up the phone.

67

I received a letter from Floyd today.

He told me a lot of things that made me sit down and think. It was like a puzzle for me to unscramble.

This was the letter:

Dear Carol Schultz:

I believe Rock Norton got paid twice for the LaSalle Street Murders and for the Microfilm.

Rock Norton always talked about a **"Doctor"** being involved in the LaSalle Street Murders.

The doctor was selling the "Microfilm" out of the Pentagon. Money. You need to read Rock Norton's letter of 1986.

Carpenter was telling William Bracy to stop the leak at all costs.

The doctor paid Norton to kill the men on LaSalle Street, so nobody would be talking. There were five men altogether that year that were murdered.

Bobby Lee Atkinson

John Terhorst

Robert Gierse
Robert Hinson
James Barker

Norton was to burn the "Microfilm". This was ordered by the "Doctor".
"Stop all leaks to the doctor."
But Norton recovered the Microfilm. He had two boxes with little cans on top of them that he took out of LaSalle Street.

The Doctor was onto William Bracy .
Norton recovered the "Microfilm." "Stop the leaks at all cost."

Before you can have Pentagon Papers, to leak out, you have got to have film! We get the film first and then we print!
Mama Hoffa and Orie Hoffa – The son went to see the President at the White House. I had the documents. My sister knows. He went to see him to free his Dad from US Prison. November/ December 1971.
The President and William Bracy used the National Union President to pick up the "Microfilm" from Tommy's Star Light Lounge in Indianapolis.
Norton was at Tommy's Lounge before we got there to drop off the microfilm of the war and the two boxes.
Norton told Hoffa about the room of Carpenter's. It told of it on the Microfilm. Plus, the doctor paying him (Norton) too.
You need to talk to the young girl at the scene of the murders. She saw the type writer. She typed a note on it for Rock Norton that night.
Then the Union President told Bracy about the "Doctor" pay-ing Rock Norton for the LaSalle Street Murders.
"Stop the leak" at all costs.
That's why the break in of the Doctor's office. 5 men broke in. On the movie "All the President's Men" you saw it. Watch the movie again.
Looking for more "Microfilm."
The C.I.A. was at the house the next morning – on LaSalle

Street. To see if we left any microfilm.

The same men that freed Jimmy Hoffa (out of prison in 1971) killed him!

The national union President Jimmy Hoffa – in 1975 – was killed.

Yet Hoffa was going to run for President of the union before 1980. Hoffa was going to run in 1976. Hello!

Yet, the President went to Nashville, Tennessee (Tennessee Bill lived there). "Don't let him run."

Tell Norton to pick up the **$500,000.**

Stop him at all costs.

1976, we picked up the money for the murders.

It's in the writing of the Mandamus. You got the case number.

Tennessee Bill and I – you know why – we had to go out West. T.L.C. Truck Lies. 1976 Green/White K.W. 325 Cat.

Bill Haze got to the house in Clearwater Florida with THE EXPERT. Susan got photos of it. We all went down to it, indoor pool and all.

In the center of the room was a S.R.1. Code Photo hook to the Pentagon, for the war ships. "S.R.1. Chandler Code Phone."

There was a pretty lady at Tommy's Starlight Lounge that night. She had just visited her family before they got to Tommy's.

The state police officer from Indiana that found John Terhorst's body. (W.) Run his name in the Bracy Library Package. They give you a list of names.

You will see, he saw the President two times at the White House. "Around the time of the Death of John Terhorst." But he was an oil man out of Indiana. That's what the White House document said. Free documents.

The date of the newspaper tells it all.

"Where the Spirit of the Lord is there is liberty."

Fifth of whiskey is what the box was for.

May God ride with you all. In His Service

Floyd

P.S. Don't forget Susan got photos of Bill Haze (in the federal witness protection program) and the Expert's home in Clearwater, Florida.

Romans 8:28

****

Floyd sent me a letter in which he confessed to being involved in the murder of Jimmy Hoffa and that he knew where Hoffa's body was buried. (See sketches in the center of the book.)

Carol received a letter from Floyd Chastain which connected organized crime to the LaSalle Street murders.

68

THE THREE EYES

I had to find the three eyes.

What are they?

They are the three hotbeds of organized crime in Indianapolis, according to the large yellow book I was reading. The hardback was titled, "SPOOKS."

"You have to get the book called "Spooks," said Peter Knapp, an international consultant on conspiracy who lives near Chicago. When I first contacted him for advice on the LaSalle Street Murders he was skeptical.

"Mr. Knapp, you are known to be *the* absolute expert on conspiracy," I told him.

"So?" he asked me in a crusty voice over the telephone.

"Can you please give me some advice about these three men who were murdered?" I asked. "I think they were killed over something they saw on microfilm."

Peter Knapp growled a bit before he gave me explicit instructions.

"Don't even call me again until you read a book called SPOOKS," he said with a gravely voice. He sounded like he'd had an operation on his throat. "Or until you find out what the three eyes are. I *know* you have no idea what the three eyes are. Do you?"

He didn't even wait for me to respond.

"You had better find out," he said.

Peter Knapp is a physically disabled, extremely intelligent radio broadcaster who lives alone. He devotes his life to exposing conspiracies-20 hours out of every day. When I first told the feisty older gentleman about the LaSalle Street Murders – and that I believed the murders were linked to Washington D.C. – he immediately insisted the case could be linked to a national conspiracy.

I couldn't help but laugh when he told me this – he was such a typical conspiracy theorist – but I knew I needed to obey his instructions. I wanted to tap into his overwhelming wealth of knowledge.

I could leave no stones unturned.

"I will help you," said Knapp, who once testified on a Watergate DC-10 airplane crash trial. He is an expert on airplane sabotage.

"But I will *not* do all of your work for you. I can't stand lazy reporters."

I told him that Rock Norton had given me a clue.

"He said the word "**747**" would help me solve the LaSalle Street Murders," I told him.

Knapp growled for a minute. I thought he was going to belch but he offered a priceless suggestion. He said it could be a clue that related to a Watergate airplane crash several years ago. A plane crash where Howard Hunt's wife was killed. She was carrying a lot of money on the plane that day.

After hearing my story – and hearing a little bit more about the Lasalle Street Murders, Knapp grew quiet.

"I think you're right about the President at the time and the

Union President," Knapp said. "Read my report on airplane sabotage. Get these books. Indianapolis has more spies in it than Russia. Call me after you do your homework and I'll tell you what to do next."

"And for God's sakes," Knapp said, warning me like I was a six-year-old in first grade. "Don't talk to any more reporters. Ever. Tell them all to go to hell."

"And you absolutely need to read something called the HOUSTON PLAN," he added. "Find it. Read it. And get back to me."

I was impressed with Knapp. His suspicion that Indianapolis was once a hotbed of organized crime proved true the next day when I read an article that was published years after the LaSalle Street Murders.

*"**Organized crime** maintains a quiet but powerful influence in Indianapolis ranging from gambling to pornography, to a variety of fraudulent money schemes."

"**This influence** is cemented by political alliances and, according to law enforcement agencies, backed up when needed by muscle and murder.

"**For more** than four decades, the catalyst has been lucrative gambling activities – private clubs, extensive horserace booking and sports parlay cards – which, although usually controlled locally, are often under the sway of persons with crime syndicate connections.

"**Unquestionably, gambling** and fencing of stolen goods are the twin hubs of organized crime's interest in Indianapolis.

"**From these** activities come other spin offs running the gamut from "legitimate" business investments to the silent backing of thefts, arsons and other crimes.

"**Rather than a** cohesive organization enjoying ironclad control, what exists here is a loose network of persons who occasionally work together, and generally know each other.

"**While one element** may be independent of each other, with each holding "connections" in different cities and with different underworld figures, some nevertheless intermingle locally for a common goal – money and power.

"**The investigation** determined that several local gamblers who enjoy syndicate friendships also associate regularly with career hoodlums who have been "arrested" but never convicted" for murder.

"**Underscoring the sinister** reality of organized crime is information from three law enforcement agencies that at least six unsolved murders here can be traced to mob-related activities.

"**These statements,** corroborated by underworld informants, identify three Indianapolis men, individually or together, as executioners in the murders.

My eyes grew wide as I read the names of my boys on LaSalle Street.

THE VICTIMS WERE BUSINESSMEN ROBERT A. GIERSE, ROBERT HINSON AND JAMES BARKER, WHO WERE FOUND WITH THEIR THROATS SLIT IN 1971. SALESMAN JOHN C. TERHORST, SLAIN IN THE SAME YEAR, burglar Robert Lee Atkinson, also murdered in 1971, and gambling club boss Ronald G. Grubbs, slain gang-land style last July.

(*footnote, The Indianapolis Star, 1971)

I thought of my recent telephone call to THE EXPERT, a man who is alleged to be one of the most dangerous underworld figures in Indianapolis. Once, we almost met face to face at a downtown Indy restaurant!

I knew it was time to press in. Not too hard. Nothing too dangerous. I just knew I had to keep digging as my gut led me.

I had to talk to THE EXPERT again. I had to get him to trust me. Rock Norton spoiled me with his attention and his interest in my book. These other bad guys were not as easy and gullible as Rock Norton was. They were much more difficult to get an interview with. They were cautious and aloof.

The next day I called Peter Knapp to tell him what I'd found. He apologized for offending me with his abrasiveness.

"Read up on President Nixon," he said.

"He was in Dallas when Kennedy was killed. It didn't seem to bother him a bit when JFK was shot down," Knapp offered.

"President Nixon…" I said out loud after I hung up. I remembered watching his impeachment hearings on my mother's television set when I was a little girl. I remembered standing in Mom's sewing room, helping her make a cotton jumper for me as we watched the news together. It was a sweltering hot season that I called a "Watermelon and Watergate summer."

"Did you have the LaSalle Street boys killed, Mr. President?" I asked out loud. I was speaking to the air, but it felt good to ask Nixon the question. I liked to think I was just like Barbara Walters or Diane Sawyer.

I imagined the deceased President giving me a calculated answer.

"If he did have them killed, where do I look next to prove it?" I thought.

As I turned the lights off and went to bed, I kept thinking about what the Private Detective, Don, told me.

"You need to stick with Peter Knapp," Don said. "He might turn out to be your best friend."

69

THE WEATHER

1996
8 a.m.

I got up and decided to call the weather.

I had been dreaming about the case when I woke up with a bright idea.

The Indianapolis Police Department's initial reports claimed that it was **NOT** snowing the night the LaSalle Street Murders took place.

Floyd, however, insisted that it *was* snowing – ever so slightly – when he was driving home after the murders were committed.

I made one phone call to the Indiana National Weather Service and found out the truth.

There was no measurable snow that night, according to a spokesman.

However, there was recorded snow just after the midnight hour.

Into the wee hours of the morning, December 1st, 1971, there was a **TRACE** of snow, the Weather Bureau reported.

Floyd was right!

70

Five Years After I Began Investigating the Murders

THE ARREST

Finally, a new prosecutor was elected in Marion County.

Justice had arrived in the form of a short, clean-cut Jewish prosecutor who promised to do everything he could to bring the truth out in the celebrated triple homicide. He pledged to help *before* he was elected.

He held true to his campaign promise.

He called a grand jury to convene on the LaSalle Street Murders in 1995.

I prepared a lengthy report for the grand jury.

The jury deliberated for one solid year.

Six men and women came back with a verdict in March, 1996.

They indicted Rock Norton on three counts of murder.

March 22, 1996

When I woke up just before dawn I had a funny feeling in the pit of my stomach.

It was a deep, nagging sensation in my gut that was my own body's signal that something was getting ready to happen.

It was almost as though a loved one was just about to die.

Even though it was the first day of Spring, the teal gray skies outside were pregnant with plump white snow clouds. Indianapolis was unpredictable this time of year – more often than not school children could build snowmen and drink hot chocolate endlessly when they were home for Spring Break. I could hear the drone of television commercials in the next room. Undoubtedly my son was already snuggled under a heavy quilt and fixed for a long day of watching television.

I pulled myself to the edge of the bed and fidgeted with my bedroom slippers with my toes. Although it had been thirteen years since a crisp, white Virginia Slims cigarette had passed my lips, my lungs still tingled with each breath whenever I was nervous. Every time I even thought of smoking, however, I thanked God that a near-fatal case of pneumonia, collapsing both of my lungs, delivered me from such a nasty addiction in 1983.

I glanced at the clock.

It was 6:25 a.m.

I was running late. I knew I had to call him soon. I couldn't ignore him one minute longer. In five more minutes he would be gone for the day. I had to call the man I had talked to every day for the last three years and nine months. I had to comfort him today. I had to assure him that everything was going to be okay – even thought the gurgling in my digestive tract was telling me otherwise.

Rock Norton was always punctual.

The 69-year-old auto racing magnate was known for precision in every area of his life. His mornings were perfectly routine: Without an alarm clock he was up at 5 a.m. every day for a brief, shocking, ice-cold shower. He then towel-dried a shock full of silver and white hair and gave himself a dry razor shave. He then padded down the wooden staircase of his 1920 Dutch Colonial mansion.

After watching the morning news and skimming the daily paper, he prepared and ate the most important meal of his day. Poached eggs, salmon, toast and strawberries were a frequent breakfast. He then headed to the refrigerator to retrieve a plate of T-bone steak, dripping with blood, that he laid at his feet on the white linoleum tile floor.

His dog, named Zack, always ate better than he did, Rock often joked.

When he answered the telephone, I could hear him washing his hands.

"You're *late* Pretty One," he said, barking into the receiver.

"I'm sorry," I apologized. I could hear a few dishes in his kitchen sink rattle as he dried his hands. I knew he was lathering moisturizing lotion in the deep cracks and crevices of his palms. After year of hard work in the Indy 500 racing circuit, he had scorched all of the hair from his thick, distinguished fingers.

Even his fingertips were scarred.

Rock Norton's temper softened as soon as he heard my voice.

"What took you so long?" he demanded. He was still short. "I am leaving in two minutes. TWO MINUTES."

"I – I – I overslept," I explained, stuttering.

There was no excuse acceptable in Rock Norton's eyes. I heard him sigh in disgust. "Oh well, I guess you'll just have to call me tomorrow morning. I'll be busy all day today," he said, waiting for a response before he scolded me again. He was baiting me. He wanted me to beg for his attention.

Deep in his gut, I think Rock Norton knew what was about to happen, too. He was one of the most intelligent men I'd ever met in my life. Admittedly, he claimed to have had total recall ever since he was 16-years-old. He could read a book cover to cover in one day, and then immediately recite every word of it out loud. Although I scoffed at him when he claimed to have ESP, a keen extra-sensory perception, I couldn't help but admit that he really did have some sort of fine-tuned sixth sense.

"I-I-I just wanted to read the Bible to you this morning," I said, stuttering. I scrambled for conversation. Rock could sense the fear in my voice. I knew he enjoyed it immensely.

Reading the Bible to him may have been a feeble attempt at conversation, but it was a powerful one.

"Okay," Rock agreed. I was surprised.

I quickly leaned over my bed and grabbed my favorite red-leather New International Version Bible from my nightstand - before Rock Norton could change his mind. I closed my eyes and the pages fell open to the book of Jeremiah. My eyes fell across the tissue-thin pages and landed upon one of my favorite scriptures, underlined with a yellow high lighter.

"For I know the thoughts that I think toward you, saith the Lord, thoughts of peace, and not of evil, to give you an expected end," I said, reading out loud.

Rock and I both swallowed the silence. It was as thick as butter melting on a hot ceramic plate.

Even though I believed that Rock Norton was a serial killer, an alleged monster, a knife-wielding sociopath, I knew that he was coming to an end.

Yet he was still a human being, and the end of a human was sad. We had grown surprisingly close to each other during these five years. In the beginning – I wanted him arrested and put on death row.

Now, after fighting the system for so long to get him in jail, I was starting to feel sorry for him.

In a *strange* way, I understood him. In an even *stranger* way, we had become friends.

And for another bizarre, unexplainable reason, I knew that, after all of these years, Rock cared for me too. Deeply. As intelligent as he was, I knew that he had to know how aggressively I had been following him for the past five years. I knew that he not only enjoyed the undercover game, but I believe he genuinely wanted to help me solve the intriguing mystery that I had immersed myself in.

Rock truly wanted to help me win the Pulitzer Prize.

"Get everything in a safe place!" I blurted out unexpectedly.

Although he said nothing, I knew that Rock Norton was

shocked at my boldness.

I could feel him raising his eyebrows on the other end of the telephone.

"Get absolutely everything in a safe place in case something happens to you," I repeated myself. "If you were to die or be arrested, the Indianapolis Police Department could never fathom what you know. They're not smart enough, Rock!

I knew I had captured his attention.

"They're not big enough to solve something that happened in the US government over two decades ago," I said.

I knew that Rock was nodding his head in agreement with me.

"It's done, Pretty One," he told me.

"Everything, absolutely everything to do with the White House and the President?" I asked him.

I knew Rock was nodding his head in agreement.

"Don't leave one morsel of anything lying around the house," I instructed him like I was a teacher at a daycare center.

"Okay," Rock agreed without hesitation.

"But what if something should happen to you, how do I get it?" I asked him.

"We need a code word," I said, without waiting for him to answer me. "We need a way to communicate if you do go to jail. This person needs to trust me to pick up the information."

"What code word do you want to use?" he asked.

"I know," I said. "Julius Caesar! That's our code word from now on."

"Okay, Pretty One," he said. "Julius Caesar it is. But I'm going to give you something you should have in case it does happen. Trust no one with it. **You must take it to Washington if anything happens to me.**"

"Do you have someone in Washington you can trust?" Rock asked me.

"Yes," I said, swallowing hard. I had to realize something could happen to Rock very soon. My stomach cramped as I suddenly realized how much I cared for this grandfather of 18 grandchildren!

"I have someone in Washington I can trust" I said quietly.

"Then I'm going to mail you something," he told me. "When you see it you'll know what it is."

"NO!" I almost screamed. "Don't mail it!" I knew there was not enough time, but I couldn't tell him that. Rock Norton might not be here in 24 hours. The Marion County Grand Jury had been deliberating the re-investigation of the LaSalle Street Murders for over a week now. Although they had reviewed testimonies for nearly a year now – rumor had it that the six men and six women were nearing a verdict.

If they came back with an indictment by morning, Rock Norton could be in jail by noon.

But I didn't want Rock to know that. I didn't want him to be frightened on his last night. He needed just one more good night's sleep.

"I – I don't trust the mail. Take it to my post office box," I said. "Do it *today*. Do it this afternoon."

"I will if I can," he said. "I'm very busy today."

"No," I insisted. "Trust me. The time is at hand. You must do it today."

"Okay," Rock said quietly. He asked no more questions.

"I'll do it today," he said.

71

The next several hours were very suspenseful. I couldn't eat and I could barely sit down. I paced every inch of the hardwood floors in my bedroom until my son yelped at me from the living room that I was getting on his nerves.

"Chill out, Mom," he said, suggesting my presence was ruining his Spring Break. "Can you go somewhere else and do that?"

I marched to the kitchen to fix him his favorite garlic fried chicken. I peeled and fried heaping servings of homemade, seasoned potatoes for lunch. He smothered them in ketchup. Afterwards, he seemed to forgive me as he lifted up his T-shirt and rubbed his protruding belly in gratitude.

I looked at his innocent blue eyes that were fastened to the television set. They were almost covered by overgrown bangs and a mop-full of brown hair glistening with natural golden highlights. I couldn't help but notice what a beautiful teenager he had become.

I waited until nearly three p.m. before I took him to his grandmother's house and dropped him off. I sped to the post office on Shortridge Avenue and pulled my car into the parking lot. I turned off the engine and sat there, facing the front entrance of the straw-colored building. Three elderly women with short and curly blue-frosted hair walked up the sidewalk and passed in front of my windshield. They seemed to inch their way along like snails before they pulled open the double glass doors to go inside. Directly behind them a young college girl from Indiana University jogged up. She seemed irritated at their slowness and jogged around them. She butted into the building and stood in line.

A middle-aged businessman, parked his Saab next to me. He slid his sunglasses on top of his balding head. He got out of his car with a large manila envelope tucked under his right arm.

"All of these innocent bystanders," I thought to myself. "You don't even have a clue." They were all part of a humdrum society, oblivious to what was going on around them. They had no idea within minutes, I may find the key to one of the greatest secrets in American history tucked in my post office box.

I got out of my car and walked inside the lobby. A pregnant woman with her hair in a ponytail was scolding a curly-haired toddler. I could feel my heart beating through my chest as I walked by them. Everything seemed to be in slow motion. Even though it was bitterly cold I was not wearing gloves. My hands were purple from the near-freezing temperatures. They felt like ice as I took my key ring from my coat pocket and fumbled for my post office box key. My hands were shaking so hard it took me a few minutes to find the right key.

I was more scared than I have ever been in my life.

I glanced in the box window and saw the mail. I swallowed hard. I knew it wasn't just a piece of junk mail. I knew it was from him. There was a part of me that hoped he hadn't dropped it off. I wanted to go back to square one, five years ago, and I wished I had never made the first phone call that hooked me on the LaSalle Street Murders.

But it was too late.

The adrenaline was too much for me. I slipped the key into the box and turned it. I saw a large green manila envelope tucked inside. That's all that was there. Nothing else. Not even a lousy pizza coupon. I stared at the folder for a moment.

Then I put my fingers on it, gently, like it was a ticking time bomb.

I tugged at it for a second, then grabbed it, slammed the post office box door and locked it. I tucked the envelope under my coat and ran out the door. I got in my car.

I started the engine and glanced around. All of a sudden I felt silly. How paranoid of me to think anyone who was watching would know what I was doing. I felt like I was in the middle of a James Bond – 007 movie. My fingers were still shaking, but I knew I had to tear open the envelope. I gently ran my fingers across the label as though I were a blind person reading the Bible in Braille.

In large black letters Rock had written with a black marker. "BETTY THOMPSON."

"What a sense of humor," I thought as I smiled to myself. Betty Thompson was the pseudonym I had used for myself when I started on the case five years ago.

Rock Norton hadn't forgotten. I doubted he ever forgot anything I did or told him.

I held my breath and tore open the envelope. There it was. In black and white. No mistake about it. Rock really did trust me. He had given me the *real* reason the three executive playboys were savagely murdered on LaSalle Street.

Yes, Rock had slit three throats over a sex game involving his ex-wife, but, just as I had suspected all along, someone had *paid* him to kill the three men he thoroughly enjoyed killing.

I bowed my head and prayed, "Dear God, why me? Why did you pick me to do this?"

I had just been handed an answer to one of the greatest secrets in American history.

Something in my life that I thought was almost over was now just beginning. With this information in my possession I now knew I had yet before me yet another, long, tedious road of investigations.

"DEAR GOD! Haven't I done enough!" I cried out in the privacy of my own car. "Why this? Didn't I do enough for you already! I've just gone through five years of hell in catching a serial killer! Why this too! I don't want to do this! I'm not strong enough! No more! I can't take anymore!"

And in less than 24 hours later I knew why.

As I stood in front of my television set, I watched live footage in horror as the elderly man, someone I believed was once a brutal, savage serial killer – the same man who let me read the Bible to him – was handcuffed and stuffed into a police car.

I wept as Rock Norton cried out my name on live television.

"Carol Schultz! Carol Schultz!" Rock cried out to reporters. He had just realized the young woman who had befriended him was really Judas. She had just betrayed him – as she had every day for the last three years and nine months. She was a spy working for the police, and he had trusted her with his life.

I sat down on my couch and stared at the ceiling. I was a heroine, but my emotions were indescribable. I knew what I did was right, but there was a part of me that felt sorry for him.

72

April 1996

"RIDE DOWNTOWN"

Doors were locked, deadbolts fastened and security alarms were activated as Rock Norton continued to make front page headlines – four weeks after the Marion County grand jury indicted him on three counts of murder.

The media had a field day when an arrest was finally made – twenty five years after the murders. Especially when the one who received the most credit for solving it was a young single mother – not a veteran police officer. Now, not only was my five year cover blown with a man I and the cops thought was a savage serial killer – but my neighbor's suspicions were now public knowledge. I was a traitor, a narc, a renegade. I was someone who liked to flirt with danger – my neighbors whispered amongst themselves. I lived in their quiet circle of safety and trust.

When I opened the front door of my two-bedroom farmhouse I noticed the neighborhood was quiet. In an area just south of Highway US 40 and Post Road, it was filled with many friendly but rowdy dogs, over a dozen pre-school children and a rooster that diligently crowed every morning.

An eerie hush fell on this tiny community just before dawn and I knew why. Although I enjoyed the usual silence I was concerned about this tight-knit community as I stood on my front porch, waiting for a ride to the City County Building. I worried that parents would never let their children play in their yards again – or at least until Rock Norton was convicted. And I knew that it could be nearly a year before Rock went to trial – a year too long to punish small children because of my desire to solve a murder. I felt chagrined as I realized that not only was my life changed, so were the lives of those that knew me.

I looked at my watch. It was 8:52 a.m.

Someone would be arriving soon, I knew. As I waited, I decided to focus on the brilliant sunrise creeping through the billowing oak trees, blooming lilac bushes and balsam pines bordering the eastern side of my two-acre property. Every tree was well over 100-years-old with roots buried dozens of feet within the soil. The sunlight seemed to illuminate my modest landscape like a candle. I loved the lush greenery, including a huge pocket of poison ivy caught near a shrine of lilies of the valley and rose bushes near my garage. It made me feel as though I lived in the heart of one of Indiana's state parks instead of a flourishing suburb in the state's capital.

Finally, I saw the police sedan.

A white, four-door Chevrolet Caprice pulled into my driveway and parked close to the street. Without craning my neck to look, I knew it was an IPD cruiser. As I waited for IPD Department detective Randy Sabens to walk through the knee-high grass and fallen tree limbs in my front yard, I noticed a gray and white rabbit raise up on its hind legs in the thick of overgrown weeds. It darted its head back and forth as though it were trying to decide whose scent it was detecting – mine or the police officers.

I had completed dozens of print, radio and television interviews and had even been flattered with invitations to fly to New York to be on Good Morning America, CBS This Morning, several syndicated talk shows. I had courted the company of several

TV Movie of the Week producers and had fielded questions from book agents from New York to Hollywood. I had even spent an exhausting three days dodging a camera crew from Inside Edition.

I didn't want the News, Rock Norton or the Mob to know I was home.

I stood on the front porch, waving to Sabens with a crisp white subpoena in my right hand and a large, navy burlap purse in my left hand. The purse was filled with ten of my most intimate, personal diaries. Although I had kept a diary ever since I was in the second grade, these diaries were special. They were all in journal form, written in empty hard back books that I had purchased at a quaint Family Bookstore on East Washington Street.

These books had kept me sane during the years of my homicide investigation. Writing in them, documenting my daily detective work, including every scrap of information I uncovered each day.

The pages not only included hundreds of incriminating statements from murder suspect Rock Norton, but they also revealed interviews with important witnesses, police and forensic experts that could corroborate the case I lived and breathed for five years. These diaries also detailed my daily fears, my anxieties, my ups and downs and other very intimate, personal aspects of my own private life.

I was still in shock.

A Marion County Circuit judge ordered me to produce these diaries to defense counsel Rick Ham, Rock Norton's attorney – based solely on the fact that they were photographed on WXIN-59, the local FOX NEWS affiliate. That's what the subpoena said. In black and white letters the highest criminal court in the state ordered me to surrender my diaries to the police – and to Rock Norton's attorney immediately. If I didn't – I would go to jail just like Rock Norton.

I was horrified!

I was more than embarrassed. I was frightened. How could I be ordered to release my LIFE for public scrutiny. WXIN news anchor Debra Zahler, a gorgeous blond with baby fine hair and a model perfect figure, was the only woman with the answer. She was the only woman with the video tapes. Video tapes that contained sound bites of my investigation that could both incriminate Rock Norton and smear my reputation as a woman at the same time.

Thoughts of the last few years ran wild through my mind…

****

Debra Zahler and I had become very special friends during the last year. She was a woman whose inner beauty was as magnificent as her outside features. She was genuinely kind, caring, intelligent, and she had a great sense of humor and was one of the sweetest personalities I'd ever encountered in my life. I had no idea this woman would some day become a very good and precious friend. I wished that most television personalities had an attitude like she did. She truly conveyed a heart of kindness and love.

When I met Debra for the first time last June, only days after a Marion County Grand Jury was called to convene on the case, I knew I'd never forget the look on her face.

I sat across from her at a conference table in the news room of WXIN FOX-59. She had asked me to come in for an interview with a press officer because the Marion County Grand Jury announced it was re-opening the LaSalle Street Murders' investigation. I had agreed to Zahler's interview – hoping that she would understand my plight to expose Rock Norton once and for all.

Her eyes grew wide with disbelief as she listened to my story. She interrupted me and waved her hand as though she were tossing a garden salad. "Your story is absolutely incredible," she said.

"I know," I said, nodding my head. "It's the story of a lifetime."

"No, no," Debra said. She was shaking her head as though I was a child who had just made a mistake on a math problem.

"Not the murder case," she said, emphasizing her point. "I don't want to do a story on LaSalle Street. I want to do a story on you – on your life. I want to interview your son, your mother and your friends. I want to do a series on your life and what you've gone through in all of this. Your persistence is amazing."

I could only stare at her. "You've got to be kidding," I said, dumbfounded. I felt the curl in my hot-rolled hair go flat. My right knee started to shake. "A story about me?" I was flattered but confused. But it was too late – Debra Zahler was already writing the script in her head. And a friendship that was to last was born in the basement of WXIN-TV 59, right next to a Coca-Cola machine and a metal dollar bill changer.

The two of us began meeting on a regular basis throughout the summer of 1995. Debra interviewed me in three parks, four different public libraries, in front of the Indianapolis Star News building and in a red-brick alley behind IPD's Southside district. Finally, in September, Debra and her camera-man, Jamie Suiter, were ready to photograph me in my home.

"Your diaries," Debra said, pointing to a corner of my bedroom office. "They catalog your personal life during all of this – don't they?"

"Well, yes," I told her.

"Then bring them out for a shot of you sitting at your computer," she said. She leaned over and started re-arranging books, folders and files in my office. "I want to lay them all out on this table," she said, pointing to a long brown fold-out next to my Pentium Legend computer. Zahler, who was just 33-yars-old, had just learned that she was pregnant. She stood in high heel pumps and arranged my diaries in three rows on top of the conference table I had purchased at a garage sale. It had a large chip on the right hand corner that I covered with a flower pot.

When Jamie Suiter panned the room with his video camera, he caught a two-second glimpse of my diaries and the flower pot.

This would prove to be my worst nightmare.

✷✷✷✷✷✷✷✷✷✷✷✷✷✷✷

73

FINAL CLUE

After Rock Norton's arrest on March 22nd, 1996, the FOX series about me ran in three segements – as headline news at the beginning of the nightly news broadcast. It was an incredible, dynamic series. It made me so nervous I could barely watch it. Seven months later, Jamie's two-second glimpse of those diaries cost me dearly. Debra's wonderful series that netted Jamie an Emmy nomination was now part of the LaSalle Street Murder trial. My journals were no longer diaries. They now had a legal name – DISCOVERY.

Now, the intimate details of my life would be displayed to the Deputy Prosecuting Attorneys Office. They would be given to Rock Norton's defense counsel to chew on like a juicy steak.

This meant that, essentially, Rock Norton, an alleged serial killer – would be able to drink a cold Pepsi, prop his feet up on a pillow and lounge on his jail cell cot to read about my sordid, sinful past. My life would be on display like an R-rated movie at the drive in theatre.

I knew that the Marion County Prosecutor's Office was angry

252

with me. The big shots there were jealous of me for getting so much publicity after Rock Norton's arrest. This was their subtle, yet powerful way of getting even with me. Their torment would be my punishment.

"It's not fair that I'm ordered to produce my diaries in their entirety, in their original form, just as punishment for the series that Debra Zahler had done," I whined to myself. "They might as well pass those diaries out to the five thousand people who work at the City County Building.

Why not?

I knew my journals would be checked out like library books.

"I can see the juiciest pages being duplicated in photo copiers by the handful. "Cheaper by the dozen....read all about it..." I wailed to myself.

But then again, a lot of things weren't fair in the infamous LaSalle Street Murders re-investigation. This was only the tip of the iceberg.

When Randy Sabens finally arrived at my front door, I handed him the burlap purse with my diaries and a black trash bag full of documents for deputy prosecuting attorney Linda Hope to review. Although he raised his eyebrows, Sabens didn't say anything. "Oh well," I said under my breath as I followed him out to his police sedan. I didn't have any cardboard boxes, and somehow, I deemed his black vinyl trash bags as inappropriate in this instance.

I noticed the clock on the dashboard of Sabens' cruiser as I fastened my seatbelt. It was about 8:50 a.m. I had to meet Linda Hope in ten minutes. It was *at least* a 20-minute ride downtown.

"Don't worry," said Sabens, a short, but good-looking gray-haired man with a neatly-trimmed mustache. "I used to race at the Indianapolis Motor Speedway."

I looked at him; my eyes wide open with anticipation. I covered my face with my hands and grinned.

"Oh no," I said, partly joking and partly genuinely scared. "Does this mean we're going to do about 120 miles per hour in the fast lane?"

"Well, not quite," Sabens said. "But let's just put it this way. We won't be late."

I thought I felt the hair on the back of my neck stand up as

Sabens put the cruiser in first gear. In fact, we had a nice, long talk during the lightning-bolt ride to downtown Indianapolis.

"What did you do before you came to the Indianapolis Police Department?" I asked him. I noticed that he had blond eyelashes and eyebrows. Trying not to appear nervous, I popped a piece of peppermint candy in my mouth to settle the anxiety bubbles in my stomach.

"I used to work in the coroner's office," he said matter-of-factly.

"You used to cut up dead bodies?" I asked. I suddenly envisioned a silver bowl full of bloody organs sitting on a gurney in an antiseptic room.

"Yup," Sabens replied with a smile on his face. "Usually right after breakfast."

I said nothing but turned my head towards him to give him a disgusted stare.

"In fact, my partner Clint could perform an autopsy with his right hand and eat an apple with his left hand," he said. He took his eyes off the road to see my response.

I couldn't help but laugh. "That's pretty sick," I told him.

"No," he said. "It's called – used to it. It's just a job, like being a school teacher or a – reporter."

I couldn't give Sabens a quick comeback, for I glanced at the dashboard speedometer and noticed that we were traveling at every bit of 96.8 miles per hour. I fell silent until we reached downtown Indianapolis.

"Will you need a ride back home?" he asked. I could tell he was afraid that he had offended me.

"Yes, please," I said as Sabens pulled the car onto the ramp next to the west-wing entrance of the City County building. "Just be back here at 11:30 a.m. I have a hair appointment at noon."

I pulled my satchel of diaries next to my chest as though I was carrying the Hope Diamond inside. I opened the door and stepped up on to the sidewalk.

"Thanks for the ride," I told him, looking at the small silver watch on my wrist. I smiled down at him. "We made it – 17 miles in 11 minutes."

"No problem," Sabens said. He didn't want me to end the conversation by shutting the car door.

"Hey – wait a minute," he said, pausing a full minute before he spoke.

"There's something you should know," he said, lowering his voice.

"My ex-partner at the coroner's office, Clint, he, uh, he did the autopsies of your three boys on LaSalle Street," he said.

I raised my eyebrows at Sabens, but said nothing.

"And, he, uh, he…." he added. I could tell it was difficult for Sabens to speak. "He still has a file at home, somewhere. I don't know where. When the coroner's office moved to the new head-quarters a lot of stuff got shuffled around and lost. Don't ask me why, but he decided to keep a file for himself."

I felt myself gulp. This time I turned around to see if anyone was looking.

"Where's Clint now?" I asked Sabens. I knew we didn't have much time. And I knew we shouldn't even be seen talking on the front steps of the City County Building for very long.

"Last I heard he's in a nursing home out west," Sabens said. He put the sedan in drive. "I'm only telling you this because I feel sorry for you. That's all I know."

I winked at Sabens and shut the passenger door swiftly and loudly.

"More evidence," I thought to myself as I climbed the stairs into the large 30-story building."

"Thank-you, God."

74

BATTERING THE WITNESS
April 1996

I sat in the fifth floor lobby of the prosecutor's office, waiting for Marion County deputy prosecuting attorney Linda Hope for nearly twenty minutes.

I was not dressed up in my usual business attire. A suit was just – me. On this warm day I wore a pair of Levi's blue jeans, black cowgirl boots and a favorite black T-shirt. I looked like I was ready to go country line dancing.

Linda finally arrived to escort me down a long, locked corridor to her small, cubbyhole office. Without even asking, she promptly took the ten diaries from my satchel and gave them to a young, twenty-something law student standing at her side. He had a military haircut and a pencil-thin nose. I assumed he was Linda's own, personal gopher. More than likely, he was an intern from the nearby Indiana University School of Law over on Michigan Street.

"Copy every single page of every single diary," Linda told him sternly as she gave me a dirty look. I could tell the stress of the case was getting to her. There were dark circles under her blue-green eyes and even her shiny blond hair looked limp and tired.

I looked at the intern as he headed out the door with the most precious moments of my life tucked under his arm. He was carrying some of the most intimate thoughts and reflections of my heart, mind and soul. And some of the most explicitly intimate details of my life.

Linda motioned for me to take a seat in front of her desk. Her demeanor was much different than it was before Rock Norton's arrest. Before my picture was on the front page of the Indianapolis Star, she treated me with respect. She seemed sympathetic to my plight to put a serial killer behind bars. In fact, she once told me how to make homemade bread from the new bread-maker she received for Christmas.

NOW, she treated me coldly and formally, like I was a prankster calling the fire department with a false alarm.

As we discussed a few more details of my last telephone conversation with Rock Norton before his arrest, Linda lightened up a bit. We joked about detective Jon Padget, and how Rock Norton had cleverly nicknamed him Detective Dick Tracy. Even though Norton had considered Padget a bitter enemy, I felt a real camaraderie with the short, plump police investigator. Padget was a good person – one of the few caring people I met while pursuing the investigation during the past five years. He was a committed family man.

I knew that Linda Hope was a nice woman, someone who had small children. But I wondered what her relationship with her children was. Were they lonely? Especially on this day, I wondered what kind of mother she really could be from the way she was behaving.

"Ham is on his way," Linda said quickly, without looking me in the eye. I could tell her dainty eyes were swollen from lack of sleep.

"He wants to ask you a few questions before tomorrow's deposition."

I nodded, but was surprised at Linda's decision. After all, I had just retained a high-profile attorney from Chicago. He catered specifically to the media. He was making a hefty dent in my wallet to the tune of $500 per hour – but he was worth every penny. I did not want to be alone with Ham. He was famous for his brutal questioning.

"I can't meet him right now, I look awful," I told Linda. I looked down at myself. "My ratty jeans, my boots, a T-shirt, for heavens' sakes, Linda."

"This is not the first impression I want to make with Ham," I said.

"Oh, that doesn't matter," Linda said. When her assistant, Deputy Prosecuting Attorney Darren Hickman walked in, she refused to look me in the eye.

Actually, it didn't matter. I might as well have been wearing a diaper and bib when Rock Norton's attorney, Ham, walked through the door. If I have ever met anyone in my entire life that looked just like Satan – it was Rick Ham. Even his fiery, red and black goatee looked sharpened this morning – in my honor I assumed.

I made my first mistake when Ham walked through Linda's door. I treated him kindly. I shook his hand and smiled at him when he walked in the room and sat down. When he drilled me mercilessly about my relationship with Rock Norton, I answered every question with courtesy, honesty and helpfulness.

But, as the questioning continued, Linda Hope and Darren Hickman fidgeted in their seats. Both of their eyes were ablaze with anger as they watched me. Hickman eyed me as though I were a prostitute arrested for street walking on East Washington Street.

As Ham interrogated me, they quickly interrupted his conversation. Linda rescheduled an appointment for him to resume the interrogation. I noticed her eyes were almost wild with disbelief as I stood up and shook Ham's hand and said good-bye.

Both prosecuting attorneys walked to the fifth floor elevators and disappeared for about 20 minutes.

Soon, I heard the methodical click of Linda's high heels and the stomping of Hickman's $700 dollar shoes as they returned to where I was seated.

As soon as Hickman walked in the small, cubbyhole office he slammed the door.

A tall, medium-built man with strawberry blond hair, his countenance was noticeably jaded with pimples and a rosy complexion. He was cloaked in anger.

Walking across the room, Hickman stood behind the desk and glared down at me, shaking a long, diamond-studded finger at me.

"Well, Little Miss Reporter, you think the whole world revolves around you, don't you!" he screamed.

I stared up at him in shock.

"You think this whole case is about YOU!" he repeated himself, as though he was afraid I didn't hear him.

"Every time I turn on the TV – there is Carol Schultz! Carol Schultz on the CBS EVENING NEWS WTH DAN RATHER!

"Carol Schultz on Inside Edition!"

"Stay tuned to Hard Copy for an interview with Carol Schultz!" he said, bellowing like a hungry lion.

I could feel my chest pulsating through the muscles in my neck. I was speechless.

Linda Hope quickly chimed in with Hickman's attack.

"You should have done just like we did! We didn't do ANY interviews after the arrest! We disappeared!" Linda screeched. "That's exactly what you should have done!"

I gathered my composure just enough to barely mouth a retort. "Well, then, why didn't you guys have the courtesy to call me and tell me about Rock Norton's arrest? You knew it was going to happen. My life was in danger the day he went to jail and you guys didn't even care. You had absolutely no concern for my safety. I had to watch the arrest on the FOX NEWS!", I wanted to shout.

But no words came out of my mouth. They could tell I was wounded.

I don't even know why I did it, but I came to my own defense. "I wasn't on Inside Edition," I told them. But they wouldn't listen.

"In fact, I literally ran from photographers when Inside Edition came to town. They stalked me at my mother's house like a bunch of vultures. I refused the interview because I didn't want to hurt the case. I had already done the interview with Dan Rather *before* the arrest.

"That's a lie!" Hickman screamed at me through his belly. His temples were flinching in his tirade. "I SAW you on Inside Edition wearing your fine, pretty little black dress."

I had taken the final blow. I knew there was no reasoning with Hickman or Hope. He would never understand that Inside Edition had bought the clip of me from the local NBC affiliate. He didn't want to hear reason. He was angry and jealous.

"And WHY did you tell Channel 59 that you were testifying before the Grand Jury!" Linda wailed.

"I *didn't* tell Channel 59," I said, through my teeth. "I told my girlfriend, Debra Zahler. Indeed, after Debra had completed the three-part series on me the previous summer, she had frequently called to check on me. We had lunched together more than once. We quickly learned that we had a lot in common. Throughout the next few months we had become very close. She was always sympathetic to my ups and downs on LaSalle Street.

"So this woman just CONVENIENTLY had a camera crew show up?" Linda asked with disbelief. She glared at me with clenched teeth.

"Number one, they were just out in the parking lot," I said, shrugging my shoulders. "It was no big deal – a shot of me walking from the parking lot up to the front door. They didn't even use the clip. That's just how TV works."

"Why, oh why did you tell her!" Linda said, stomping around the room, chanting in an Indian-like babble.

"Because she's my friend," I said simply. Warm tears spilled down my cheek. "Debra is my friend."

"She is NOT your friend," Linda yelled, twirling around on her toes like a witch about to cast a spell. For a split second, I thought she was going to spit on me.

I started to cry like a first grader with a scraped knee.

"She *is* my friend," I wanted to say, but instead I pursed my lips in dry silence. "She cares about me."

Linda meditated on her next round of attack before she spoke.

"From now on, you don't talk to ANY reporters!"

She commanded me like a military captain.

"DO YOU UNDERSTAND ME??!!! She bellowed until she echoed.

"That will be impossible," I replied with respect yet absolute precision. "Ninety percent of my friends are reporters."

Linda Hope wasn't listening to me. She was beyond listening. "And don't tell anyone – I mean ABSOLUTELY ANYONE – when you come down here!" she said.

Instantly I felt that Linda Hope was breaking the law by forbidding me to tell anyone about my whereabouts. That was for places like Russia. My son and my mother were entitled to know where I was, especially when my mother was watching my child. I felt like Linda was abusing her authorities as a deputy prosecutor.

"And cops," Linda continued. "You don't talk to any more cops. From now on you're not allowed to talk to any more policemen. PERIOD!"

I couldn't believe my ears. She was threatening me!

I suddenly felt like a Jewish concentration camp prisoner. What Linda Hope was saying was 100 percent illegal. She could not make life time demands like this on me!

"So…." Linda said, changing the subject. "Just what exactly have you sent Floyd – that lunatic prisoner in Florida?"

"What a stupid question," I thought to myself. It all finally made sense. I realized what was going on.

"You guys are under so much pressure you're losing it."

"I've told you this a million times," I said out loud with subtle sarcasm. "I have never sent him ANYTHING, absolutely ANYTHING, except for the one newspaper article that appeared in the Indianapolis Star when I met Floyd in September of 1992."

"And I already gave you a copy of that specific article, a long time ago. To the district attorney's office."

Linda flipped out again.

"I DON'T BELIEVE YOU SENT HIM A GOD D - - - newspaper clipping!" she thundered.

"I can't believe this is happening to me," I thought to myself. I told her over a year ago – before the grand jury ever convened – exactly what I had given to the state's star eye-witness.

But it doesn't matter!

"If you guys would just contact the Sheriff he could show you Floyd knows things that NEVER appeared in any newspaper article!"

It was Hickman's turn to yell at me again.

"YOU THINK YOU SOLVED THIS CASE, DON'T YOU!" he screamed as though he were a referee on a softball diamond.

I said nothing, blinking my blue eyes in rebellion.

"DON'T YOU!!!" Hickman screamed again as the jugular vein in his neck turned purple.

When I remained silent Hickman looked at me with disgust. "Well, you DIDN'T," he yelled, content that he had overpowered me.

"And this case is not about you and your F - - - -ing little book anymore!"

Linda took the platform away from Hickman. "What kind of police evidence do you have in your possession?" she asked me as though I were a bank robber.

"I told you, I don't have any," I said flatly.

She walked around the room, grabbed my purse and started searching it. She looked at the insides for a minute, then threw it back down on the ground.

"Well, how's come you know so much about this case?" she clenched her fists and paced across the room. "Just how in the HELL do you know so much about this case?"

Without even waiting for an answer, Linda marched on for battle. "And Detective Jon Padget! I don't get this friendship you have with him – with ALL of these cops in the last five years!!!! HOW DID YOU GET THEM ALL TO GIVE YOU SO MUCH INFORMATION?"

I remained silent.

"You were sleeping with Detective Jon Padget, weren't you?" Linda said, accusing me in a belittling voice that was raised above an intercom speaker's potential.

"How many of the other police officers did you sleep with to get information?" Linda asked. "How about the Sheriff? You seem to get along with him pretty well. Mike Ryker? And how about that other cop – what's his name? Don Campbell?"

I felt like I was locked in a room with Satan himself. I refused to answer her degrading questions.

She walked around behind my chair and folded her arms

across her chest. She leaned against the door, blocking me in like I was a fleeing terrorist. I had never been so insulted in all of my life. I felt the tears welling up in my eyes again.

"Well, you had better get it in your pretty little head that you're not the star ANYMORE" Hickman said, pounding his fist on Linda's desk. The tiny framed photographs of her children rattled with his anger.

"This trial isn't going to be a TV circus. It's the real world! When you meet Ham tomorrow, DON'T BE NICE TO HIM! DON'T EVEN SHAKE HIS HAND!"

"He is *not* your friend," Linda added. "He is the enemy. Don't be nice to him."

"Now, what about movie offers, how many have you had?!!!" Hickman was still yelling like he was at an NBA basketball game.

Before I could answer him, Linda asked, "And book deals?"

"I – I – I don't have any movie or book deals," I said. "But —

"YOU AND YOUR G—- DAMN BOOK!" Linda screamed in a high-pitched voice. I wondered how high her blood pressure was escalating by now.

I wanted to bawl. I was so humiliated.

"I don't care if you're writing a book about F - - - -ING JESUS CHRIST! She yelled, slamming her fist down on her desk like it was a brick. "I don't want to hear it!"

"YOU ARE NOT THE STAR ANYMORE!" Hickman said. He decided to chip in again.

"DO YOU HEAR ME???"

Hickman's words suddenly became nothing but an echo in my ears. He seemed like he was in another dimension. Getting yelled at did something to me that I couldn't explain. Why were they being so mean to me! I didn't understand.

I looked up at the clock. I had already missed my noon appointment. Detective Sabens was no where in sight.

"May I use the telephone?" I asked.

"Go ahead," she said, repulsed with my voice. She left the room with Hickman trailing her. I could hear them whispering for a few minutes before Hickman walked back in and confronted me.

"We're done with you," he said, disgusted with me as he

turned and walked away. "You can go. Get out of here."

I just stood there, waiting for Sabens to appear. Instead, Linda walked back in. She would not even look at me. She shoved a yellow voucher in my hand. "Here, go on," she said. "Take a cab home."

As I bent over to pick up my purse, tears streamed down my cheeks and spilled onto the zippered satchel I was carrying. I couldn't believe what was happening.

"Oh, and by the way," Linda said. She stopped me as I walked toward the elevators. "I did NOT tell you that you can't talk to any reporters. You may not discuss anything we discuss that is pre-trial testimony."

I thought she was threatening me, in a subtle way, but I wasn't sure. I took the cab voucher and folded it up. I put it in the back pocket of my jeans and stretched my black suede jacket over my shoulders. I was in a daze as I stumbled through the hallway to the stairs. I hadn't eaten all day and I could tell my blood sugar was low.

Before I knew it I was outside the City County Building. I didn't see any cabs so I just started walking into the steaming noon-day sun and the rush hour traffic. I heard a horn blow and tires squeal as a truck driver slammed on his brakes. As he yelled profanities out of his window, I continued walking, headed south on Alabama Avenue.

"What a joke," I thought. I didn't feel like waiting for the cab. All I wanted to do was get as far away from the City County Building as possible.

When I finally reached the steps of the Marion County Jail on Maryland Avenue and Alabama Street, I heard someone call out my name.

"CAROL SCHULTZ!" the male voice cried out. "CAROL SCHULTZ!"

I looked up and saw a young, long-haired man with a mustache standing in front of a canary-yellow cab with a dented grill and dirty fenders.

I smiled weakly and headed towards him.

"Are you Carol Schultz?" he asked.

I nodded.

"Come on, get in," he shouted. "I've been looking every where

264

for you!"

Knowing that I had little more than 15 cents on me, I hesitated for a moment, then opened the cab door.

"Take me home?" I said weakly.

`Yeah, hon," he said, holding up a pink voucher. "I'll take you home. Marion County's paying for it."

I climbed in the cab and shut the door. As soon as I collapsed in the black vinyl seat I started sobbing out loud.

The blond-haired driver climbed behind the steering wheel and stared at me, looking equally miserable.

"Where do you live, honey?" he asked gently.

I was sobbing so hard I couldn't speak. I had kept my emotions in all morning. Now, the salty tears flowed like a river, washing away all of my makeup. I lifted up my right hand and pointed east. "That way," I said, choking back sobs. "Just drive that way."

My low blood sugar was causing me to tremble. Crying on top of it was making it worse. For a second, I couldn't remember where I lived.

The cab driver spoke with a soft, comforting voice. "Did you just get out, honey?" he asked. "Were you in long?"

"Oh, my God," I thought to myself. "He thinks I was just released from jail."

I looked down at myself. I couldn't blame him. I was dressed more like a convict than a reporter. I looked over at him and couldn't help but smile.

"No," I said, blowing my nose on a wrinkled tissue.

"I'm a witness," I said.

He nodded as he drove. "To what, a robbery?" he asked.

I shook my head.

"No, murder," I said bluntly.

He became quiet for a minute. Then he said, "I been there."

I looked over at him and softened. "Really?" I asked.

The cab driver, who wore faded black jeans, a green jacket and a three-day old Tom Cruise-style beard, explained how he once witnessed a murder. "Saw one of my buddies sliced up over a bottle of Jack Daniels over at Mustang Sally's." he said.

"The police treated me like sh - - ," he said. I wanted to help them and they acted like I wuz the one who killed my own friend."

He paused for a moment, lost in thought. "I got out of it," he said. "I'll never help the police again."

I looked at him and instantly felt sorry for him. Suddenly I realized we had been driving east on Washington Street for nearly 20 minutes. We were about to pass up my street. "Wait!" I said as he drove by Post Road, the intersection next to my house. "I live down there!"

He turned the next corner and within moments we had pulled into my driveway. He parked under the shade of an Oak tree and turned off the engine. "You gonna be okay, honey?" he asked.

"Yep," I said with my right hand on the door handle. I hesitated and turned to look at him. "You know, I don't even know your name," I said.

"I feel like we know each other. You've been very nice to me."

"My name is Duane," he said, grinning. I noticed three teeth were missing on top. "Does that mean you want me to come in?"

I laughed at him.

"No," I smiled. "Thank-you for being so kind to me. I really needed a friend just now."

Something kept me from leaving the car.

"Duane?" I said.

"Yeah, hon?" he asked, looking intently at me.

"You know, when you pull out of this driveway, and get back on Post Road?" I asked.

"Yeah," he said, looking puzzled.

"What would you do if a semi-trailer ran a red light and broadsided this cab right into a telephone pole?" I asked.

"And you were killed immediately?" I added.

A look of horror crossed Duane's face. He said nothing.

"Do you know if you'd go to heaven or not?" I asked him.

"Yeah," he said. "I know for sure I'd go to heaven."

"How do you know that?" I asked.

"'Because God wouldn't let me down like that," Duane replied.

I smiled at him.

Duane gave me a puzzled look and I reached over and held his

266

hand. His grip was strong and his fingers were scarred with knife wounds. I held his palm in my hand for a moment.

"Duane?" I asked. "Do you mind if I say a little prayer for you right now?"

He shook his head. "No, not at all," he said.

Duane bowed his head and closed his eyes. I closed mine and started praying. I remembered an old fashioned prayer I'd heard growing up at my mother's country church. It was a red brick building near a creek and a deep woods.

I recited it out loud to Duane. Amazingly, he recited it back to me. It was a Kodak moment.

The 1800's hymnal, "On the Old Rugged Cross" suddenly came to my mind. I got goose bumps all over. It was the same song they played at my Daddy's funeral. When I looked up, I thought I saw a tear coming down Duane's cheek.

"God be with you," I told Duane. I jumped out of the car and waved good-bye.

I watched Duane back out. He had a really strange, peaceful look plastered on his face. He was smiling as he drove off.

At that moment, I felt relief.

No matter what grief I endured in the upcoming murder trial, this extraordinary moment with Duane made it all worth while.

I felt like I'd made a difference in someone's life – even if it was just the cab driver.

75

TWO YEARS LATER

AFTER THE MURDER TRIAL

ROCK DIES

January 3, 1999

It was about 10:30 a.m. and only three days into the New Year as I sat at my mother's mahogany kitchen table in front of a large plate glass window. I watched the snow fall and make deep trenches under her patio's ledge.

Large crystal flakes layered her backyard, covering everything tangible with a blanket of white. Overhead, a cloud of gray appeared to hover over the adjacent neighbor's naked landscape. It held a menacing promise to dump nature until infinity was over. I knew we were in a snowstorm like my family hadn't seen since the blizzard of 1978. It was the year paramedics had to ride snow-mobiles to our front door to rescue my father who had a massive heart attack during the snowstorm of the century.

Although Daddy survived the heart attack when I was just a teen – when my mother's telephone rang abruptly before noon - I learned others weren't so lucky. It was a day that mother nature was running its course with notoriety.

When I answered the phone, I learned that a dear friend, Tammy, was in the hospital agonizing in hard labor with her second child on the way. She and her husband had fought a dangerous battle on the icy, snow-covered highways to reach the hospital before they were snowed in without medical help.

No sooner had I hung up the phone, it rang again. This time the news was riveting. One of the pastors at my church, Rick De'Armond of Hagerstown, Indiana, had just died of a massive heart attack while shoveling the morning's mounting snow in his driveway. I was crushed to hear what happened to him.

Ironically, as soon as I hung up the phone from the fatal news, it rang again.

This time, it was a call I never expected. I could hardly believe my ears.

ROCK NORTON was DEAD!

"No!" I cried into the receiver. "He can't be dead." I ran into a back bedroom and threw my head and my long curly blond hair into my hands. My mind raced to the 72-year-old Indy 500 racing mechanic's voice the last time I talked to him.

"There, there, Pretty One," Rock had said into the telephone the day he was arrested for the LaSalle Street murders. There was unbelievable patience in his voice that last morning.

"Everything's going to be okay," he said. "You'll see. You'll solve these murders and I'll help you do it. Don't be afraid."

It was the last time I ever talked to Rock Norton alive. It was almost bittersweet. Rock had predicted that I – his nemesis – would someday retrace his footsteps after his death.

I didn't believe him when he said it – and I didn't want to believe him now. Rock was one of the strongest people I ever knew. He had a reputation at the INDIANAPOLIS 500 for being a man who had steel emotions and a steel body. He was invincible.

How could he be dead?

This news was unbelievable!

But the truth melted over me like water cascading across Niagara Falls. I was told the paramedics had to pry Rock's cold, stiff body out of his home. From the massive amount of blood nearby, I was told it appeared Rock had died a gruesome, painful death.

He died while sitting in his favorite recliner in the living room of his Irvington, Indiana home – sometime between 9 p.m. on New Years' Eve and noon on New Years' Day, 1999.

Instinctively, I wondered the worst.

Did Rock's greatest fear come true?

Was he murdered?

Did the people he was afraid were looking for him find him? He told me he thought someone was following him in 1996. He thought they wanted to murder him because he knew too much about the LaSalle Street Murders. Did the people he told me he thought were tape recording his telephone calls intercept his personal records – and finally catch up with him?

I couldn't help but remember the countless conversations I had with Rock about how afraid he was that someone was stalking him.

I pleaded with him often, "What do I do if something happens to you, Rock?"

Rock insisted he would leave me a clue of some sort if he ever died. He said it would be in the form of either a package, a letter, a file of documents, or some other souvenir only I would recognize. He said it could possibly even be a lock box. But it would definitely be a message from beyond the grave. It would be something he would leave hidden for me. It would be somewhere that only I would find it. Something only I would know what it is.

Somehow, in some morbidly twisted, unpredictable, "Silence-of-the-lambs," type way – I knew Rock Norton would communicate with me.

In spite of my grief over the death of an elderly man I once put in jail for murder – a man I relentlessly pursued for five years - a sinister man I had surprisingly grown close to – I knew I had to find it.

Someday I would have to find what he left behind for only me to find.

76

SIX YEARS LATER

NINE YEARS AFTER ROCK'S
ARREST FOR MURDER

April 25th, 2005

After clopping down three flights of stairs in a pair of black high heels, I reached the place I needed to be in – Room B-2 of the Marion County City-County Building.

For a brief second, I had an eerie flashback of my past. This was the very room where Robert Gierse and Robert Hinson did subcontract microfilming work for the City of Indianapolis. I shuddered for a moment, then shook off my chill.

It had been almost a decade since I last investigated the most sensational murder case in my state's history. I hadn't had dinner with a serial killer in years.

A lot about me changed after the LaSalle Street Murders trial. I moved to California to "get away from it all." It was there that I worked for a national magazine and composed one of the best stories of my career, an excellent piece about former President William Jefferson Clinton. I returned to Indiana to be near my mother. I met a wonderful man who treated me like a queen. We got married and I changed my last name from Schultz to Sissom.

I gave up reporting because I couldn't ignore my passion for solving murders. I immersed myself in a civil rights case where two youths were violated in Las Vegas. I solved another homicide in Florida and finally met the rigid requirements to become a Private Detective, licensed by the State of Indiana.

As a modern day private eye, I went up to the microfilm counter to look up some files.

I spoke to a very attractive, well-dressed black woman who was eager to help me. I was impressed when I heard soft gospel music coming from behind her desk. It sounded like Ron Kenoly was singing in the back room. The work area was peaceful and conducive for studying.

I showed the lady the folded up piece of paper I had in my hand.

I told her I was researching a family genealogy.

She looked at my notes for a minute, then disappeared for a while. She brought a few canisters of film to me and loaded them onto the machine.

After all these years, the sight of microfilm still gave me goose bumps. To me, the word Microfilm meant Murder.

"What are you looking for?" the woman asked me.

"I – I am researching a family tree today," I replied. "But, while I'm here – just out of curiosity – I want to look up a man's marital history. He died about six years ago."

The woman gave me a sympathetic look and started unwinding film onto the machine.

"Can you look up another name for me, even if it's not a family member or relative?" I asked politely.

"Yes, of course," she said.

"Can you look up a man by the name of Mr. Rock Norton?" I asked her.

She stared at her long delicate fingers unwinding the skinny black tape.

"He died in 1999," I continued. "But I think he had several wives in Marion County while he was alive."

It had been over nine years since the trial – but I couldn't resist the temptation to look into Rock Norton's past.

After all, I was sitting right there. The information was at my fingertips. Besides, Rock was dead. It wasn't like he was going to care if I was down here looking into his scandalous past.

Within half an hour and with much help from the assistant, I found what I was looking for.

The woman handed me several printouts. Apparently, Rock Norton had been married at least 7 times.

"Seven wives," she said out loud. "Goodness, the man was busy."

Goodness!

I pulled up each file and read it carefully. On one of the applications, Rock wrote that he had been married three times – and that was on his second marriage application in Marion County! This was 1946! It showed Rock could have been married at least 9 or 10 times! I wondered what the names of his other wives were! I couldn't even find his marriage to Diane Norton – and I knew for a fact they were married.

What a twisted life Rock Norton led!

The next printouts showed his divorces. These confused me.

Rock had a divorce record from a Mary on April 10th, 1948 and again on April 27th, 1949. On his application for marriage to Marilyn on March 22nd (the day he was arrested) 1960 – he wrote down on the application that he had three previous marriages. He was divorced from Evelyn on May 9th, 1957.

There was a divorce filed from Hannah on December 1st, 1982. It was later dismissed because they reconciled on January 21st, 1983.

One of Rock's wives committed suicide.

What a history!

I looked at Rock's divorce record from Norma Norton – filed June 6th, 1973.

"Wait a minute!" I said out loud. "How can this be? Norma

filed for divorce in 1973 while Rock was still married to someone else!"

"Was Rock Norton a bigamist?" I asked the woman – assuming she would know the legal answer to my question.

She shook her head.

"I don't know," she said. "It looks like he had a lot going on. It was just too much."

I read further.

There was no record of the divorce from Norma ever being finalized.

I saw that Norma had filed a restraining order against Rock, but I could not read the file – it was not accessible.

"Why would there be no record of divorce from Norma?" I asked out loud. "It shows that he married Hannah in the 1980's, and it sure looks like he was still married to someone else while he was in the middle of a messy divorce with Norma!"

"If she died there didn't have to be a divorce," the assistant pointed out to me.

"Died?" I asked out loud.

All of a sudden, everything around me fell silent. It was the same feeling – the same gnawing in my gut – I felt 10 years ago when I was working so hard to get Rock in jail. I had the unmistakable intuition of death.

And murder.

"Was Norma murdered?" I asked out loud.

I had to find out more.

I picked the papers up and told the woman I was headed down the hall to do further research. I needed to find out more about Rock's wives. How many of them died mysteriously?

As I walked down the long, murky hallway I felt the eeriness of my surroundings creep around me. There was a terrible thunderstorm going on outside – and the lights in the hallway were flickering on and off.

I was reflecting on who Rock had been married to at the time of the LaSalle Street murders when I walked into the records room.

I had no choice but to do a manual search….to find out if Rock was a bigamist or not. Before I started pouring through the large, olive green marriage and divorce books – all written by hand – I reviewed all of my notes. I tried to organize Rock's wedded life before me.

I attempted to get everything in chronological order.

For a brief second, I looked across the room and to the darkened hallway. I saw a row of prisoners – all dressed in orange jumpsuits – passing by on their way to the elevator. They were peeking in and looking at the few of us in the room as they walked by.

I felt a little uneasy, but went back to my business.

Only a few seconds later, everything went dark! The power had gone out and we were all in pitch-black darkness!

I tried to breathe and not panic.

Suddenly, the lights came on again. I felt the eyes of a man seated at one of the tables dart up and look at me.

When I looked over at him, he looked away.

I was becoming more and more nervous. The room was chilly. I couldn't find the book I was looking for.

I walked up to the counter and asked the clerk for help.

"I need to look up a divorce for a man in 1986," I told the woman.

"Do you have the exact date?" the woman asked me with a friendly, Victorian smile. She had freckles and soft, silky hair. She looked like a candidate for a shampoo commercial.

"No," I apologized, trying to be helpful. "I'll just do a search by name. What's the man's full name?"

"Rock Norton," I told the woman.

"Seven wives," she commented with a sigh. "Was that man crazy?"

I smiled as I watched her look at her screen intently and then look over at me. "Oh, I found him," she said.

I looked up at her.

"Well, I see here that he just got married again very recently. In February of this year," she said.

"WHAT?????" I almost shouted at the woman. "I thought he was DEAD!"

The woman just stared at me.

I had to repeat myself.

I THOUGHT ROCK WAS DEAD!

All of a sudden, my life flashed before my eyes!

I always wondered if Rock Norton weren't really still alive. I had found no one to confirm they had actually seen his body at his funeral.

There were reports of a cremation. Someone said they saw his ashes in what looked like a cookie tin. There was an official obituary in the Indianapolis Star. But not *one* person could tell me they had actually seen Rock Norton's dead body.

I turned around to see if anyone was watching me.

I had let my guard down – ever since I received the riveting call that Rock Norton was dead. I had quit looking behind me every time I walked in my front door. The nightmares had stopped. I felt safe again. I came out of my seclusion and started living a normal life.

The last time Rock and I talked was the morning before he went to jail for murder.

He gave me bitter glances from his seat where he was hand-cuffed – at the LaSalle Street Murder trial in 1996.

He made it public. He hated me for what I had done to him.

He called me a traitor and a liar.

Afterwards, I received death threats, but I didn't know who they were from. All four tires on my car were slashed in the middle of the night. I couldn't confirm who had done it, but *I knew it was him.*

When I heard he had died, I felt safe again. I began to come out in public and live a normal life.

Now, I nearly fainted at the realization that Rock Norton was still alive.

Was he out there somewhere – still lurking – in Indianapolis?

"Was he looking for me?" I wondered.

To be continued . . .

Epilogue

In March, 1996, Rock Norton was indicted on three counts of murder after a one-year investigation by the Marion County Grand Jury. On March 22, 1996 he was arrested and spent five weeks in jail. After a miniature trial – a Marion County Judge declared the charges against him were preposterous and she ordered Rock Norton to be let out of jail. The case was never allowed to go before a criminal jury. The Marion County Prosecutor figuratively "unarrested" Rock Norton and freed him to the streets of Indianapolis.

He was the only person to ever be indicted or arrested for The LaSalle Street Murders – in the entire history of The Indianapolis Police Department.

In 1997, I received tips that Rock Norton had killed again – after being let out of jail by the prosecutor.
*One tip was he killed his own housekeeper.
*There are still unconfirmed reports that there are bodies buried in the backyard and the basement of his former residence.
*The Indianapolis Police Department seized 90 percent of my book research about the murders, including over 200 tape recordings, mostly of Rock Norton and I talking. They have never given it back.
*Upon the publishing of this book, I approached the Prosecutors Office and asked for the return of my material and my tapes once again. The answer was "No." When I asked why, the answer was "When we took them they became ours and since they are ours we will not give them back."
*Mike Ryker was suspended from work for his role in helping me write my book about the LaSalle Street Murders.
*Jon Padget was reprimanded and received disciplinary action from IPD for his actions in assisting in the LaSalle Street Murders investigation.
*The Sheriff had all of his files and any information he had about the LaSalle Street Murders taken away from him by The Police.

Afterword

In 2005, an unidentified source inside the Indianapolis Police Department told me IPD received a confession from Rock Norton for committing the LaSalle Street Murders. This confession was never publicized or released to the public. This same police officer told me IPD has officially "cleared" the LaSalle Street Murders from their files.

I asked him what "cleared" meant.

He told me, "Cleared means it's been solved."